A NATIVE'S TONGUE

MICHAEL D. DENNIS

OCEAN STREET PRESS EDITION, SEPTEMBER 2023

Published in the United States by Ocean Street Press.

Ocean Street Press

ISBN-10: 0-9960964-2-6

ISBN-13: 978-0-9960964-2-3

Ocean Street Press

Author's web address www.michaelddennis.com Printed in the

United States of America

Library of congress control number: 2014908583

33 12 1001

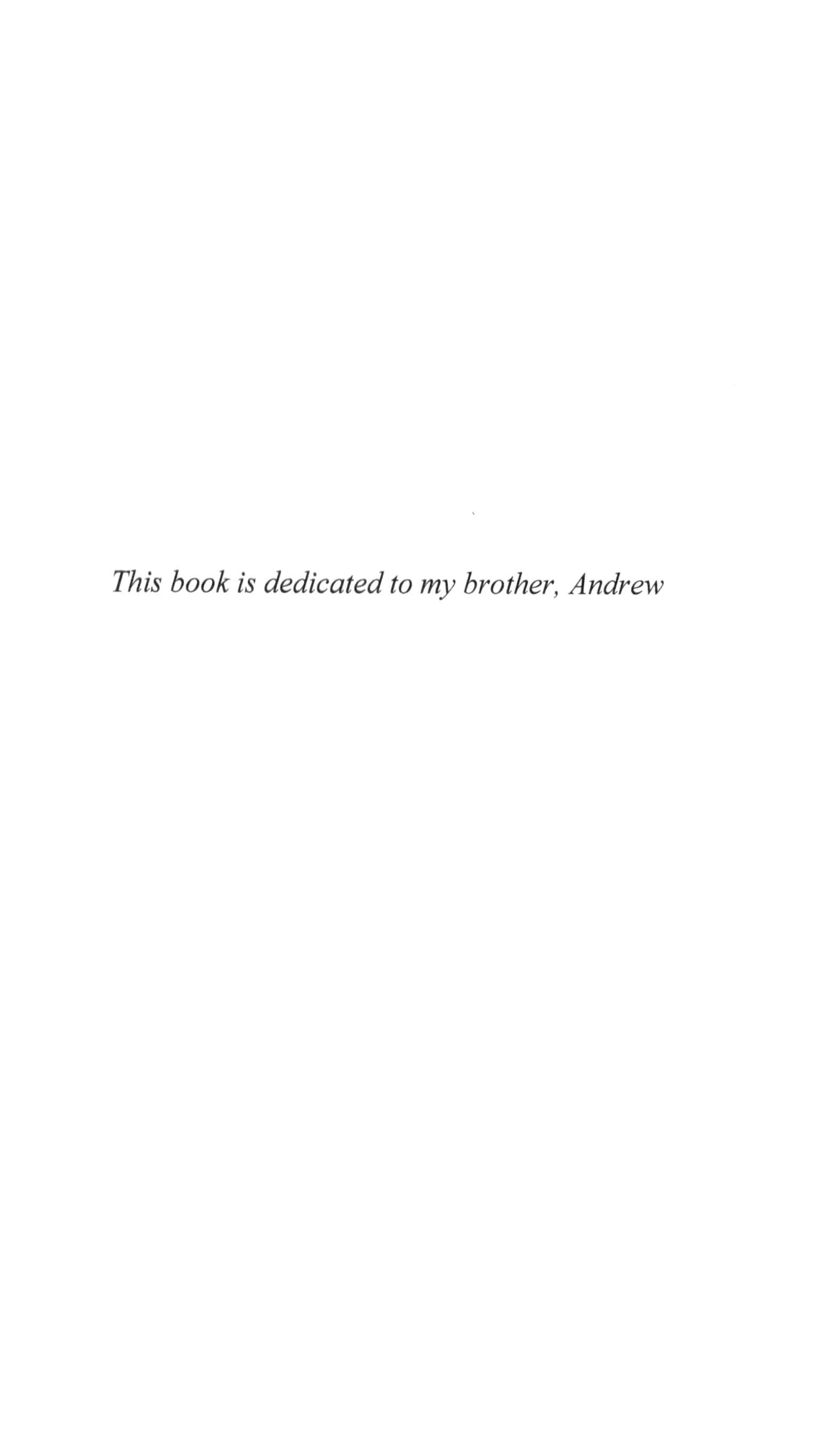

This book is dedicated to my brother, Andrew

CHAPTER ONE

Jennifer Bannister's footsteps echoed down the hall. The uniforms of the inmates dampened the sound. Her ears tried to follow the faint sound, if only to affirm that she was still moving forward. There wasn't anyone to hold her hand. She just trusted that each sign would guide her in the right direction.

I'll get there at some point, Jennifer thought, trying to convince herself that she was doing the right thing. *You can't get lost in here; they don't let you go off course.* Her words slipped away. She felt the cold air settle over her skin. She glanced at a placard marked Visitors Only.

In the cool air, her skin tightened. Jennifer shivered and wished she were somewhere warmer. Seeing Violet for the first time was going to be hard enough. She was going to look the woman she hated most in the world in the eye. She didn't want to be shaking from the cold and covered in goose bumps.

Jennifer peered through the bulletproof glass at Violet. There were markings embedded in the glass, swirls that made it harder to look directly into Violet's eyes. Jennifer picked up the phone and listened. Violet grabbed it and began to speak, "It was never you that he loved. You know that right?" Violet's voice was raspy.

Her expressions and mannerisms changed from static to fully engaged. She stood up and waved her hands maniacally at Jennifer, and then she slammed her fist against the glass.

Jennifer hung up the phone. Her blonde hair got caught in between her hand and the receiver as she placed it back on the black hook. Turning, she slid out of the red plastic chair and down the corridor, guided by the exit sign's green light. In the stale air of the prison, she searched for a pack of cigarettes, unsheathed a Parliament, lit it, and smoked nervously.

Two overweight guards carrying guns in nylon hip holsters directed her to the parking lot, where they offered her matching robotic waves good-bye. The midnight blue 2005 Jaguar xk8, which her parents loaned her for this visit, was the only vehicle in the parking lot row. Her parents thought she would feel safer in their car rather than her own bright red Honda.

In either case, she seemed to fit this car, or the car fit her a lot more. Her lean physique matched the lines on the Jag, and it made her feel more mature. She was constantly trying to act older than she was. Jennifer went around to the passenger side of the car and opened the rear door. She set her oversized black leather purse on the back seat and took out a translucent orange bottle filled with tiny white pills. She slung her head back, popped two, shut the door and walked around to the driver's seat.

The heat had melted the surface of the Jaguar's leather seats, reducing the fabric to a buttery texture. Jennifer's blonde hair clung to the sides of her shoulders, heavy with sweat. She retrieved her car key from the passenger seat, pressed the key into the slot, and burst into tears, suddenly unable to move.

Jennifer hadn't eaten all day. The heavy dose of Xanax caused her to feel excessively nauseous. She blacked out and fell forward, hitting her forehead on the steering wheel. The car increased in temperature with the late afternoon heat. Her powder-white skin grew red.

“Miss. Are you alright? Miss?” A young guard, Bill Marsh, had spotted the car, and decided to go in for a closer look.

When Jennifer didn't move, he took out his club and smashed the window. She woke up from her temporary coma and lashed out.

“You Fuck!” Her voice was barely audible, even with the window smashed. Her energy was gone.

“Miss—I, I'm sorry you didn't look okay.”

“I am! What business do you have involving yourself in my business? Do you know what you did? You just fucked up my car, you moron.”

“Look, I just saw you from my station.”

To Bill, her face looked familiar, though he couldn't place where he had seen her before.

“You have no idea. Sitting in your stupid box, behind that intercom.

“I'm sorry, I know we'll pay for the window. Hell, if the prison won't, I personally will.” Bill said.

“That's great. I know where to find you. Now take your hand off of my car.”

Bill stared, trying to remember where he knew Jennifer. But the year he had spent on facial recognition back at the police academy didn't pay off. His only memories were from his years as a rookie in the field, doing ride-a-longs, days that seemed like part of a past life.

Jennifer started the car abruptly and revved the engine. The Jaguar shifted into gear and jerked in a half-moon shape across the asphalt. She put the car into drive and went flying past the young Officer Marsh, who was staring unabashedly, and out onto the open road.

"That was such a waste of time… what was I thinking?" The thought circled in her head. She glanced at the scenery; colored billboards splashed across Sherman Way. It was a road she had driven a thousand times. Unless you were driving to the jail, you never stopped at any off ramp in between Burbank and Calabasas.

This trip to the prison left Jennifer questioning her existence and her sanity. What did Violet have that she didn't? How did she trick her, the cops? Everybody? The walls were coming crashing in. She just wanted answers, no matter how much they cost.

Back home, at her desk, Jennifer began to write. Immediately, the tears fell. They drifted down her face, pooling in an indentation on the right hand corner of the desk. The lower right drawer opened with an awful squeak, a sound that pierced her every time. In the drawer was a box full of newspaper cutouts and hand writtenletters. It was all she had left to piece together the mystery of the last few years of her life and the days spent with Charlie.

Jennifer read the headline from one of the newspaper clippings, 'Menace in the Valley; a Modern Tragedy'. She drifted away from her chair to the white cotton-covered couch that divided the room. Falling with graceful symmetry, she lay down on the bed. But trying to sleep only produced a state of consciousness between waking and dreaming. Her eyelids were heavy, and her eyes were almost too swollen to open.

I cannot last another day like this, *she thought.*

“Why am I mixed up? I can't, no; I don't *want* to be into him. I want to love him forever, have a family in his memory.”

She wanted to continue talking out her feelings, but she fell back into her thoughts.
Doesn't mean anything, I need to know what's going on with me. Everybody is fucking clueless. How can they help me? They don't understand us. *She picked up a photograph of Big Sur. She stared at it.*

“Enough! I just don't want to live like this, without you. Knowing you were never who you said you were. I still love you, but I will never forgive you.”

Tears drowned out her final words. She rubbed her stomach and went over to the refrigerator to grab some leftovers. All she had were condiments and a few pieces of pita bread.

Jennifer wanted to get away from Los Angeles for a while. She thought about the thousands of places in Eastern Europe she wanted to visit, like the home of Czar Nicholas in St. Petersburg.

She didn't know what drew her to Russian royalty. Perhaps it was the many Dostoevsky and Gogol novels she had read in high school on her lunch breaks. The grim portrayals of Russian elitism and social hierarchy left her as the outsider. Jennifer thought about trying to talk to her parents.

No they will just lash out and ridicule me.

Jennifer's mother was always off trying to participate in the next best charity. Her father, Rupert Bannister, a B-movie producer in Hollywood, had achieved success with a series of movies that had reached cult status. He was always attending movie premieres, wrap parties, and other related soirees. Occasionally, Jennifer was able to go with him, but back then she had been so young that she only remembered being clutched closely to her father's chest as he shook the hands of many different people wearing elaborate costume-like clothing. It wasn't the Hollywood of now, where celebrities wore sunglasses and black on black clothes at night and vintage-looking clothes in the day, proving they were famous by trying not to be noticed.

Jennifer's parents' absence had infringed upon all of the relationships she tried with guys her own age. They all seemed to fail, due to Jennifer's lack of independence. Her only real relationship had ended in mystery, a surreal phenomenon that left her constantly guessing, picking up clues with dead ends.

Did the endless portrayals of love and romance in novels really exist? Or was it the grim reality that no man would ever love her more than the remaining ounce of love she felt for her own being? Jennifer undressed in front of a long black maple wood framed mirror she had taken from her parent's room.

She had witnessed her body grow and change in this same mirror. Her powder-white breasts had increased into their 32C form. Her nipples had gone from shallow pink into a darkened brown. She turned and looked at her back in the mirror. Jennifer's mother had waited to have her until her mid-forties, and Jennifer had been born with a birth defect. Her spine was twisted under her skin, already starting to curl over at the top. The black thong Jennifer had on barely covered the stretch marks on her legs, from her skin getting bigger from trying to fend off a teenage eating disorder and then going back to her binge and purge routine. Her legs still had traces of peach fuzz, naturally bleached white, containing the last remnants of her childhood physique.

She straddled the black leather Eames chair. The metal crossbeams protruded from in between her legs and reflected the recessed lighting above. She showed no curiosity. The metal felt dull, blunted by the factory that had forged it.

"Gimme one answer," She said. "I know you loved me Charlie. Do you still want me, like this? Do you remember me before—what I looked like?"

If she really had been in love, it was over now. She wanted to know why she had fallen for a man who she didn't have time to really get to know.

Can you really love someone who you don't know the first thing about?

She wasn't usually this confused. Jennifer wanted to find her own sexual energy, through love, but lacked the resources. She was now stuck carrying on a new and troubling legacy.

Her dimly lit reflection bored her. Men always lost interest in her shortly after they began dating her. Was it the lack of eroticism? Her fear of sex?

I'm still sexy, right? She thought to herself.

Her insecurity carried itself over into every relationship she had. She had never been with a man for more than a few weeks, even with Charlie. And now even that relationship was in contention.

Each night before Jennifer closed her eyes, cucumber- scented candle flickering, she would say a prayer: When this life ends, give me back my love. Make me comforted by my actions. Let my parents truly, deeply love me. Let me know that he really loved me, that he wanted me to do this for him. I miss you nana, papa… Good Night. *She would blow out the candle and roll onto her side to face the window.*

Jennifer felt stupid dreaming about other men. But Charlie was gone now and she couldn't help it. Flashes of all the men she had known moved in and out of her mind like ghosts. They were of different ages, and they wore different outfits, but they all moved towards her with one motivation.

Memories of her sexual experiences continued to churn, coming as fast as the pages of a flipbook. The chapters grew cartoonish, convoluting her true experience, persuading her that the men she was with had not really been human beings at all, but characters or robots. They had their own program, hardwired to do one thing only: Please themselves with sex and leave the same way they had come in, never to return again, save for in Jennifer's memory.

Her visit to the prison had proven that nothing is ever as it seems. If seeing Violet today at the prison could fill-in any gap, if her conversation through the glass had given her any glimpse into the truth about her own life and what it meant, it was buried now beneath memories of Charlie, the only man she ever loved.
"It's fate," he used to say to Jennifer. Those memories, the moments she shared with Charlie washed away any chance of Jennifer believing Violet's claims about her own relationship with

Charlie. And Violet making up the stories about Charlie writing real love letters for her?

Jennifer believed in her own intuition at this point. How hard would it be for her to pick up minute details glossed over by the police and the authorities, paid to do a job, and get it done under budget and on time? Her neurosis was more like a heightened sense of awareness. It gave her a prophetic ability to foresee the outcome. Had she foreseen this scenario as the end to her vision? Charlie gone, off into some other realm, a parallel universe, and her completely alone to continue gathering the stale breadcrumbs? This convoluted plot that replayed over and over again in her head.

She shook her head sideways and realized she would rather have continued following the story, speculating about what the narrator left out, what information the characters had intentionally misplaced to encourage her to look beyond to see if the whole phantasmagoric experience was somehow more real than the continuous monotony of the picture painted by her childhood perception of the ideal life.

CHAPTER TWO

The shadow of last night revealed itself in the bags beneath my eyes. The red lines that sprawled across my eyes were barely a shade lighter than the candy-apple colored muscle car of my dreams. I was driving my 72' Nova, which was far from the beautiful red color I was dreaming about. In fact, it was more of a shit gunmetal black and grey.

I had purchased the Nova down South from an ex-Israeli Mossad gone civilian in a trailer park near Lomita, CA. When I went to pick up the car, I was displeased to find its already sub-par black paint job damaged by a rather substantial dent in the hood. Most of the metal logos and ornaments had been removed, so it looked more like a demolition derby car that lost its competition privileges. The mobile home park was like driving into a mothball airfield, where salvaged airplane parts were sold to bargain bids offered by foreign countries. When I met the Israeli, his complacency about the stripped identifiable logos on the car gave me the sense that he may have used the car to smuggle drugs in from Mexico, but that was a question I had no desire to ask, considering the vehicle's $250 price tag.

I needed coffee. I was sure by the time I reached work, I wouldn't be able to get out of the car without either vomiting the Southern Comfort I'd had with my pancakes from the 24-hour diner the night before, or getting some of that black sludge that coffee franchises call Java. The abbreviation is just a nice way to describe the Javanese coastline in the French Polynesia, where some underpaid and enslaved laborer picked the beans. I used to rely on the Puerto Ricans in New York to ship my coffee beans. But when the Polynesian government made promises to the United States to have Pea berries harvested and delivered for a fraction of the price, my favorite Puerto Rican coffee company was priced out of the competition.

I was sympathetic to the Puerto Ricans. They didn't have the same sensational surf as French Polynesia, but they were beautiful people. I remembered the long haul we made to Polynesia as teens without fear of the big waves. I had met up with a few locals and ran into an old Malibu local Bennett Harby who gave me a tour of the local spots. Sitting on the beach in between sets drinking Hinano beers and chowing on incredible shellfish hand caught by the locals. It was definitely paradise. I could see how they had priced out the competition with their coffee too. Every morning behind the canvas covered beach shack, we would fill a large glass basin with divine coffee. It dripped through a filter made from coconut pulp and left the coffee full of rich oils that you could see floating in little bubbles on top of each cup. It was the only trip I ever took outside of the U.S. It made me feel more at home than I ever did in Los Angeles. My memory of the beautiful surf made me forget about last night and why I was so compelled to scrounge up some unique Puerto Rican coffee.

I was walking up the white staircase of an apartment building near Westwood. I bumped into this beautiful brunette who had just entered the country illegally and was staying with a group of UCLA exchange students. I passed her in the hallway, and she smiled and giggled a bit. I smiled back, and continued upstairs to go sell a bag to some dropouts.

When I finished the deal, I walked down stairs and knocked on the door where the brunette went into. A short Asian man answered.

“I'm looking for—” I said.

Before I could finish, she came out from the back room.

We spoke broken Spanish to one another and smoked her stale marijuana out of a handmade wooden pipe she smuggled from Puerto Rico. We laughed about our inability to communicate. She accented every laugh with her hands, which she used to conceal the clear braces that she'd gotten while in the States. The habit only made her more attractive. She started to show me her photo album of her and her friends in Puerto Rico on a nude beach, and I nearly lost control. I kept my cool. Her tanned skin against my pale torso was enough to leave a soft spot in my soul for anything Puerto Rican.

Which may have been why I searched for Puerto Rican coffee on a daily basis, motivated by the belief that the perfect taste and aroma of a sandy beach, combined with the scent of her brown skin, would come back to me with each sip.

When I reached the counter, and it was my turn to order, I blanked.

"One black. Double black if you have it."

"Double-black? That's not one of our daily roasts," said the counter girl.

"What?"

It became clear to me suddenly that I was one step behind my life. I took the coffee she gave me, spilling some drops on the top of my wrist.

I got back in my car and revved the engine. The music began and I started the day. The local 88.9 FM KXLU station played an old Slim Harpo track, and it brought some peace back into my soul. Today felt like it was a real beginning to an end. Not just the typical haphazard bullshit. The DJ came on and started their bi-annual fundraiser. I always gave a few bucks and one year even got some concert tickets. It was too early for sales. I switched the station, which was a bad idea.

"Shut up asshole!" I shouted at nothing.

Stupid movie trivia. I hated it when a great song got cut short, and on came some out-of-work actor with a good voice, shouting about contests and giveaways designed to exploit the hope of strangers.

"Looking at people like their fucking ears are suction cups, and fuck if he doesn't get paid that cock!" I yelled. The traffic light turned red, and I sped aimlessly through it.

I was driving like most Angelenos who pretend they have to reach an important destination, speeding in intermittent stretches of open road. But I actually had a job that I could never make it to on time. I would speed, causing minor fender benders, and use the shoulders on freeways for my usual transportation to circumvent traffic jams. The best way not to get caught using the shoulder of the road is to lean out of the window and pretend you're throwing up. If you have a passenger have them spit water or any other beverage out to increase the dramatic effect.

Most of the time, let's face it, you sit on the 101 smoking too many fucking cigarettes and wondering how you even got to this hell hole in the first place. Most responses to this question involve a silly acting career: You did a couple of plays in high school and bang! Hollywood or Bust.

Well, my dear friends, we are in the same boat. Only you want to get into this city for an absolutely ludicrous reason, and I want to get the fuck out even worse.

I finally arrived at the food court where I worked, in the Sherman Oaks Galleria. The restaurant served steak sandwiches and was called "The Best of Philly." *I sure hope not,* I used to say to myself whenever someone asked me where I worked.

That was of course if I wasn't lying to them. Most of the time I would make up something elaborate like I worked as an Account Executive with some big advertising firm. I had a friend who really was an ad executive so I always had some type of factual information to draw from in case I was quizzed. I was only quizzed once, and still remember that time, because I lasted for at least an hour with this overweight punk rock girl in Reseda, who just wouldn't swallow my story.

The mall was a trek from anywhere in the city, but at least I had a job. Manny, my boss, didn't care when I showed up. As long as he saw my smug face a couple of times throughout the day, he figured I was working. Manny had emigrated from Thailand twenty years ago with almost no money. He bought a franchise here in the mall, and within two years, had enough money to bring his whole family out here from Phuket. I never really knew how large his family was. It always seemed he was introducing me to his niece or nephew for the second and third time. His expressions never changed and his answers were always "yes" or "no," which made conversation short and simple, a rare occurrence in most interactions these days, and rather refreshing.

At the back of the restaurant was the deep freeze, where I spent my time after 9 pm. It was the only place where I could think without interruption. I'd try and read some esoteric books here and there, but never finished them. The business was never inordinately busy, and yet there was always something for me to do.

Every night at approximately 9:58 P.M., two minutes before closing time, there was a homeless man who used to come to the register when there was no one left but me. The first day he showed up wearing gas station sunglasses, a black ball cap with an exaggerated bend, a filthy soiled green army jacket and a black shirt. I told him we were closed. I thought about it twice, decided it couldn't hurt, and asked what he wanted. Prepared to offer him a free meal, I was hit unexpectedly when all he asked for was a cup of coffee. That should have been easy enough, but we didn't have any coffee made. I told him I would have to brew a cup.

"Never mind," he said.

"It's not a problem," I said, "I could use a cup myself if I've still got to finish cleaning up the mess in this hole."

He agreed and laid approximately $1.62 cents on the stainless steel counter where the register rested. To my surprise he knew exactly the amount it cost with the tax. Had he been here before? I didn't remember seeing him. Had he calculated that in his head? He must have been some eccentric genius or something.

The following day, he was back right before closing.

"What's your name?" I asked.

He looked at me, puzzled, and said, "Tommy."

I had a feeling Tommy hadn't been asked anything about his life in a long time.

Tommy looked me in my eyes. He removed his dark glasses and stuffed them into the front pocket of his army green military jacket. His last name, embroidered above a 101st airborne patch from Vietnam, was Greene, Tommy Greene.

“Thanks for the coffee. I-I- just wanted to make sure you don't have to go digging through the machine that's all, so with tax, it's always the same.”

“It's not a problem. But I appreciate you thinking about it.”

“Yeah, no problem, um… what is your name?”

“Charlie.”

“No problem Charlie.”

He muttered with a half-smile, turning up the side of his unshaven face.

Tommy walked off. I returned to the smell of overused Canola oil, abused after frying bag after bag of tempura battered fries. My hallowed ground was a short order shack in a mall. Tommy had comrades that died. I only had one friend besides me who had seen a dead body. I was alone, finally, as I was at the end of every night. I heard the faint sound of other stores sliding their metal closures down to secure their products for the following day. Tomorrow, I would repeat this day again without any deviation from the normal operating procedures tomorrow.

The day was over, but in the mall you have no way of identifying the exact time without a watch. The architects and designers make sure that you can't discern the time of day for a reason. This intentional distraction from the earth's rotation around the sun tricks the average consumer into eating more and spending more on food and items they don't need.

I saw a subtle flicker in the eye of every customer. It was deep inside each soul, and it just barely burned, keeping the last remnants of each person's humanity alive. *Strip malls and plastic dolls,* I used to say. No one wanted to think they were made from a mold, but without any purpose or movement beyond the typical routine of the 'give and receive' motion that occurred at the register of every store, it was difficult to distinguish who was selling whom. They both looked like suckers, at least that's what P.T. Barnum always said, "There's a sucker born every minute, and two to take 'em."

I could smell the stench from the forty Philly cheese steaks I had served to these dismal remnants of humanity in the final rush at closing time. That moment when the smell overwhelmed my thoughts; I knew it was time to leave work.

It was the hour of night before true black sets in. A time when you suspect the possibilities left for you may still be endless. Where to go? What to go do? There was always some void, something missing, when I got off work. I wiped my hands with the soiled white terry cloth rag I had tucked in my apron.

Maybe my lack of direction was because I wasn't following my passion.

Passion was a question that pervaded society, especially in this city. The theatre kids who come came to Los Angeles to "make-it" were not following their passion. They were following fame. Fame was the attention they never had as a child. Fame was the undeserving encouragement their parents gave them to follow their dreams. Even if that meant working as a waiter or waitress, spending their tip money at social events networking, and snorting cocaine with obnoxious phonies who promised to cast them in their next productions.

As I walked out under the Los Angeles sky, the possibility of becoming something more than a short order cook, living in the valley, and resenting my dysfunctional family had occurred to me. Now I thought of the ancient ritual that occurs in India every twelve years, a festival called Kumbh Melah. Hundreds of thousands of people crossed the desert sands on their bare feet for hundreds of miles. The pain and agony was almost more than anyone could handle. At the end of the journey the people bathed in the Ganges River. It cleansed all of their pain, all of their suffering, and was a rebirth.

CHAPTER THREE

Violet sat motionless as she spoke, enveloped in a dark cloud of smoke from her clove cigarette. The essence of cinnamon and cardamom choked the life out of the air. With each inhale, her vocal chords let out a soft purr, producing a sound so faint, it was nearly inaudible to her psychiatrist.

“Charlie used to dream he too was in a kingdom,” Violet said.

“Did Charlie ever act out this role? Was there any indication he believed — I mean, truly believed — what he told you about this fictional story?”

Violet nodded, sending ashes tumbling from her cigarette.

“In the dream, there was a king who would enchant the people of all the surrounding villages with songs, as if he were the Pied Piper. In the end, the king gave his life for the castle. It was the only way for him to stay sane.”

“Did you ever picture yourself as the wife of the king?” the psychologist continued, struggling to interpret the imagery.

“No, I didn't. The King's wife he said was a humble Christian woman who was all poor and destitute, but a natural blonde beautiful girl. That's right; that's how he told the story. She was a peasant. Actually, more like a prostitute, if you ask me.” Violet's voice was flat. “The queen always did everything for everyone but herself — or so she wanted you to believe. She called herself the most generous woman in the entire city, but those who knew her saw her true colors soon enough. She longed to control the loyalty of others," Violet felt her frustration build. She decided it was time to talk about herself.

Violet wasn't crazy. And even if she was, it wasn't without reason. She had harbored rage for years after surviving a childhood filled with neglect. Throughout her life, Violet had convinced herself she was an object of male obsession. The reality was that she had only had a few relationships in the years between her teens and late 30s, none of which had matured into any sort of long-term partnership.

Her style was professional and alluring, fashionable blazers and capri pants yet all her clothing was made in low-end Asian factories that sent the garments en masse to eager U.S. franchises. Her body was compact at just over 5 feet. She had pale skin and dark hair that clung to her shoulders. She caked make-up on in layers, and accented it with maroon lipstick. Her protruding nose made her face both attractive and off-putting.

Violet attributed her last few years of success to the real estate boom. Nationwide, unqualified people were being approved for million-dollar loans. People like Violet, who were in the right place at the right time, capitalized on the faulty bureaucratic process. Violet had worked in the real estate business for 10 years, since the day she graduated from a lycée school in Cheviot Hills. The bulk of her experience came from working as an administrative assistant to a prominent developer who had swept up most of the commercial properties in Bel-Air and Beverly Hills during a buying frenzy in the late 1980s. She had been a reliable assistant, funneling money into different entities and doing as she was told with the speed and efficiency of a blitzkrieg. Execution was all part of the game, and if there was one thing she knew, it was not to ask questions. So, Violet kept her mouth shut and became second in command to the firm's two partners. The day she got her own license was the day she stepped out from under their wing and began to make real money.

Making that first substantial chunk of change transforms a person, for better or worse. In Violet's case, success made her the object of her sister's jealousy. Her twin was a more majestic version of Violet, with elongated features, a thinner frame and a more seductive personality. Her name was Christina, but the family always called her Destiny. They thought she had so much going for her she would make an amazing life for herself. Violet saw it differently and had always found the nickname fitting: Her sister was lost in fate, with no firm grasp of anything that involved responsibility. She was really only interested in sex and causing drama. Violet's success only upset the balance. And what was Destiny's response? She went and had a child with a man she wasn't married to. That gave the family another life to think about and yet another reason to ignore Violet's well-deserved success.

Underneath every silver-lined cloud of success was a tale of misery and self-deception, watering the soil below the money tree. For Violet, the story boiled down to excessive partying and drug use. Smoking crack and inhaling massive amounts of marijuana each night led to torturous 6 A.M. wakeup calls and unbearably long days in the real estate game. “That was my 20s,” she would always say, “I could never do that now.” Somehow, Violet made it through the wave of drugs and debauchery without ever feeling as though the behavior defined her.

But even now, Violet wasn't happy. Not having a companion who loved her chipped away at her confidence. The most unattractive element in a human being is desperation, and Violet wore desperation like a mink coat in the middle of a New Orleans summer. It was obvious to anyone of either sex that the aim of all her hard work was to attract a man who would love her.

The prison shrink stood up and walked to the window, where he twisted open the blinds. The light revealed the full features of Violet's face: A rim of sweat glistened on her upper lip, her expression a mixture of anger and denial. The psychiatrist looked closely at Violet, never suspecting narcissistic rage to be the cause of the inmate's actions.

He had long ago diagnosed her as bipolar. He had prescribed a cocktail of drugs with Lithium as the central binding force for an array of colorful pills. Violet took them willingly as an alternative to taking responsibility for her own pain. All she wanted was to get back to her house in the hills, eat a large, rare steak, floss her teeth, and pet her two old dogs.

The psychiatrist's voice interrupted Violet's thoughts.

"Is there anything else you can tell me about what happened?" he asked.

"No, I think everything I have to say they already took down in my statement for the police. And what's the point of saying more, when the media is distorting it to make me look like some crazy old rich bitch? I assure you I'm anything but that. He loved me. I know he did. You should see the letters he wrote me."
"I'm sure they show exactly that."

"What?" she asked.

"Love. I am sure they show that he loved you. But —"

"Love? It was more than love! We were soul mates. Just because I was 12 years older than him doesn't mean that our souls weren't connected," she said.

"I know, Violet," the psychiatrist said quietly.

"What do you know? All you know is what I tell you!"
"That is true to certain degree. If there is something else you want to share with me, then please do."

"Nothing else," she said. "Not today."

And with that, the session ended.

The psychiatric office was quiet again. The energy started to return to stagnant. Violet threw her hair over one shoulder, rested her chin against her chest and began to sob. Her arms wrapped around her body, as if she was holding an invisible child. Violet's tears soaked through the top of her white undershirt, revealing the outline of her bra. She threw the top of her jumpsuit back over her torso.

CHAPTER FOUR

December in Los Angeles is never chilly. It's not cold, and there's no snow. One year, a fluke storm hit Compton. The snowfall was such a shocker that the *Los Angeles Times* wrote an article called "L.A.'s Perfect Storm." They quoted a team of UCLA meteorologists attempting to explain the phenomena. These are the random, surreal events that occur in this twisted, magic mystery box.

The most authentic part of winter in Los Angeles is the wardrobe. People here wear elaborate jackets, flowing furs, scarves and gloves as though a blizzard is going to pop up miraculously over the Pacific Ocean and bury all of us. It was during one of these false L.A. winters that I met Violet.

Ventura Boulevard is a never-ending wasteland of retail boutiques and sushi restaurants. My oldest childhood friend, Tennessee Sterman, lived in a condo right off Winnetka. A little gated community filled with porn stars and actors (not that I'm putting them in the same category), just up the street from Mike Tyson's private boxing studio.

The side street was dark. I pulled up in my 1977 Chevy van—it looked like the *Scooby Doo* van, only blue, with a thin red-and-white pinstripe running alongside the diamond windows—and rang Tennessee.

"Hello? Yeah, I'll let you right in. Hold on," Tennessee said. I waited next to the small waterfall that flowed over the well-lighted building sign: Winnetka Willows. The van climbed the steep driveway, and I parked around the back of his place. Tennessee waved me into his condo. I could already make out the blurry image of an animal in his hands; whether it was a feline or canine was undetectable at this point, but it was an animal nonetheless, and I didn't remember him having a pet. I inched myself onto the edge of my cushiony captain's chair and strutted over to Tenny with an exaggerated, excited gait.

I think it had been almost 5 years since I'd seen him. We had known each other practically our entire lives, had been practically raised at each other's houses. His parents had divorced when he was young. His father was a successful real estate developer and his mother had been a supermodel. Apparently, there wasn't along-term relationship belief system in place back in those days. I think half the marriages of the 70s worked out, and the other half didn't. Either way, Tenny's parents were a product of a combination of luck, drugs and unexpected childbirths, following Hugh Hefner's example. As kids, we would spend weekends in the pool consuming quesadillas one after another, and washing them down with ice-cold cream soda at his father's premier property on Carbon beach in Malibu. The weekdays we spent at my house with my mom, or at his mother's place off Mulholland.

Tenny had been there for all of my experiences as a child. He saw my slow, awkward progression from innocent child to corrupt, ambitious teenager with an overzealous, creative mind attracted to trouble. My motto was, "What doesn't kill you only makes you stronger." If an authority figure said there was something you weren't supposed to do, I made sure to put it at the top of my list. Last time I saw Tenny, he reminded me that he still blames me for getting him hooked on cigarettes.

He had the same conviction talking about those cigarettes as he had when he told me about how he couldn't get any girls to go out with him. He finally settled on a girl named Sung-min, but everyone called her Stella. She seemed sweet at first. Stella controlled the shit out of him, and took advantage of Tenny's generosity. Always making him buy her the next Louis Vuitton bag or bracelet. He would talk to her on speakerphone, and just roll his eyes. Every once in a while when he got really mad and didn't want us to know what he was saying he would use one of the few Korean phrases he knew to incite fear in Stella. She would go quiet after that. Maybe it was a cultural thing, but whatever it was it worked.

I knew Stella was part of the reason we had not seen each other in so many years. She was always telling him how I was a bad influence and thought we were doing drugs together. It's true I had shipped him quite a few drugs to boarding school over the years. Tucking bags of hallucinogenic mushrooms or dried San Pedro cactus inside stuffed animals. He was always happy to get a care package that had some random Hollywood, CA address on it. Despite all the drug use and rehab we had maintained a pretty decent friendship.

Tenny seemed to be doing well. He had a nice condo and a foreign luxury automobile in a neighborhood filled with porn stars. If you were into that sort of thing, then you had to admit he was making a stake for himself here in the Valley.

"Hey, Charlie. Great to see you," he said. He grabbed me and gave me an awkward hug.

"It's been too long," I said.

"Yeah, fucking shitty times. Between my girl's bullshit and my Dad's cancer. But, well, we gotta keep trucking."
"That's for sure," I said. "Whose dog is that, man?"

Tenny lifted up the animal closer to the light near his door.

“Oh, it's not a dog. Come look,” he said. “I have these chinchillas that crap all over the place. They were me and my girlfriend's out in NY, but now that she's out of the picture — I got stuck with these things.”

There wasn't much to say in response to that. I couldn't stop staring at the weird furry animal Tenny was holding.

“Doesn't matter,” he continued. “I'm going to sell them to some poor fucker who hit me up after I posted an ad online. He'll probably make earmuffs out of them, but hell if I care. Once he sees how much crap these things produce, he won't want to keep ‘em around.” Tenny paused as he shifted the chinchilla in his arms. “Point is, I left her behind, but these little varmints were like her way of getting in the last big ‘fuck you.' “

“Damn, man. Well, it's good to see you regardless, and you look good.”

“No, I feel like garbage,” he said.

I thought back to our days downing quesadillas in hot tubs in Malibu. “Let's change that. You have any Mexican restaurants out here? I could go for a couple ‘margs' and whatever else they serve. Maybe some Carne Asada or something.”

“Umm… yeah. We have, like, an El Torito.”

“Man, that's it? No little hole in the wall spots.”

“Not as far as I know.”

He was still holding the chinchilla, and the smell was beginning to get to me.
“Fuck it. Let's go,” I said. “At least you know it's the same as all the rest.”

“Yeah, gotta love a franchise. Most of them are my anchor tenants, so I don't complain. Support your clients, I guess.”

“Alright, cool. You want to drive?” I asked.

“Let's take your van. That thing looks like fun — or funny. I think I've seen some of the porn stars that live here hump in those.”

“Hey, don't knock it ‘til you try it. That's my 70s rock ‘n' roll van.”

“Looks like a rapist van.”

“Funny, dude. Let's go.”

I thought we were heading out then, but Tenny insisted on locking the

Chinchillas in the bathroom and bolting the door. Tenny claimed they always escaped, but I didn't see how, unless they had some way of reaching under the door and using bolt cutters on that lock. Nonetheless, that was what he claimed, and, if the faint smell of animal shit mingling with the scent of cheap melon candles was any indication, he was telling the truth.

Once we were in the van, I saw Tenny swiveling in the blue cloth captain's chair. He was loving the freedom of the seventies in my all-American Chevy van, and I couldn't blame him He reclined, spun sideways and laughed.

"This is fuckin' great, man. I feel like I'm on Mars in a porno shoot back in the day. Shit man, it even smells like drugs and sex in here," he said.

"Thanks."

"No, seriously. You know when you walk into a tattoo parlor and it's clean, but you can feel the filth in there? It is like that, only soft, and there are a lot of sexy young girls in it. I like this," he said. "Make a left up there on Balboa."

"Alright, I'm telling you though, someday this van is gonna have, like, a plaque for the number of chicks I lure into this baby."

"Yeah, if they don't run off screaming 'rape' first."

"Very funny, dick," I said as I rolled up to the Mexican joint. "Same old mother fucker I remember, but I love you."

I turned sharply into the parking lot. The suspension was still a little busted, so the front of the van took a nosedive and sparks flew from the white painted metal bumper as if someone were shooting fireworks. Sparks flew onto the puke-green El Toritosign, and almost set the damn thing on fire.

"Let's do this."

A feeble old Hispanic man with an exaggerated Stromboli mustache escorted us, carrying slippery plastic menus smeared with last night's salsa and guacamole. He pointed toward the center table, which had a carved, fake wood backrest and a stapled pleather bench.

“What are you having to drink? A blue Cadillac?” I asked Tenny.

He looked at me confused. “What the hell is a blue Cadillac?”

I looked at him long and hard to call his bluff. I was sure he was pulling my chain. “Dude, you grew up eating quesadillas in Southern California, which has more Mexican restaurants than Mexico, and you don't know what a fucking blue Cadillac is? It's like your life went on pause when we stopped hanging out.”

It didn't take any more convincing. We ordered blue Cadillacs and started drinking, pounding the tableside guacamole. I was so excited to be with Tenny again and reminisce. Whenever we got together we felt like a couple of delinquents without any responsibilities. We just wanted to party. I pictured the amount of cocaine we were going to do later that night. Just as I successfully repressed the wild urge to do a few bumps of coke right then and there, we wrapped up our third round of blue Cadillac margaritas.

“So what are you thinking about doing later?”

“Nada mucho, my friend. I'm just here to hang out with you. Life has been a little dodgy lately, but I mean I'm down to party… you know me!” I said.

“Yeah, well let me call this girl I've been hanging out with and see what she's doing.” He drank the last few drops of his margarita.

"Is that the older girl you've been seeing?"

"Not, like, seeing her, dude. She used to work for my father. She's pretty crazy, but she has a lot of parties at her house."

"Is that where you were the other night when you called me? It sounded pretty fuckin' crazy."

"Yep. You would've have liked it. A lot of weirdoes, and like all older. There was this one, like, washed-up musician rocker dude. I gave him your number because I thought you should be the one talking to him," Tenny said.

"Are you serious?" I asked.

"Hey, I didn't understand what the fuck he was talking about, but I knew you would."

"Thanks, I guess."

Days later, I received an hour-long phone call from an overweight, dubious character with false promises of record deals by big-named guys in the business. He was a telesales rep by day, rock producer by night, and was still clinging to the shredded pages of rock 'n' roll history. So I suppose there should have been no thanks involved in having this card passed my way. I would have preferred a plate of $4.00 fried chicken and gravy from Denny's off Route 40, with a heart attack attached for ninety-two cents extra.

But the phone call with the washed-up rocker didn't much matter at this point. Tenny had convinced me that this party would be a good time — not that I needed much persuading to roll into some high-rise condo in Beverly Hills for a party. We scrambled outside into the cold Valley air. Once in the van, it was time for us to put on some jams.

"Hmmm. How does The Rolling Stones sound?" I asked, ready for some classic rock.

As soon as I popped in the CD, an error message came up on the screen.

"Fuck!" I shouted at the radio. I had purchased it from some underground shop downtown that was really just a warehouse of stolen property. Tenny took another disk out.

"Play this," he said with a grin from ear to ear. Without question, I popped in his disk and threw the scratched Stones CD out of the window.

Tom Petty's voice filled the car. I should've known; Tenny loved that one Heartbreakers song. What the hell was it called? They've been overplaying on the radio for decades, but I always forgot the title. Tenny scrolled through each track, waiting to hear the recognizable chorus kick in. "No, I won't back down," it started. He sang it over and over again. I didn't have the heart to change the song, and he wouldn't shut up, so I joined in.

I could feel we were on a path to a dark place, but I ignored the danger signs and proceeded down the 405 freeway.

We arrived at a white high-rise in the middle of the Wilshire corridor in Westwood. So it wasn't Beverly Hills, I thought. Oh well, Beverly Hills adjacent was close enough. In California, people always describe the crappier area as “adjacent” to a nicer one.

I pulled past the entrance to the building just off Warner Avenue and drove by slowly, scouting the parking situation. I figured they probably had a valet service, but it was too risky given that the van smelled of drugs. Besides, they probably wouldn't figure out how to get the van into gear, anyway. The shifter was a little temperamental and without the proper technique, one would fail miserably. Yes, it was too risky, and I could already see the overweight doorman eyeing the van like we were contemplating robbery. I pulled down a small side street and parked under a tree. The blue metal doors creaked as we got out of the car.

The warm air in the lobby felt good around my torso. The security guard behind the desk muttered something to Tenny, who quickly gave him a back-story that convinced him to let us pass. The metaphorical bridge lowered and we walked to a second set of stainless steel elevators in the North tower.

“So what's the deal with this place, anyway?” I asked when we were in the elevator.

“I don't know. But the chick throws crazy parties, and her friends are pretty strange. I told you about that one weirdo.”

“Yeah. Great,” I said.

“This guy is a producer for television shows, like those reality shows where they make people do things they are afraid of, or live on an island with nothing. I forget the name, but he lives in the penthouse here, so he isn't doing bad."

When the elevator door opened, all I saw were a lot of olderpeople. I didn't recognize a single face, but I figured if I owned a television set, I might have had a clue. A stooge of a guy came over to greet us, and some skinny, half-naked cocaine whore wearing red sequins offered her warmest of welcomes. "I'm Destiny," She said, almost drooling on herself. It was a horrible sight, but I was somewhat intrigued. It was a decent way to start a party that I had low expectations for.

I got ready for the woman to get on her knees and kick-off our royal entrance properly. Instead, a short, plump, dark-haired man pulled her away. We found out later that the man, Trevor, was her quasi-husband. After Trevor yanked his girl into another room, a curly, black-haired guy introduced himself as Adam Lonnergan. Apparently, he was the producer and this was his penthouse. (A note of advice: always make sure you're overly pleasant to the host. He will be the one to determine if you get thrown out later in the evening for doing something excessively stupid or trying to have sex with someone's girlfriend.)

In the case of this host, I charmed him by offering him a flask I had been keeping in my coat. Yeah, I know what you're thinking — a little déclassé of me. But the shocking thing was that the peace offering was accepted. We bonded over slugs of 18-year-old Macallan.

Tenny and I were standing against a long white wall that led to the living room. The space was decorated with a black iron birdcage, but I didn't notice anything living inside of it. I once had a friend who kept his younger sister's poodle inside that kind of cage. I also know a couple strippers who would have fit inside this one, which had to have been about five feet tall. I was fascinated by the thing, but I kept walking into the living room.

The whisky in my blood was warming my brain so that every light I saw glowed. My tongue was unprepared to phrase sentences properly, but I wasn't afraid. I welcomed discomfort. After all, I was the fountain of youth in the middle of all these old folks. My vintage tan jacket and silver flask were the youngest things in the room. They glowed like a beacon attracting attention from anyone around.

After I had been sitting for what felt like hours admiring my own youth relative to the rest of a party, a woman wearing a fancy silver turtleneck walked up to me.

"We meet at last. Tenny has told me all about you. I feel like I've known you forever."

I looked at her, puzzled. "Is that right?"

So this was Violet, the party animal. Tenny had told me about all the crazy shindigs she hosted at her house, but this did not look like a woman who partied hard. Maybe she had partied a little too much the night before, but the sense I got from her was that she was a mature chick with a superiority complex. It must have been her age. She looked about 35. Her makeup was thick and her lips were coated in dark maroon lipstick. I couldn't look at her anymore, so I let my eyes travel to the balcony and through the large panels of glass that let the light of the city filter in.

Out on the deck, pockets of people were ingrained in meaningless conversations, self-obsessed and not looking for any new friends. I pulled a smoke out from my pocket and found a joint buried next to it. I figured one comes before the other, so I went for the joint first. I sensed half the guests downwind were intrigued, longing to take a puff and restore their childhood sense of wonder. The other half were disgusted by my juvenile habits.

"Have some to spare?" This guy was down to smoke, but he seemed so disconnected from the scene, he might as well have called it grass.

Oh well. I figured I'd throw the poor guy a bone.

"Sure, I always have enough to go around."]

I could not escape my own curiosity about the producer, and thought my new smoking buddy might know something. "So who is this guy?" I asked.

I was enjoying this view that thanks to some TV show that people across the country salivated over stupidly. The guy didn't say much, so I posed the question to the small group of people nearby.

"What type of shows does this guy make?" I asked.

"He does a lot of the big reality shows. I think the last one he produced was *Survivor*. I'm sure you've heard of that one," said an Asian girl.

I nodded my head. "Oh, sure that's a big one."

I had no idea what she was talking about.

I decided to conceal the fact that I didn't even own a TV. With this group, it wouldn't matter that I thought the whole television enterprise was diabolical. The typical ‘oohs' and ‘aaahs' I get when I put that card on the table weren't worth the energy. I let the city lights soak into my red eyes and wondered how to get out of the conversation I had started.

I was fading fast, and fortunately the night was beginning to wear down. I went back into the living room. There were only a couple strangers left. As I neared the finish line to this indigenous journey through the lower echelon of Hollywood culture, I was sideswiped by Violet in her silver turtleneck again. She approached with vigilance, and a motive I was too oblivious to uncover in the brief. “*Au revoir*,” Tenny said as the two of us tried to exit. I felt her shadow behind us. Then came the breathing. Tenny and I turned simultaneously, like clown heads in a 1950s funhouse, to see her on a collision course with us. I hadn't picked up on any kind of bond during the broken conversation I had witnessed between them earlier. Apparently, they were better friends than I had thought.

The back-story was that she had worked for Tenny's father 10 years ago and had since gone on to start her own business in the same industry. I'm not sure if that was real estate, because given the crowd at the party, I assumed she posed that she ran some small production company. I could picture her manipulating people into executing the vision of a subpar director from the Northeast. I looked at the layer of crème makeup and deep maroon lipstick again. They were a dead giveaway that she was nearing the big 4-0.

I was trying to figure out exactly how old she was when she started interrogating me.

Where do you live?"

I decided to joke with her.

"I live in my van."

She was taken aback, but not thrown off. "Yeah right, I'm sure you have an inheritance or something."

I couldn't believe it. Yet another jaded woman thinking I was loaded and couldn't possibly live in a van. Her prodding was a litmus test for dating in this godforsaken city. She wanted to find out my housing situation, my car, my bloodline, and my whole genetic makeup to judge whether I was worth breeding with or just good arm candy. I didn't want to acknowledge her interrogation, but for some reason, I gave her answers, anyway. My honesty left me naked. The elevator doors opened abruptly, and we got out simultaneously.

The building's elaborate trellis made our existence feel finite as we exited the party. I sighed as the air touched my face, thanking some imaginary God for that coolness. When I'm around people, I can almost smell their sweat. I can feel it, too: that heat raises the temperature of the local atmosphere by at least 10 degrees.

I thought Tenny and I had made it out unscathed. That is, until Violet gently ripped into my back with her nails.

"So do you guys need a ride to your car?" she asked, knowing we had not parked with the valet.

"Oh, no, it's ok," I said. "Thanks, but my van is right around the corner."

“Yeah, right,” she said. “I forgot you drive a van.” She winked.

Tenny answered in his Johnny Carson voice. “Yeah, a 70s rapist van. I love it.”

She laughed, intrigued, but disbelieving. I'm not sure what compelled me to ask her name again, but I did. I could tell the gesture made her feel flattered.

“Violet,” she said, “But you already knew that.”

There was only one thing left to do: escape her piercing stare. Her words seemed to drag on and she wasn't moving her mouth. Tenny and I said our goodbyes and walked quickly up the stale Westwood corridor. Around the corner, I spotted a Sycamore I hadn't noticed before. Its branches clung to the roof of my car, camouflaging its true scale. As we were climbing in, we saw the lights of another car passing in the distance. The pale glow of the halogen beams glided over us, pausing as if a foreign object had crossed in front of its eyes.

We heard a cackle. I looked up and couldn't believe what I was seeing. Sure enough, it was Violet again. I can only assume she was stalking us because she didn't believe what Tenny was saying about my car. Either that or, as my instincts told me, she wanted to know the truth about me. I gave her a polite wave, and muttered something along the lines of, “See, I was telling the truth.” She laughed again, this time slightly subdued as she continued driving up into the hills of glitzy Bel-Air.

The early morning air crept into the windows of the van as we drove back to the valley, home to far less luxurious hills than the ones beckoning Violet. Tenny and I said goodbye as if we were in a dream state, nodding and confirming that this experience we shared was actually reality. I had no idea when Tenny and I would see each other again; my only hope was that it wouldn't be too long.

The time that had passed between our visits was filled with bullshit and memories that left a barrier to our friendship. We entered each other's lives again that night for a purpose, but we were completely unaware of what it was. All I know is that it's in human nature to follow your heart to destiny, whether you're aware of it or not. Maybe it's just my romantic mind, but Tenny had lost his father, and I had lost pretty much everyone I loved except my mother. We shared a bond. It was the look of knowing we had this deep sense of sorrow, a hole that would never be filled.

"It better not be another chunk of years before I see you again," I said, nodding to reaffirm that I was speaking the truth.

"It won't." Tenny's response was completely sincere, but I knew he would never be able to live up to that commitment, at least not for some time. He had a ton of paperwork to deal with after his dad's passing, and was leaving back to NY in a few days. I gave him a hug and slid away. I shook his hand again and hit him on the left shoulder. I walked back to the dark parking lot and into my van.

I reclined in the captain's chair and slid the purple velvet curtain to cover the back seats and bed. I started the engine, gave the shifter a shimmy to slip it into gear, and left the parking lot. Then it was back to Ventura Boulevard and the wasteland of strip malls that led back to civilization. Los Angeles spread out around me, filled with dull-colored office buildings, half-rented apartment buildings, and overcrowded schools. The entire city was illuminated by a cosmic mass of fluorescent fast food signs. I always had a strong feeling that I should leave, pack up and see the world. But every time I got close to leaving, I realized I was stuck in the perverse reality of Los Angeles. No one ever gets out of Los Angeles without sacrificing something.

CHAPTER FIVE

Even working two jobs, I barely had enough money to pay for an apartment in this hellhole. I had moved in temporarily with my mother in Reseda, in her house on Etiwanda Street. She was alone, and I knew she wouldn't mind having me around. Plus, between the pills and television, I knew the actual time I spent talking to her would be minimal.

Everything was temporary in this city. It didn't make sense to plant your feet and get a place of your own when half your money went to rent and the other half went to food and gas. The budget here was bulging, and the State had no money. Literally, no money. A friend of mine who was still unemployed—his college degree was in economics from USC—told me once that California, under its Constitution, had to stay out of bankruptcy by whatever means necessary, even if that meant taxing the hell out of its residents, or cooking up schemes like we were in a drought.

I woke up buried in my boyhood comforter, covered in a pattern of 1970s –era trucks. In the La-Z-Boy next to my bed, my mother slept, a best-selling romance novel still in her hands. She had always loved to watch me fall asleep, especially after my father left us. Even before he was always away traveling to a city on the other side of the U.S. or the world. My mother's only love stories were in the fairy tales she read. My father was long gone, so she only had me to watch over now. When I looked at her, it was as if I had the power to read her thoughts.

My sister died four years ago in a car accident. She wasn't riding in the car. She was running to catch the bus to school and got hit.

She was everything to me. After her death, time disintegrated. Each second pulsed through my body in passing immobility: my lungs ceased to expand and I curled like a contortionist in the circus of my own dreadful reality. I was a captive to this pain and the memory. All I wanted was for death to inject me with a taste of its poison. Take me instead. Death would be less mentally traumatic than the wretchedness that swelled inside my heart after losing Wendy.

My feet did not want to work. The tendons in them seemed warped. My toes struggled to fan out on the floor like they did every other morning. Last night, I had one too many margaritas. Then again, I'd had too many margaritas every day last week. I looked over at a stack of bills. They seemed like nothing in comparison to the pain in my stomach and the sadness I felt. My lack of money to pay back my college debt wore heavy anyway, and anchored me with monthly payments to my credit union. The debt stared at me with those awful black eyes, the way TV captivated my mother's soul. I did not let it get me down. I just pictured the margaritas; that unnatural green serum that soaked my blood with sugar had always numbed me out pretty good. And now, just the thought of it allowed me to get up and move a few feet down the hallway and drag myself into the shower.

The showerhead poured cold water over my skin. We probably forgot to pay the gas bill again. I didn't care. I just needed to rinse off the tequila smell. My dreams last night had left me sweaty. The white bar of soap was covered in hair, but I used it anyway. It scraped against my skin, wiping the traces of alcohol from my body. Green apple shampoo squirted out of the bottle and into my hand. I skipped this part of the process most days to avoid the extra 10 minutes; especially when the water was ice cold. Sure, it was nice to smell like a citrus lollipop for the next couple hours, but then again, no one was going to notice.

I gripped the cheap linoleum tile with my feet to stop myself from slipping and cracking my head open on the fogged glass. I removed my toothbrush from its cup, its worn orange-and-white bristles were dull. I scrubbed the deck of my mouth, scraping away the sour taste of tequila and lime. I staggered out of the bathroom and into the hallway — my equilibrium shifted, and my shoulder brushed the wall. My mother emerged from her chair. "She must be hungry," I thought. I hadn't even made it to my room yet when my mother called out to me.

"Honey, did you pick up the salami I wanted from the grocery store?"

"No," I said quietly. I knew she was going to be disappointed: the salami was a staple of her TV diet.

Then, I remembered the leftover Mexican from the night before. "There are a couple of Carne Asada tacos in the fridge, Ma."

"Oh, thank you, Charlie. That will be my lunch for the day."

I knew that wouldn't be lunch in its entirety. Sadly, my mother had been gaining weight at an exponential rate since my father left us. It was uncontrollable. At first I thought it was a symptom of her depression, but lately I've been realizing that her addiction to eating that had taken over as an independent entity.

There were all kinds of diet programs on that television she was glued to. She used to order them, back when we had some money left over from my father, but with every diet, she seemed to gain more weight. She wasn't getting any thinner. My mother was content consuming a variety of prepackaged foods throughout the day.

It was nearing 9 A.M., so I figured it was about time to head over to the mall for work. That meant putting on my acid-washed jeans, converse hi-tops and white shirt with a nearly unnoticeable stain from last night. I grabbed a bottle of Brogruire's chocolate milk from the fridge and took a swig. *This stuff is either the perfect cure for a hangover, or it'll make you throw up. Either way you'll feel better*, I thought. I walked out the door.

“Bye, Ma! See you later.”

My mother hardly looked up from the television. The show she was watching must have been about psychic mediums. Those shows really drew her in. I never believed that psychic mumbo jumbo. The majority of those commercial actors were just making money from other people's misery. How were they going to tell me what my dead relatives were saying? Sure, I believed the soul existed eternally, but c'mon! Everything on TV was a hoax.

I used to love magic as a kid. I suppose it was because it allowed you to produce something that appeared real to the audience but that the magician knew was false. I loved Houdini, too. He was another one of my idols growing up. But think about it: His death was caused by a punch in the stomach. A young, jealous meathead hit him in the sternum and he died. The small hole in the solar plexus is also what the martial artists in the East refer to as the spot for the ‘death touch'. I wondered if they were talking about that on the show my mother was watching. *Ha! I doubt it.* I wished I could have given the death touch to that TV instead.

I ducked out of the apartment and went down the stucco-lined hallway. As I dragged my palm against the wall leading to the garage, flakes of paint chipped off into my hand. I saw a note on my car and I thought it must be one of our whiny neighbors complaining about my parking job. I had left the van slightly sticking out because the nova was up on cinder blocks. I had to take a look at the undercarriage; the right rear differential seemed off.

I unfolded the piece of paper and saw a woman's handwriting. It was in script, which I thought showed some form of higher education.

You are so funny. I really didn't believe you about your van; that turned out to be a pleasant surprise. I really want to hang out with you guys again, and by "you guys," I mean "you." I am having a party next week, and I hope you will come. Here is my address: 1719 Stone Canyon Bel-Air, CA. Call me if you want to hang before: 310.224.6677.

Oh, fancy, I thought. I felt flattered, but unimpressed. After that, I didn't give the letter much thought.

I got in the van and convinced myself to skip work today to hang out with an old friend.

CHAPTER SIX

Cindy Walker was in town from New York. I didn't get to see her often. She was a staff photographer for *Vogue*, but that wasn't what impressed me about her. I liked her photography and her spirit. We had gone to high school together, but in a school of over a thousand in each grade, you didn't really get to know anyone unless they were in one of your classes. I got to know Cindy when she asked me to be in one of her photo projects eight years ago. The shoot was avant-garde and sexually explicit. Typically, I would have made a move on her, but I had a girlfriend at the time. I was young, but I believed in loyalty.

Despite my resistance, Cindy was aggressive with her camera lens and rubbed white paint all over my body, including my genitals. But we never touched each other beyond the setup for the shoot, and I suppose that's why we stayed friends. Once you lie naked with someone and neither person instigates a sexually perverse gesture, it's pretty safe to say they can be trusted.

We bonded over our lack of sexual attraction toward each other, sharing pie and burgers together at Polly's Pies, a restaurant in Santa Monica that went out of business, thanks to the yuppies who had moved in and sent the rents sky-high. Polly's had a pecan pie that was world class, and their lemon meringue was so fluffy and buoyant it could have floated down a river. With Polly's shutdown, we had to resort to The Apple Pan, which was a trusted Los Angeles landmark in its own right. The place had been deemed historic some time ago, and since then, had been passed down through several generations. A lovely blonde woman named Bunny ran it now. She was great, always sweet and welcoming —

if she happened to be around. The place cranked people in an out like an old Ford assembly line. "This is a serious machine!" I would say every time I entered the holy burger house.

I took Sepulveda Blvd over the hill from the valley, as the 405 freeway looked like a shooting gallery full of parked cars. Sepulveda is a windy road that connects the two sides of Los Angeles, and for some reason no one ever drives on it. I used to wonder why. I took the road with my mom countless times when I was a kid traveling to see some of my friends who lived in the affluent neighborhoods on the Westside. There were always a few accidents on Sepulveda, an ambulance with its lights on, or one driving down the road in anticipation of what was to come. That didn't seem so bad; you got that on the freeways, too. I never really thought a thing of it. That all changed the day I saw a bloody corpse slip off a stretcher on Sepulveda Blvd. That was the day I decided people were better off not driving this road of horrors. But for some reason, I took it today, anyway.

Cindy stayed with her mother whenever she came to town. Her mother had lived alone in Santa Monica on 11th street since their old St. Bernard mountain dog, Claudia, died years ago. Pulling up to the craftsman house with blue trim and the white picket fence, I noticed the neighbor's daughter walking a dog. She was a petite blonde with a serious eating disorder. I had already seen her naked skeleton in a black & white photo series Cindy had taken years ago. I could almost use my X-ray eyes to picture her skinny pelvis and breasts with the small light pink nipples. I thought it must have been illegal to take those photos, but I guess in the name of art…

My thoughts were interrupted by a gardener who decided to use his leaf blower at full force right beside my van window. Debris spurted into my front seat, but for some reason, I wasn't angry.

I turned off the engine and walked to the gate with a skip in my step, still somewhat aroused and creeped out by the images that had flashed through my mind earlier. I closed the white gate behind me, fastening the broken metal latch before knocking on the front door. Cindy gave me a big hug and a polite kiss as if to convince me she really had missed me. I walked in, admiring the photo on the wall from Cindy's 'Beaches in France' series. Aside from the photos, the décor was pretty drab. I could smell chocolate chip cookies, which provided a much-needed contrast to the house's grim interior. Cindy's mother gave me a frigid hello and I gave her a kiss on the cheek. She offered me a cookie, but at this point I was still holding the chocolate milk in my throat. It sure would make a chocolaty puke mess if I let go at this point, I thought as I declined the cookie and went with Cindy to her childhood bedroom so she could grab her sweater.

I looked at the picture of her father and three older brothers she kept on her dresser. Her father left her mother when Cindy and her brothers were still young, but that was nothing new. Practically everyone I knew in this city had the same story: They came from a one-parent home, and were shuffled between the mom and dad if they were lucky enough to have both living in the same city, or if they were unlucky enough to have both parents battling for their favoritism. I didn't ask Cindy which was the case with her.

We pulled up to The Apple Pan and went around back to find parking. It was a tiny lot, but there always seemed to be a spot if you went during off-hours. Maybe the lot operated on the same philosophy as inside the restaurant: get them their burger, and get them out of the seat, a tradition ingrained in the joint's well-paid staff.

As soon as we walked in, there was Cindy, camera in hand, as though it was 1950 and this was a real drive-in. But then again, I had on my Ray-Ban glasses, so it seemed appropriate. We took a few photos outside by the main sign. I tried to imagine what kind of shots she would get once we actually started to eat those sloppy burgers. Picture a clown applying his makeup before a show in a public restroom; that's how the sauce would get painted around our lips.

We walked in through the screen doors, an image that brought back strange memories of eating at a diner with my mom in the valley. I think that's when I said my first word, "Shit." Cindy and I waited a couple minutes for a table. An obese man and woman vacated two seats near the rear of the diner. We stampeded over, next in line and eager to beat out the other people waiting at the back of the restaurant. Seated on the uncomfortable stools, we got down to business.

"So what's going on with you?" she said. "You totally ditched me the other day, but that's alright."

"Well, there's a story behind it," I said.

"There always is."

I relived the sequence of events at the party, telling Cindy about the older woman named Violet who would not leave me alone.

I could not tell if she believed my story. In fact, I'm pretty sure the majority of the time; Cindy doesn't believe a word I say. Cindy had never really experienced anything traumatic or quasi-interesting growing up in the Westside. The closest she had ever come to adventure were her family vacations in Europe. The first time I admitted I had been arrested when I was 13, she looked at me like I had disrupted a religious ceremony. Regardless of our differences, our conflicting universes colluded at some point.

I told Cindy about the note, and how Violet had found my apartment and somehow navigated her way over the gate to leave the note on my van.

“She left it on the van!” Cindy said, shocked.

“Of course. She doesn't know I have other cars I'm restoring, especially not the Nova. I mean, I hope not. She's already in way too deep. And now I have to make a painful confession: The other night when I blew you off, it was for this mysterious older beast of burden with painted lips and the sweet smell of Chanel perfume.”

“Oh no. What did you do? Wait, don't tell me,” she said.

“I didn't have sex with her, if that's what you're implying.”

Typically denying it means I did have sex with the girl, and Cindy knew my sarcastic tongue well. But this time, at least, I was straight-shooting.

“Her car was a death trap, but you know me. I'm always up for the experience.”

“Yeah, I know you,” she said.

“Well, tell me the full story then. Are you going to make it out alive from this one? This woman sounds like major stalker material,” Cindy said.

“Stalker material.” I repeated.

The words bounced around inside of my head for a few moments. I had no idea if Cindy was right, or whether I should take her warning as an enticement or a red flag. In the moment of the pursuit, it all feels new. The normal reluctance seems to die somewhere between the words "hello" and the first time you have sex. I didn't know how to answer her, so I just cocked my head and smiled.

CHAPTER SEVEN

I decided to call the number 310.224.6677. I wasn't sure what to expect, or why I did it, but I did.

"I knew you would call," she said.

Her voice started me. "Yeah, hey what's going on?"

"We're going out tonight. You are coming."

"I am?"

"It'll be fun. I know where you live. I'll pick you up in an hour. Be outside." She hung up the phone.

I liked a woman to take charge, but this was over the top. I decided to comply with her demands anyway.

Violet picked me up in her gold Lincoln Navigator SUV with her friend Steven in the back seat, and drove us to the Malibu Inn. The night was as frail as the ninety pounds of skin sagging gracefully over Violet's bones. At every stoplight, the rear view mirror reflected the ocean. The air poured in through the open windows and over me. Salt fragments collected on the blond hairs of my arm. The expanse of it all, and the mission to Malibu appeared to be the result of a vast miscommunication. Somehow, I had actually volunteered for it.

“Here, listen to this.” Steven, the balding, overweight out of work actor wannabe muttered from the front seat as he turned the song up on the radio. I didn't trust him.

Violet finally spoke. “So what do you want to do?”

“Let's just park over there,” Steven said.

We spotted a Mexican man in a red vest holding a stack of one-dollar bills in his hand. We pulled forward. Violet passed a couple of dollars to him. He had obviously had too much to drink, because he could not correctly count out her change. At least, I assumed this was the reason. Why else wouldn't he be able to count out eleven dollars when it was his job to count out small change?

When we parked, Violet and Steven laid out a few lines of relatively decent cocaine. The smell of ether and ammonia filled the car. They offered the tray to me and I declined, I needed to stay alert.

I entered the Inn and walked past the sepia photographs of the old Malibu pier. Surveying the landscape of the bar, I knew I wasn't in the right place. I loved the Malibu Inn growing up, but the crowd had changed.

“Are you hungry?” Violet asked me. That's pretty considerate I thought, considering she had just snorted a couple lines of coke. The last thing I would be thinking about is food. I nodded, eager to leave and go anywhere else. On our way out, her friend, Steven, called out that he wanted to go with us. She bribed him with a bag of blow. “That'll keep him busy.”

We stepped out onto the dimly lit street and back through the makeshift parking lot where the attendant had been only moments before.

We drove together in the darkness up PCH and headed to Cross Creek. We stopped at a restaurant tucked one side of the strip mall. One of my oldest rules is never to trust food from a strip mall. It had evolved from a suspicion I'd developed as a child that franchise restaurants were out to poison people who couldn't afford the luxury of fine dining. I should have listened to my instinct right then, but I walked right in. A dark-haired local Malibu rancher's daughter greeted us with what looked like a cum stain on her dress.

I didn't know then that she was the owner's daughter. I also didn't know that a few minutes before, her boyfriend had broken up with her in the parking lot and then proceeded to fuck her brains out. What she didn't know, on the other hand, was that she was now pregnant, and her ex-boyfriend was leaving the next day with her best friend since kindergarten. They would move to Klamath Falls, Oregon, where he would deal methamphetamine. Don't ask how I knew this, but Malibu was a small community and word always made its way all the way to the Valley. The Valley was a small place growing up, a microcosm of Los Angeles, and we kept tabs on all the attractive girls in our neighborhood.

We ordered Cadillac margaritas She demanded that one of the waiters dim the lights. The control she exerted over the waiter was attractive; although, the lighting never changed. I think, subconsciously, all men want to be dominated by women. The reason most men wind up abusing women verbally or physically is that they are afraid to admit it. Meanwhile, those who do submit feel violated. “I agree, it would make this place feel a lot better with the lights lower; especially, after a couple tequilas.”

“Yeah, do a shot,” she insisted. She snapped her fingers and over came one of the waiters. He was already intimidated by her, so he did not hesitate to come to her beckon call. “Yes ma'am?” He said, his accent getting in the way of the ma'am part making him sound like he was from Texas not Mexico. “He needs a shot. Get him some Patron silver and a few limes.” She waved her fingers for the waiter to get on with his task. He bee lined it to the bar, didn't even stop when another diner tried to flag him down. The tequila was back in no time, and the waiter put down the shots. “I didn't want one!” Violet said. “It's on the house misses.” The waiter placed it in front of her. “I don't want it, you have to do it.” She pointed at me in the face. A rude gesture, but since she was insisting I imbibe more tequila I complied willingly. After the second shot I started to feel a little nauseous. The only thing to stave off the drunkenness was to gluttonously consume the food.

“This is fun. Glad we got out of that hell hole, now I can look at you,” she said.

I just nodded, acknowledging her failed pass at me. It was hollow, but the attempt was there. We continued to make small talk.

Violet snapped her finger at another waitress. I was uncomfortable with the rude gesture, but I let it slide, as her intention seemed to get us more alcohol. In addition to the extra-large margaritas in blue glasses, she added two more shots of tequila to the order. This moment was the tipping point, and the cocaine in her bloodstream gave her an unfair advantage. There was no way to win a drinking contest with someone who had been snorting cocaine. Even if the other person was relatively high and drunk, they would appear coherent without displaying their true motives.

The check came. She paid. I was shocked. That's definitely not something that happens in LA very often. Why had this woman taken the check? Did she think I was for sale? I excused myself to go to the bathroom.

The bathroom was covered with photographs of Mexican Haciendas. One photo made me think of my Uncle Leonardo, a real *vaquero*. He had been raised in a family of six in Oaxaca. He rode a horse named La Luna. She was larger than life, and my Uncle was the only one who could ride her. The taste of tamales from my cousin's wedding in Mexico City filled my mouth for a moment, before the memories were washed away by the smells wafting from the bathroom. My stomach started to hurt from the few bites of the tacos I ordered. I could hear it bubbling up inside and I wasn't sure now was a good time or place to give in to the growling.

Staggering out of the bathroom like I was the *vaquero* riding La Luna I could hardly recall where our table was. From across the room, Violet's fingers, adorned in heavy gold and diamonds, waved me back to the table. I angled my body in her direction, and proceeded with extreme caution, trying not to fall.

"So, Steven called me. I hate to say it, but we have to pick him up on the way back into town," she said.

"Okay. That's fine with me." As much as I didn't like Steven, any extra company would ease my nerves.

"Are you drunk?" She asked me.

"Just kind of buzzed." I was pretty wasted and didn't want to appear immature.

“We'll get you drunk by the end of the night. Don't worry.”

Her phone started ringing. She answered it on speaker and put her finger up to her mouth gesturing me to be quiet.

“What is it?” She said rudely.

The voice on the other end was softer, but sounded raspy and similar to Violet's.

“I am not coming tonight,” She said.

“I figured you would flake.” There was a long pause.

“He beat me.”

“What the hell! What are you talking about?”

“He said I cheated on him and he hit me,” The voice said.

That motherfucker. I will kill him.” Violet started to get enraged.

“It was in front of Jason,” she continued.

“Is he ok? God that asshole.”

“Yeah, he's fine just locked himself in his room.”

“I can't talk right now. I have to call you back.”

They hung up. Violet was silent. She looked at me and then adjusted the rearview mirror.

"That's my twin sister. She's all fucked up."

"I think I met her at that party."

"What party?"

"At your producer friend's house. The one where we met."

"Oh yeah. She was there. Probably whoring around then too."

"I'm sure you'll get to see her again at some point. Just ignore her, whatever she says. She's crazy. And she will probably try and fuck you."

I didn't know how to respond so I just stayed silent. That was the last we talked about her sister.

We got in the car and rode back to the Malibu Inn, mostly in silence. Violet raced down the street causing the tequila's effects to amplify my disorientation. Where was I and what the hell was I doing?

"Steven better be ready. I'm not waiting. "

"There he is." I pointed to where Steven was standing under an overhang.

The sky over the Pacific Ocean was red as we drove back toward town. The combination of liquor and the overly sweet margarita mix swirled in the crevices of my brain. Some of the sticky concoction must have leaked, because the world shifted, moving sideways. I almost vomited.

I interrupted Steven and Violet's conversation.

"Does anyone see the cosmic red trails across the sky?"

They looked at me with disbelief. I wondered why. Sure, my description wasn't that of an acid cult leader like Tim Leary, but that's what I saw.

Violet pretended to understand what I said. "I feel like I am on acid when I look at the colors."

"Yeah like trails," Steven followed up.

I realized that the silver line of dust that reflected the red in the sky was caused by missile testing. The military was conducting tests about 5 miles off the coast of Santa Monica. If they only knew the toxicity dropping into the water and onto the flesh of millions of beachgoers every weekend in the bay. Surely some city council do-gooder would raise an objection, at least once.

I was out of breath from thinking about all the people who would contract an illness from the water. *Cancer is probably the least of their worries*, I thought.

The thought of death crossed my mind, but only for a moment. In Los Angeles, knowing someone who died was a medal of honor. For some reason, few people even believed dying was possible in this city. The fountain of youth flowed so freely that no one ever talked about lying down in the earth forever.

I had the badge. It was tattooed on me after my sister died. What it netted me wasn't sympathy, exactly. Only a nod, the flutter of the eyelashes, acknowledgement from those who had come face-to-face with seemingly elusive death.

You rarely saw the eyes of those who had felt rigor mortis beneath their palms, on the forehead of their friends, family members and loved ones. But every so often you met someone who gave you a certain look, like a secret code shared by the members of a cult of tragedians.

In my opinion, there were those of us who feared death, those who had experienced it and still feared it, and those, like me, who welcomed its presence.

CHAPTER EIGHT

I woke up, and could hardly remember what had happened. Faint sunlight pierced the room. Birds of Paradise shaded the window from the late afternoon sun. The stench of tequila emanated from under the sheets and hung over me like steam.

How did I get here? How long have I been here?

I was at peace. I felt a serenity that had not existed in my body since all of my family was together. I could picture my sister standing on the side of the bed, watching me. It was as if her spirit saw that I had returned. I tried to talk to her, but she dissipated into the air.

I put my feet down on the floor. My shoes were filled with sand. The pebbles mixed with the powdery white granules felt like boulders. I remembered driving along the beach, but I did not have any memory of walking on the shore. Fingers wriggled their way around my waist. I fell back down onto the cream-colored sheets, my head caught between two pillows.

Violet snuggled her twitching nose against my chest, trapping me on the queen-sized mattress. She whispered her thanks, feeding my pride.

This morning I felt empathetic towards the previous night's marauding. It had brought me a woman. I still couldn't help, but feel remorse. Whenever I was in a state of euphoria and regret I would think about my sister.

Violet kept nudging me. I couldn't manage to hold a thought in my head for more then a moment. Her consistent physical contact demanded my attention.

"You want me again," she said.

My body was satisfied. My mind's curiosity about the immediate physical world had been replaced by an innate desire to suspend myself in my imagination.

"Yes," I said, "I would like to taste you again."

Then, my eyes caught sight of this grim reality. Her arms gripped my body, half her face hidden behind the plush down pillows. Her nose was disproportionate, and her eyes were a sullen brown that looked closer to black in this light.

I moved my hands over her breasts, which were firm, but fell slightly outwards towards the bed. Her scent was deep and musky. It reminded me of my grandmother's closet, oddly alluring because it made me feel nostalgic.

Before I knew it, I was inside of her. I could tell how good I was making her feel by the way her body twisted up with every thrust. Within moments, she thanked me for satisfying her. She rolled back over and started to snore.

When I woke up the second time, my stomach was grumbling and I knew it was time to eat. I didn't know how long I had slept, but definitely more than usual. I wasn't sure whether it was day or night.

Am I supposed to be at work? I thought. I realized I wouldn't be able to get there even if I tried.

I smelled sesame oil. I reached down and pulled on my jeans, and looked in the bedside mirror. My eyes were swollen, my face was bloated, and my hands were sore. I mashed my hair from the back over my forehead.

I walked out of the bedroom and into a long white hallway decorated with photographs of forest landscapes. A worn yellow metal toy with red targets and white spirals on it had been mounted at the end of the hall. My footsteps creaked on the polished hardwood floor. I reached the kitchen, where the smell of the sesame oil washed over me like a sponge bath. Violet was sautéing scallops.

She handed me a beer. It was ice cold.

"Sit down."

She pointed to the beige leather couch. I decided it would be appropriate to sit down and eat informally. I still wasn't sure what was going on.

"Alright," I said.

"Don't make me force you to have a great dinner with me," she said.

"I'm game."

"Good."

The smell of the sesame oil and rice made me lose my appetite, but I nodded in agreement and sat down on the couch. Violet's coffee table was a restored Louis Vuitton steamer trunk set beneath a pane of glass. Violet slid her slippered-feet over the wood floor, and placed the steamy plate of Saigon noodles, rice, shrimp, and scallops the size of hockey pucks on the side of the dish.

I finished the beer in a couple sips I was so thirsty. “You have anything stronger?” Violet pointed over to the bar. I poured a healthy glass of twelve-year-old scotch and admired it for a brief moment before taking a swig. The liquid made my mouth tingle. Alcohol was a cleanser, and for me and every other AA alum, a way to bury pain. It also brought me that much closer to my sister. She would surface, her angelic voice whispering in my ear, telling me I was wasting my life obsessing over the past. *You know what you're doing to me*, she would say. One more sip, then another. I was on my third glass, when Violet spoke.

“So you want to go get a drink somewhere?”

“I'm having one.” I motioned to the glass.

“Don't you feel like getting out?” She asked.

I felt the visions coming again. I looked up. There was my sister, staring at me from behind the bar. She walked around and took my glass of scotch from me, and poured it down the drain. I knew she was doing me a favor. I tried to reach out and touch her skin, but she just floated by.

I followed her, thinking of everything I wished I could say. All the apologies I wanted to make for all the mean and inconsiderate things I had done. I could have protected her. I could have saved her. If I had, her death might never have happened.

I wanted to buckle over sideways and throw up all of the undigested food in my stomach. I wasn't used to eating so much rich food. I didn't want to be rude. I decided to swallow a few times instead, and convinced myself to go out with Violet.

Violet stood in the doorway in a deep purple dress. I didn't know whether she had come to seduce me, or take my soul. Either way, I knew the game was for keeps. My mind turned into jelly, and I couldn't say no.

“Okay, cowboy, are you ready to get on the horse and get out of here?” Violet said.

“Umm, why not?” I grabbed my black leather jacket and slung it over my shoulder. We wandered out of the house, got into Violet's car and sped out of the driveway into another night in Los Angeles.

The air felt good. I was warm, and needed something to cool me off. I had no destination in mind. I was a passenger on a wild ride with no end, the centrifugal force I felt pulling me around every corner convinced me there was a bigger plan for this evening and my life wouldn't end on this winding road.

Violet looked at me, shook her head, “Are you alright? You don't look so hot. Are you sick?”

“Yes, thanks for noticing,” I muttered.

She swerved off Mulholland at a pull-out area. I jumped out of the car, stumbled and threw up. The redness of the puke made it look like chum on a shark hunt. I wanted to stop heaving, but couldn't. I started to feel better, reached my hand under my shirt and held my belly. My own touch felt foreign. My hand was ice cold. My eyes were swollen shut. The smell of vomit coated my lips and evaporated into my nostrils. I fell down into the dirt, rolling in it.

CHAPTER NINE

I woke up and looked around, disoriented. I knew I was still in Violet's car. I remembered that I vomited over a dirt inlay overlooking Los Angeles, but that was as much as I could compute. My surroundings were stifling, concrete. There was a warning sign that some of the building materials might cause cancer.

Of course!

“I am in a fucking parking garage!”

This was a reassuring thought. I was safe here. At least, I was safe as long as there wasn't an earthquake.

I decided it was time to go exploring. I got out and straightened my vintage leather jacket, brushed off the dirt and smudged the few pieces of food still affixed to the lapels. I thought I looked all right. Certainly better than a man who had just thrown up, blacked out, and woken up in a parking garage had any right to. I nodded to a few of the valet drivers, and walked out onto the street.

I was ready for some more alcohol. I wanted to use it like a mouthwash. But the only bar down the street was flooded with people. If you build a modern bar, get some single women and expensive alcohol at a location in Los Angeles, you could be sure that everyone in the area would go and pretend to have fun at least one day a week. That was of course until either gender met their prey, and sunk their teeth in. They would bite down and keep them for a few months, or until the monotony of routine set in, and both partners went on the hunt again.

I had taken home so many wounded beasts, I had become a beast myself. I was content now to watch the other hunters and their prey, to sit back as the kill strategies unfolded. Tonight, the objectives were to find a place to wash off my face, douse it in cologne and chew a hundred bathroom mints.

A woman in a tube top, mini skirt, and a blue vest walked by. I couldn't help myself. “Miss, Do you happen to know where I might find a bathroom?” I asked in my finest Manchester accent. I must have distracted her from my horrible smell, because she nodded and batted her eyes. She pointed to a hotel in the distance.

“Thank you kindly.” My accent had begun to fade, but she had already taken the bait. She took my hand and led me inside.

We approached the two bathrooms. I thought we would break from our huddle and go our separate ways. To my surprise, she had a different intention. She continued pulling me down the corridor to the single bathroom on the right. I could not say no.

The bathroom was empty. We stumbled in. As we fell into the hollow porcelain well, I thought I heard my name called in the distance. *No, couldn't be. No one knows my name is this bourgeois cesspool.* I went straight for the sink to rinse my mouth out, but before I could, she had cut a few lines of cocaine on the sink.

She motioned for me to go first, while she took a bump from her key. I thought how lucky I was to find a savior, someone to ease this suffering and restore my focus. Cocaine always put me right back in the game. The coke wasn't very good, but I snorted it hard to make sure it got past all the mucus stuck in my nose from earlier. The drip hit and I knew I was good. My nose was cleared, it burned my nausea away. Until, I inhaled and realized the smell of the bathroom was putrid.

She cut a few more lines, and I shook my head. My new bathroom buddy paid no mind and helped herself to finish the two huge rails. My body contorted again. I knew there was nothing inside my stomach to throw up anymore. She saw me writhing and holding my stomach.

"Are you alright! You look fucked up man," she said.

"What is it?" I said, knowing full well what she was referencing.

Oops. I'd dropped the accent.

"What the hell? Where are you from?"

"Nowhere." I tried the accent out again, but she didn't believe me. The mood was dead. My mind was getting mushy, and the ammonia-saturated cocaine was dripping down my throat. My body went numb, and I knew there was more then a cheap cutting agent like baby laxative in these drugs.

I reached in to kiss my new companion, but by the time I leaned in she was gone. I was alone in the bathroom, and the door was cracked open. An innocent bystander peeked in and saw my condition. She politely shut the door again.

I could still smell the girl's hair products and her perfume. Her scent could barely cover the smell of the bathroom. I wanted to slide the bolt on the door again and keep the room closed, but the smell of the toilets overcame my desire to be alone. It was time to leave.

The door opened. Violet peered in at me. "How did you get here?"

I was baffled. "You drove me here."

"But how did you get in the bathroom?"
\
"I walked up from the parking garage."

"You were in the fucking garage?" She was surprised. I was not sure why, after all she had driven me there.

"I told them to leave the car parked on the street! Those assholes." She was infuriated. She still seemed drunk, so I didn't want to interrupt. She patted my head like I was a dog, and left to the street to go yell at the valet.

The crowd outside the hotel looked mostly European. I smelled Gauloise cigarettes. The second-hand smoke left my throat dry. I caught a glimpse of a girl slinking into the hotel lobby. I could only see her head of natural blonde hair bounce past the other bleached-blonde women on the sidewalk. I had to see her face, to know her, if only for a moment. And then I would know whether she was everything I perceived her to be.

CHAPTER TEN

"The reservation is under Jennifer Malone," she said.

"Malone, Malone... here it is." The concierge waved and snapped his hands to the bellman to show her to the elevators.

"Oh, I don't have any bags, and I think I'll grab a drink before I head up to my room."

"Yes, of course," the concierge said.

Jennifer was only twenty, but she had been through this before. Check-in to the hotel, pay the nightly rate if she couldn't find some poor schmuck to pay it for her, casually walk to the bar for drinks, and charge them to her room. The routine was formulaic. She and her friends had been following the blueprint since her seventeenth birthday. Tonight was the same formula. She was on the third step of the plan when she faltered.

"Sure, just charge them to my room," She instructed the young bartender.

"What room is that?" He responded.

"209."

"Got it." He finalized the transaction, but he was suspect. Usually women who looked like her were escorts, but he had never seen one this young. She looked almost too innocent.

“Can I get you anything else?” The bartender asked.

“No. I'm meeting someone.” She told herself that this was true. She didn't want to be alone. The glow in her eyes was not predatory. She only wanted to be saved. She let one of her legs sweep the ground beneath the stool. Usually the perch at the bar was an ideal crow's nest when she was looking for a man to take her home. But tonight, the bar was stale.

Jennifer's Balenciaga pumps scratched against the bar floor one more time. Steadily, and with ease she walked along the bar. She walked carefully, elegantly. It took a keen eye to pick up on the insecurity beneath her veneer of confidence.

She looked at one man and then another, performing a delicate ballet. The floor beneath the bar was translucent. The sky wrapped around the building in all its abysmal existence the moment I saw her.

I approached her. She turned and sensed me. I knew she felt my gaze.

I felt a magnetic pull.

“Sometimes you don't know which way to go,” I said aloud. My mumbling word concoction was layered so thick with admiration that I could have said any combination of letters to attract her attention.

The problem was, I knew I didn't have the plan. The plan. You know, the one that includes a house and kids, and a dog named Fletcher. I didn't have the plan. It never crossed my mind. I didn't want to even know the plan, because to me the plan was a farcical, intangible dream out of reach. It existed, sure. It existed in one place, which was in the books of fiction with Dick and Jane and a cat named Marmalade, and yes sure enough Fletcher would always surface in the second chapter. I didn't want the dog, cat, or family. I just wanted to love her spirit wisely.

“Is it stupid to love someone you hardly know?” I wondered. One blink and the frame skipped, and she was in front of me sitting in the chair.

“Were you talking to someone?” She said.

“Me?” I looked confused, but also concerned that she actually knew I was talking to her in a hypothetical conversation.

“Yes, of course I meant you.” She continued, gesturing with her angelic hands at the two chairs.

“I suppose you're right, we're basically the only ones here.”

“There are plenty of people here, they're just distracted all looking for something.”

“What are you looking for?” I asked. “I'm sorry that sounded cliché.”

“I am looking for something, maybe. I don't think its here, so it doesn't matter,” she said.

“It's never here when you want it. “

“I always liked the green one.” Pointing to an antique plate on the wall.

“Green is best.” I stirred my drink diligently.

“If you hold the straw too tightly, I think the plastic will melt on your hand.”

“I don't know, but I'd believe it if you said it.”

“Would you?”

“Sure.”

“You seem so businesslike and old.”
“Thank you,” I said sarcastically.

“Not, like, in a bad way.”

“Businessy and old cannot be good for someone my age.”

“Let me guess: Producer? Just got out of a relationship? Or better yet… actor!”

“If that's what you want to believe.”

“Ha! I'm right.”

“Far from it.”

“Really? I'm pretty good at this game.”

"Well, maybe your game doesn't work on me."

"Oh, right on, spaceman."

"I am a Spaceman… the Kinks. Besides I'd rather be a damn astronaut…"

"Than… what? What's the alternative?"

"A not-astronaut?"

"That's a double not. I think you're in the void."

"Anti-matter."

"Science term?"

"That's right, the Universe all probably formed out of nothing."

"Sure, completely believe you. Hey, wait a second, I got it… Scientologist."

At that moment, I felt like it was Halloween, and I had on a really obscure costume that was also completely subjective. The only thing I was wearing was my fascination with her.

The conversation continued, but I couldn't hear anything. I could only see her smile, the eyes that squeezed together every time she let her inhibitions stop crippling the connection she had to me. She would say a few words, take a sip of her drink, which was down to the last olive, and then flap her blonde eyelashes like albino wings. I couldn't help myself, I wanted to lean in and kiss her lips. I didn't. I just waited, and watched her every movement. The green stripes in her eyes crisscrossed the indigo blue patchwork woven under cinder brown speckles.

I was lost in those carriages of colored harmony. They straddled me and took me on an out of body experience to a farm in the midwest outside of Wisconsin, where I had always desired to know the secret of a simpler life. If she could get me out of here, I would dedicate my life to her worship.

CHAPTER ELEVEN

Our connection was shattered when Violet screeched like a banshee across the outdoor fireplace. Cocktail glasses resonated on the verge of breaking into sharp fragments. I knew the insatiable experience I had with—

“Wait! What's your name?” I asked, knowing I needed to follow the banshee cry before the horrid beast reaped terror on the only promise I saw for life in this city of darkness.

“My name?” She said.

“Yes, please your name… I need it to find you.”

“Why? Are you leaving?” She was surprised.

“I promise, I'll explain.” I just wanted to protect her, but she didn't know about the wretched creature that would soon have its talons dug deep inside my moist palm, peeling back layers of skin like paint with a chisel.

“I'm Charles, Charles Winters,” I said.

“Ok, I will give you my number. That's all you want.”

“That's not all I want. I want to know you. Everything about you.”

“That's sweet I guess. Ok, my number is 323.418.99—”

The last numbers trailed off as Violet grabbed my hand and yanked me from my irreplaceable connection with…

“Your name. Please, tell me your name.”

She saw me being dragged away by this older woman. Maybe she thought it was my sister or something. I prayed she didn't think Violet was my girlfriend or anything. I tried to reach out for her hand to kiss it goodbye.

“Next time.” She turned away, coy and confident, denying my lips the opportunity to touch her powdery skin. I could smell the pores on her hand, the subtle hint of lilies earthly and elegant. The bittersweet aroma of nail polish remover, from a recent self-procured manicure left a slightly acidic floral bouquet in my nose.

“I'll see you again,” I said.

My words trailed off and she was gone.

“Who the hell was that girl?” Violet's words hit me.

I ignored her questioning. The fresh scent of talcum powder filled the air. I wanted to live in this innocence, apart from all the banal meanderings and squalid interactions I was preparing myself for with Violet. Without warning, the fantasy capsule I swallowed was destroyed by her. She reached her bony fingers underneath my shirt and grabbed my pelvis. She intended to arouse me with the gesture, but her nails pierced deep into the marrow of my bone and sent a poisonous tingling sensation down my leg.
With one leg slightly paralyzed, I staggered to regain my balance. Stammering, descending, back into Hell, I surpassed Dante Alighieri's nine divisions of purgatory into the utmost helpless

suffering. The safety in her clutches was the type of shelter that only a mythical maternal creature can provide. Her face was not reminiscent of any Greek frieze, but the carved cheekbones sculpted from grinding her teeth repetitiously sent her jaw line angling down forty-five degrees.

“So, are you going to tell me who that girl was or not,” she demanded.

“I don't know her name,” I recoiled.

“It looked like you were into her,” she said.

“What does it matter?”

“Because you are my guy.” The words were an awakening. I tried not to answer and turned my head to look out the window.

“Yeah, whatever.”

“Don't say whatever. You are. Whether you like it or not.”

I can't remember the rest of the drive back to her cave. The only memory I had from the evening was this mystery girl. She captivated me. Every centimeter of my skin was coated by her. The feeling inside me was fading, I wanted to hold onto it by consuming a sweet fruit. I couldn't prolong the true warmth she gave me. She knew my name. That was all she had of me.

It was the only chance that we would somehow meet again in the labyrinth of Los Angeles. I knew the Minotaur named Violet was tucked behind every corner, every wrong turn. I would stare into the eyes of that stinky brute, following the mucoidal droppings left in a track from the pursuit of this treasure.

Violet stood in the doorway. The light reflecting from her curls projected a shadow where the horns could faintly be drawn in the silhouette. I knew I was in for a ravaging. She mounted my body. I smelled talcum powder and petroleum jelly. The specific fragrance swirled like a vortex inside me. I inhaled deeply, paralyzed. The only organ that worked effectively was my penis.

I knew it was there, but couldn't bend my neck to see what shape it took. I only knew that all my blood was rushing from my brain. This was not what I wanted. I wanted to hold onto the memory I had from only moments before. Let my overwhelmed senses process the idyllic notion of fate. Instead the memory was pierced repetitiously with no mercy. The consideration was for one purpose, ownership. She wanted to possess me.

How does someone own a human being? How was it possible to capture a human spirit? My body had separated and my spirit had gone somewhere, wandered off into a distant space, like a specter or wraith. I was owned. My body belonged to someone. She had taken what was, innately, the only real property I had.

“Thank you for my ‘O', Popeye,” she said getting off of me. I wondered how many times she had said this to men in her life.

“Uh huh.” I just nodded not knowing her exact meaning. I only knew that she was done.

“Don't tell me you didn't like it?”

“I did.”

“I know… it was amaaaazing.”

I rolled over and stared at the wall. The panels of white wood had a few scuffs from black rubber soled shoes, or moving furniture. Violet slapped my bare ass and said, “You sure did good.” I could almost throw up, but I knew my only choice was to go numb.

The lace on the sheets was tucked between my right leg and hers. I pulled the barrier taut.

“The sheets are too tight, move over?”

“Damn,” I thought to myself. She had figured out my angle. I was lost at sea. I knew there was no one on deck to toss me the day glow orange life preserver. I guess I would have to stay here with her. I didn't know how long, but I didn't want to go home. It was still nicer here than the apartment. I figured I would have to continue to please her and make her feel good, get rid of my remaining pride, and sacrifice whatever I had left of my ego.

I swallowed the salty tears. I tried to believe I deserved this. I would never live my dreams. It was all a fantasy from a 1980's MTV advertising campaign; the one with the attractive blonde standing behind a corvette and she looks super hot and then the camera goes in for a close up and the hot girl is smoking a cigarette and turns into a beastly looking creature.

Violet mounted me for the last time. It was at that moment that the futile ball of remaining pride inside me unwound. I could feel the strands whipping across the inner lining of my stomach wall, freeing a sepulcher of inhibition.

I slid out from the sheets and put on my hooded sweatshirt and oversized Puma track pants, grabbed my jacket, slid on shoes and stepped out of the bedroom. I paused in the bathroom mirror to take a look at what I had become. The hood over my head enhanced the dark circles under my eyes, the guilty sense, and the lack of responsibility was the only traits I reflected. I had nothing left. No job since I hadn't shown up in about a week now, no shelter from the storm; left solely in the custody of my new patron who I paid with guileless sex, numbing my heart.

"I think it's time to go old friend." I spoke to myself in a whisper. I would be better off out in the streets, in the alley behind the Lamplighter diner off Van Nuys Boulevard, than here. But for some reason I couldn't just pick up and leave. I felt tied to her. Like I owed her something and that was to add some courtship, my duty as a man. I hadn't really felt this before. It was surely from the guilt. The same guilt and obligation you feel to your mother because they raised you.

CHAPTER TWELVE

"How did that make you feel Violet?"

"I was enraged." Violet spewed the words that were still contaminated with an anger that was common in prison, but unrecognizable to civilians.

"Why are you still angry?"

"You think revenge for the love of your life leaving you is enough? Do you? It's not." Violet broke into a sniveling tear episode.

"You have to forgive him."

"What? Forgive him? Never. I know he still loves me, and that's what's so fucked up. He is just young. He doesn't fucking get it. He thinks with his dick right now."

"Is that what you think she was to him? Just a sexual interest?"

"Sexual interest. I think he fucked her yes. He wasn't interested; he just wanted someone younger. He tried it, and then he should've come back to me."

"Did you give him a chance to?"

"He had plenty of chances."

"Doesn't that say something about his own will?"

"Enough questions, you just keep leading me to the answers you want to hear, but it's not doing me any damn good. My poor boy. He was so skinny last time I saw him."

"When you…" A knocking on the two-way safety glass mirror that separated the private counseling room from the viewing area interrupted the doctor.

"Please give me a moment."

"Take your time." Violet leaned her head back, stretching her spine back over the stainless steel foldout chair. She exhaled and rotated her head in a clockwise semi-circle, cracking each vertebra.

In one motion Violet turned to see her reflection in the mirror. The woman that stared back at her was hard. The exterior was sharp, rigid cheek lines, but in her eyes was a glaze of inner hurt, the unbearable weight of feeling unloved.

"Am I still in love with him?" Her words fluttered from underneath her breath, shallowly escaping and going unnoticed by the doctor, who was still consumed with an issue with another inmate. Violet took her hands and wiped them on her pants, trying to erase the age lines in her palms.

She couldn't alter her perception of the past. *When life is colored by love, what else do you think about?* Her answer was in the memories, but what did Charlie remember? She wanted to climb inside of his head and search around, see if there was a flash of positive emotion for her. The drunken drives home after a candle-lit epicurean dinner on Ventura Blvd in her convertible Mercedes Benz sports car. She remembered it so vividly. Winding through the ancillary streets near the top of Mulholland, pulling over to stare at the lights. Sliding up her dress, slipping her underwear to one side, and climbing on top of Charlie. Overlooking the glitter of white and red city lights below, as she rode him, cumming wildly with the taste of red wine and lamb shank in her mouth. It was a dinner she wanted to replay over and over.

He couldn't have forgotten the love, the love he shot into me when he came inside of me. Violet pulled her legs up to her chest contorting into a fetal position, embracing them like they were Charlie's body. The warmth faded when the doctor walked back in carrying with him the sterility of the treatment room.

“I apologize, Violet. I had to tend to a few problems we had in another sister facility of ours in Fulton.”

“I'm not going anywhere.”

“Did you think about anything that may help you to see the lack of love that Charlie had, I mean his debasement from the experience?”

“Debasement? If you're saying that he couldn't give a shit about me you're fucking wrong.”

“That's not what I'm saying, but even the testimony from the trial?”

“Lies. That bitch lied, she fell for an act, like a show. You know when you go to a play, how, if it's really good you forget you're at a play? You're right there, watching it happen, the actors… they convince you it's real.”

“You're saying Charlie did this to Jennifer?”

“To everybody.”

“And the love he showed you was not an act.”

“You have no idea. I told him I would have his baby, and I hate kids.”

“Why do you hate kids?”

“My sister Destiny has three with two husbands, and I can't stand any of them. Besides when I was a kid, my parents couldn't stand me. They always favored my sister.”

“So this is deep seated.”

“If forty-two years is considered deep seated, then, yeah I would say so.”

“The sarcasm doesn't help.”

“Sarcasm?” Violet gave a glance around the corners of the room, holding back the tears. She studied the doctor, who in all his years at Yale couldn't understand where the synapses had ceased to fire in Violet. He had taken on many patients since he joined the penal system after getting his medical degree, but none that displayed such anti-social personality disorder. If he could pin-point the lynchpin beyond the fictitious existence of this character she had created in her mind, then he would be able to reconcile the way she used Charlie as a scapegoat for all her own insecurities.

Violet was growing hostile as the doctor rehearsed his diagnosis in his mind. His plan was to use her psychosis as a basis for a new mental disorder. He didn't want the associations of violent outbreaks to be symptoms of previously established diagnosis. He daydreamed about the future conference discussions and panel talks he would lead about the symptomatic expressions of Violet's delusional condition.

Violet got up, spit at him, and paced to the corner. She pulled on her jumper, rubbed her chest, and leaned in the corner of the room. The doctor's daydreaming ceased as he wiped the sticky spit from his unshaven face.

“Are we done?” She stammered. She was exhausted, but still full of fight.

“Yes. One hour.”

“Good,” She said.

“I would like to continue this before our regularly scheduled meeting on Thursday, if that's alright with you?” He wanted to break through the distorted version of her reality and grasp at something more psychologically tangible.

“Sure,” Violet whispered. Her mind had slipped back into the past.

The doctor had only witnessed this form of astral projection briefly while studying under a Shaman in Panama, but now he watched the same type of physical transference in an untrained patient at a prison. The most training she had in this area was alcohol, drugs, and the occasional mushroom trip, but this current episode was without any intoxication or aid from hallucinogenic substances to induce the experience.
The doctor froze. He only wished he had neuron sensors to monitor the activity areas in her brain. He watched for signs of involuntary

movement in her facial features. He watched her right eyebrow, then scanned to her nose. He noticed her ear twitching slightly. Her eyelids flashed in random movements, opening and closing as though in REM. Her brown eyes looked like solid black marbles, the brown tint was absorbed by a well of darkness.

The doctor knew he should awaken Violet. She had begun to convulse spasmodically, but he wanted to see where this journey would take her. He speculated on the lucidity of this experience: Could she see God? Was she going to speak in tongues? Was she looking at a different version of herself? Perhaps she was reliving the love or the spiteful moments of her past relationship with Charlie or her childhood? Curiosity was killing him.

After another two minutes, Violet came back to the present and stretched her arms like she had awoken from a nap or a daydream.

"What were you dreaming about?" The doctor asked.

"Dreaming?" She was perplexed.

"Weren't you just asleep?"

"No, I've just been here? Why am I not in my cell?"

Violet wanted to get up and run back to the safety of her eggshell white cell.

"It's been a long session, you're right. We can talk about this during our next meeting. Tomorrow?" He said.

"OK, fine!" Violet was restless. She wanted to be alone with her memory.

CHAPTER THIRTEEN

It was a strange day. I woke up in the morning and Violet was gone. I'm sure she was out showing houses to a new client or something work related. I got up like I usually do and wandered into the shower. Half asleep I sat down in the large tub and let the water hit my face. It felt so good. I daydreamed a bit and then it hit me. I needed to leave. My time here playing houseboy was up. I needed to finally get out. It had only been a few months I thought, but I was lost, tired, and drained. I got out. I heard the slider open and close in the living room. I figured it must be the maid. I started shaving the ugly beard I had grown while staying here. I couldn't decipher exactly how long it'd been, but it was too long. I was sick of writing her little sweet notes everyday, having sex with her on demand, and eating such rich foods. It might have seemed like paradise for someone who was retired, and wanted a domineering woman to run his life but I was far from it.

I walked into the bedroom and there in front of me was a woman I recognized, a spitting image of Violet, only very attractive. "Hi, I'm Christina. But everyone calls me Destiny," she said.

"I know. We met before at the party. You're Violet's twin sister," I said, stating the obvious.

"Yeah, that night was shitty." She started to look around and broke eye contact with me.

"Are you alright?" I asked.

She looked at me for a second; ignoring my question she surveyed my skin and then continued to go through one of Violet's dresser drawers.

"I know she's out, but she said I could come get my top she borrowed last week."
"Yeah, cool with me." I didn't care.

"Don't mind me." She walked by me really close and I could smell her. She smelled of lilies.

"Why don't you ever come by?" I asked trying to make conversation.

"Do you want me to?"

"Yeah, you should come by more." I was being nice.

I walked over to the part of my closet where I hung my clothes up. I grabbed a pair of jeans and dropped my towel and put them on. I didn't really care that she might be watching me. Before I could pull my shirt over my head I felt her hands on my hips.

"Do you like fucking my sister?" She asked me. I was completely taken aback. I didn't know what the hell to say to something like that.

"Sometimes."

"Then you would really like fucking me," She said.

I was still in a state of shock. I was planning my big escape today, being methodical, taking my time not to upset the energy and now

Violet's twin was seducing me. I didn't feel right doing it. It was too late. My jeans were around my ankles and I was thrusting myself into her. Each time I opened my eyes and looked at her face I saw Violet. Her body was so different and she had fake breasts. We had sex in every different position until we both came at the same time. “It's okay my tubes are tied,” She said.

That was the last thing I was worried about. I knew it was a real slap in the face to Violet. It was bad enough I was leaving. She had been good to me. She also warned me about her sister. I wasn't thinking straight. It just wasn't right that Violet and I were ever together in the first place. We didn't love each other. She just wanted a young stud. And I… just wanted someone to take care of me.

I replayed the rest of that morning I left Violet's house. Destiny and I talked while I grabbed my belongings and put them in my duffle, “Why are you leaving?” She asked me.

“It's just time. We decided.”

“Violet knows you're leaving?”

“Not exactly.”

“Your secret is safe with me,” she said with a wink. She now had some serious leverage against her sister, which she was contented by.

“Thanks.”

“Just don't tell her how good our sex was.”

“I won't.” I scribbled a little note on the letterhead Violet had on her desk saying ‘good-bye' in so many words.

“Will you come by my house for dinner?” Destiny asked me.

“Aren't you married?” I asked.

“We're separated.”

“I don't think that would be a good idea.”

“Don't turn me down. I'm an amazing cook. I'm vegetarian too.”

“Yeah, sure I'll come by some time for dinner.” I was willing to say anything to end the charade. She knew I would never come by. Why was she playing this game? There was the sound of a car in the driveway. I recognized the noisy fan of Violet's radiator. “Shit! You have to get out of here,” I said in complete panic.

“It's fine she knows I'm here.” Destiny said calmly. “You should put a hat on, though. Your hair looks like you just had crazy sex.” I ran and grabbed a beanie even though it was eighty-five degrees out. The guilt I had on my face actually hurt. The note I had written on her desk in black sharpie came into focus. I needed to hide it. She would find it later. I ran to the window and threw my duffle out. I would have to grab it later. I gave her dog, Jung, after Karl Jung a final pat on the head. No more games, I decided. Living as a well-paid male escort in Bel-Air had its advantages, but ignoring the consequences was unconscionable. Sure, she offered me safety, but I had the rest of my life ahead of me. I wanted to make somcthing of it. Not retreat into her home in the hills. Violet walked in.

“What in the hell,” she said as her dog Jung vied for her attention.

“We were just talking,” Destiny said.

“Your sister stopped by. I'm just on my way out.”

“You're not going anywhere,” she ordered.

“Yes, I am. I have to be somewhere.” I tried to visualize a place to go to make the lie seem believable.

“Why are you here?” She asked Destiny.

“I was just picking up that shirt remember. I told you I was stopping by.”

“Did you let her in?” Violet asked me.

“Ummm… yeah I did. She said you knew and it was ok.”

“Whatever. I don't like this. Something feels wrong.”

“I have to get going sweet pea.” I used the one thing I could to dissuade her from cutting both our throats right there, affection. She purred and released me.
The moment I hit the open road I could feel the memories coming back of when my sister was alive. This time, I didn't see an apparition, but I felt her inside of me. The hairs on my arm stood on end as the music embellished the experience in a crescendo of melodies crashing into one another at the apex.

Winding down Mulholland, headed back to the Valley, I could feel the temperature change. Despite the smoke wafting from my cigarette, the Valley air seemed cleaner, newer, and fresher than I had ever noticed before. When you headed home after being away, there was nothing like it. I could imagine it now like a plush mansion, a castle even, with a butler waiting to offer you a glass of brandy when you walked in.

I could feel the paisley Victorian print curtains, the handmade hallway rugs imported from a loom in Persia, and the scent of royalty flooding the stairway up to my parent's bedrooms. Our family could have lived like that. My parents would have stayed together, my sister would be alive, and my mother would be a queen graced by all the company she desired if we had any money.

I pulled up to our complex, and decided to park on the street. It was completely empty. I went up the front steps. I punched my code into the silver keypad, ignored the obnoxious computer generated noise that granted me access. I opened the glass door and headed straight for my apartment. I had hope, hope that I could give my mom some of my joy and restore a sense of life to her. I fiddled for my keys in my dark blue Levi's, found the key ring, pulled it out with my finger on the right key for the front lock and opened it.

CHAPTER FOURTEEN

"Mom?" I waited for a response. I didn't hear anything. I figured she must have been taking her afternoon nap. I checked my watch. It was 2:12 pm. I checked her chair, but she wasn't there. I walked around the apartment, but found no trace of her. The scent in the air—faint traces of fruit punch and Opus perfume—told me she had just been there. When I headed over to the fridge to grab some milk, I saw a note affixed to the fridge with an apple-shaped magnet.

Charlie, call me! Your mother is in the hospital! 818.555.2146.

Janet

I was suddenly unable to breathe or swallow. My legs felt paralyzed.

In the hospital?

I called Janet. No answer. I jumped back into my car and sped off in the direction of Van Nuys Hospital, the closest emergency room. Ventura was a zoo of tourists. I weaved in and out of traffic, almost causing two or three accidents, and barely missing a pedestrian who tried to cross against a yellow light at Woodman.

The hospital was a square white building that stood out. A beacon of sickness on Van Nuys, hiding my mother somewhere in its walls of dry wall and plaster. That awful hospital smell filled my nostrils as I pulled into a loading zone marked by yellow paint on the circular drive through area. I was probably going to get towed, but

I didn't care. I was obligated to make sure my mother didn't get pumped full of unnecessary pharmaceuticals by doctors looking to make an extra dime.

The doors to the ER hissed open. The misery in the waiting room was almost tangible. I saw rows of blue plastic chairs, and heard sobs of pain. I made my way to the receptionist.

“Name?” She said.

“Winters. Marla Winters.”

She flipped through her admittance records sheet, scanning each page with her zebra patterned nail extensions. “I don't have a Winters. Would she be under another name?”

“No. No that's her name,” I said.

“Well, you may want to try the main hospital reception to see if she's been transferred.”

“That doesn't make sense. You mean you can't tell me where my Mom is?” “Look Hun, I don't know. They don't give me patient's transfer records once they're outta' the ER.”

“Thanks.”

I found the main lobby receptionist by following the brown wall signs to an information desk. I waited until she finished answering a barrage of calls.

“I'm looking for my mom. Marla?”

"Last name?"

"Winters, like the season. With an 'S' at the end."

"Let me take a look." The receptionist scrolled through the endless list of patient names and room numbers.

"Your mother is in the OR. She won't be out for another few hours. Please take a seat over there."

Her words echoed against the desk and sank into the plywood pressed faux-wood paneling. I felt a hand against my back. It was my mother's friend Janet. Janet was an administrative assistant in a Dentist's office in Woodland Hills—a prestigious job for our apartment complex—and she still had her nametag on. Beneath it, her white button-down blouse had a coffee stain on the lapel. I saw her pudgy stomach flop over the waistband of her black polyester blend pants. There were tears in her eyes. She tried to put her arms around me.

I couldn't cry. I couldn't even look at her.

"What happened?" I could feel my eyes swelling now. The pain crept in.

"She had an aneurysm."

"She what?"

"She was watching her afternoon program—"

"Which one? *The Price is Right*?"

"She started pounding on the wall to our unit. I came running over immediately, and banged on the door. Your mother opened it, and then collapsed onto the floor."

"Uh-huh."

"I thought she was dehydrated. I tried to give her some water. But when I realized she was starting to lose color in her face, I called 911."

"Jesus," I said. I had given up on God a long time ago. I knew if God existed, then he or she would never have forced me to watch everything I loved disappear. I was not a religious man, but right then I wished I had some higher spirit to ask for forgiveness. I couldn't help but think this disaster was my fault.

Can't I just have some fun here and there? You stole my sister, let my father walk away from us, and now....

Janet and I were sitting down, huddled in the corner of the lobby. The seats were uncomfortable. The blue linen cushion covers were spotted with flecks of bright color. I kept trying to situate myself between the two adjoining armrests, but the arrangement made it near impossible. I was certain this was intentional on the part of the designer to make sure no one slept comfortably across multiple chairs and seats opened up.

"Do you want some coffee, sweetie?" Janet asked.

"No, I'm fine. Actually, yes. Coffee. Coffee would be good. I'll get it though."

I needed to get up and walk around. The stagnation was constricting my muscles and they were becoming restless.

CHAPTER FIFTEEN

Instead, in the last hallway was my sister, clear as day. She was watching the two double doors that led to the operating room. I walked up to her, placed my left hand on her shoulder, and peered through the rectangular double pane glass into the room. Inside doctors and nurses moved in symphonic perfection. The staccato pace of the surgeon's movements seemed surreal, until I saw the blood. The redness of it, like Knott's strawberry jam, congealing to the edges of blue surgical napkins outlined the area of the patient's skull that was exposed.

I looked into my sister's eyes. They were wise well beyond their years. And then she was gone. The image of her faded into the air, her silhouette barely visible beneath my hand. When I looked up again, I was staring at the coffee machine.

“You gonna get something man?” A voice broke the silence. A tough black guy in his early 20s. His eyes hardened as he stared at me.

I stepped back away from the machine. “Go ahead,” I said.

He inserted a five-dollar bill and pressed the button for hot chocolate, which I didn't expect. I associated hot chocolate with weakness. Maybe, I thought, he was feeling vulnerable, going through a tough time and looking for comfort. Maybe he was getting the drink for his little sister, who had just woken up in her hospital bed. It was hard, after sitting for so long in the hospital lobby, not to wonder what everyone else was waiting for.

Doctors have to give bad news all the time, so they know just how to couch it, making it sound hopeful. *John Doe was very strong through the surgery and it all went just fine. He's recovering and should be out of here in no time at all,* translates to a botched quadruple bypass surgery during which the surgeon allowed his second-in-command the opportunity to perform the graft, and he blew it, forcing the head surgeon to open Mr. Doe's chest cavity up a second time. Now if the Doe's family were told the truth, they would probably flip out and castrate the surgeon. I'm not arguing with the politics of biomedicine, just saying that ethics seem to have no place here.

I started to cry. The guy with the hot chocolate placed his hand on my shoulder. "You want the rest of my hot chocolate, man?"

I was paralyzed. I wanted to thank him, but the words drowned in my mouth.

"It's cool, man. You look like you need something good."

I was still shaking my head, baffled. He looked like an old-timey gangster, but there he was, drinking hot chocolate, and sharing it with me. He put the Styrofoam cup in my hand.

"Go on. Have some."

I did as he insisted. The warm sugary fluid felt good in my throat. The rich clumps of barely dissolved powder were like tiny flecks of gold. "I needed that."

"See? I knew it man. She's gonna be alright you know?"

“What?”

“It's your momma, right?”

“Yeah.”

“Shit man. I've been here two weeks now.”

“What?”

“My ma, she's been in ICU almost two weeks.”

“What do you do?”

“Just hold on to hope man. Gotta trust these docs to work their magic. The rest is up to God.”

“Yeah, I guess.”

“Well, be cool.”

He walked off down the hallway. I held the cup of hot chocolate, frozen in the middle of the air. My arm was like a rusted lever. It hinged on my elbow, but would not lift the cup to my mouth.

I wished I could be as confident as the hot chocolate guy, but I still didn't know what was happening to my mother. I only had the vision my sister had given me to gauge the scale of the operation. The vision was only partially accurate, I hoped. I wished there was just a clear chamber they put my mom in like they do in a sci-fi movie, where the barometric pressure inside it would somehow cleanse and purge her of her sickness. The chamber would open and she would slide out, smelling like talcum powder and walking in her hospital gown like an angel in heavenly light.

I knew the grim reality was nothing more than a calculated mess of blood and ventricles, but putting my confidence in the doctor's 'magic' I let my attention wander around the lobby. My eyes settled on the two black metal doors of the elevator. They opened, and I recognized the eyes that stared back at me.

Violet had somehow tracked me. Maybe she was here to give me the chance to walk or ride with her to the taxidermist to be stuffed alive. She approached me, stalking with decisive footsteps. Her glance made me shudder and tapped the well of fear that bubbled up inside me.

"What are you doing here?" I said.

"I heard what happened. I wanted to be here for you."

"Not now."

"But you don't have anyone."

"Yes, I do." I motioned to Janet who was reading an old issue of *Home & Garden* and shoving Funyuns into her mouth with one hand.

"Who's that?" Violet said. I sensed an unwarranted jealousy in her voice. I forgot that Violet was almost the same age as Janet.

"I think you should go," I said. I directed her back toward the elevator.

She tried to kiss me. Her lipstick was fresh, and the smell of her breath was a fragrance similar to hydrogen peroxide, chemical and frothy. She must have been rinsing with Listerine right before. But her scent also reminded me of my mother, back when she had been able to take care of me. She had tried, she really had. Until Violet's scent wafted into my nose, I had forgotten that. I had buried the moments where my mother held me, and comforted me when I was scared or saddened by the realization that life wasn't fair. This was probably the best gift Violet ever gave me, and it was completely unintentional.

I kissed Violet on the cheek, and she twisted her head so that the corners of our lips connected.

“I'll give you a call when this thing's over,” I said.

“You promise?”

I nodded. The elevator door shut. She reached her arm and stopped them from closing. She grabbed my flannel shirt in her hand, pulled me close and kissed me, shoving her tongue sloppily into my mouth. It thrashed around, leaving a trail of spit down my lips.

In a daze, I wandered back toward Janet. She had become my scapegoat, an easy excuse to get away from Violet. The hour was getting late, and we still hadn't heard anything from the doctors. I wanted to pray to the gods, but at this point in my life I knew they weren't listening.

CHAPTER SIXTEEN

I had curled into a fetal position next to Janet, one leg dangling off the side of the cushion. The silver armrest poked into my back like a needle. I felt a tugging on my shirt. I looked up and saw a doctor, his eyes blurry behind a set of black-rimmed glasses. Next to me, I could feel Janet tense, waiting to hear the doctor's news. I braced myself.

"The operation went well," he said.

"Is she conscious?"

"Your mother is going to be just fine."

I wondered if he looked into my cranium, whether he would see all the ways my brain looked like my mother's. He must have seen a thousand brains throughout his life. Did they all look the same?

"So what exactly happened? I mean what'd you do in there?" Janet asked.

"We had to insert a small spring into one of the blood vessels that leads into her brain. The spring, essentially, will keep the vessel open to reduce pressure. We had to put in a suture to ensure that the leakage did not continue."

"Leakage?" Janet asked.

"The vessel did not pop completely, which was a good thing. It was leaking blood, and that's why she got so dizzy and ultimately lost her balance. She should recover fully."

The doctor walked off, wiping his hands.

I tried to mimic his gesture, wiping my hands clean. But I couldn't discount my mother's close call that easily. I had to hold back the tears. If I let myself cry, to the others in the waiting room, I would only be a cliché, another neglectful son, grieving his mother. Pain resonated throughout my body, but I refused to let myself cry.

Janet put her arm over my shoulder. "Do you want to go up to ICU now?"

I was frozen. The lobby air was cold enough to cryogenically preserve the scene.

"I'll go—yes, let's go there," I said. I took Janet's hand.

We headed towards the elevators, made a left and continued down to the East Wing. The doors sealed and I felt the G-force pulling me into the ground. The elevator ascended floor by floor. The sinking feeling in my stomach caught up to me when we stopped at the 5th floor. The door opened to a flood of beeping noises, stale smells, and nurses in starched scrubs.

"Are you ready for this?" Janet asked.

I nodded. "I guess so." I had no choice. I had to walk through this door and see what my future held.

Behind the third curtain was a portly male nurse with a shaved head. He had a chart in his hand. I knew that underneath the numbers and marks he had made on his graph, the life of my mother hung in the balance. I slid closer to the bed. Her face was still. The left side of her head had been completely shaved, exposing a row of incisions. A clear tube taped to the side of her skull made a sucking sound and a yellowish substance mixed with streaks of blood siphoned into a blue box machine hooked over the edge of the bed.

The Native American creation myth my mother read me as a child, about an Indian woman who cried so much for her child that she created enough water to irrigate the fields and feed the entire village now seemed false. I wished that I could cry enough for my mother to bring her back to life. I could feel the pain in mystomach, like an ulcer. It kept pumping, pumping, in perfect tempo to the beat of my heart.

I took my mother's clammy hand sticky with remnants of adhesive tape. I tried to think of something meaningful to say. I knew she couldn't hear me, but I wanted to believe some part of her physical being would recognize the bass rhythms of her son's voice.

Janet was in tears at the foot of the bed. She couldn't even look at my mom. But I felt strong. I always thought the closer you get to a person you love who is dying, the more you will get weak, curl up, and just crawl inside yourself. It's not true. The closer you get, the more love you have, and the more strength you give. When you are standing holding your own mother's hand and watching the excess blood being pumped out from her brain, you don't think about yourself or the fear. You think about her well being, the memories you share, and how you'll make everything better in the future.

CHAPTER SEVENTEEN

Back in her cell, the words of the prison psychologist bounced around in Violet's head.

And the love he showed you was not an act.

She spoke each syllable aloud to herself, and lay on her back, staring into the cinder block visible through the cracks in the drywall.

To her left was a picture of the Virgin Mary. Violet was not religious. Her grandmother had been Jewish, but her parents had been vehement atheists. Her lack of spirituality ate into her soul. Now, she had begun to feel a connection with the Virgin Mary. As much as Violet thought she had a tangible sense of love, sex never gave her the satisfaction that the idea of love did, but it pacified the feeling.

Violet caressed the lower portion of her stomach, ran her pointer finger over the centerline of her abdomen and put her hand into her pants and underwear. She didn't touch herself for very long, just until her tense body relaxed. The moisture seeped through her sailor-blue uniform and evaporated almost as quickly as it formed.

After lights out, Violet stood in the corner on top of the toilet hoping to be struck by an immaculate light from the Virgin herself. She wanted a child only to provide a reason for she and Charlie to be together again. She remembered threatening Charlie the last time she saw him.

“You're stuck with me. We were meant to be together you know that right? How do you know I didn't freeze your sperm?”

Charlie had been confused. “You can't place sperm in an ice chest and expect it to survive. That's why they have sperm banks scientifically designed to preserve the tadpoles,” he said.

She laughed to herself, still standing on the toilet in the cell. The image of Charlie laughing warmed her. She stopped shivering, and lifted her shoulders to hold on to the temporary feeling of warmth. She needed the sensation to go on. She wished she could bottle it up. If she could have sold this feeling to any of the other girls in the cells, she knew it would be the best rehabilitation program the State had ever witnessed.

But she couldn't keep it, and if she could have, Violet refused to share any of Charlie with anybody else. Her desire to possess him was what had driven her into prison in the first place.

Charlie's explanation for the scientific preservation of sperm sparked her imagination. She had, in fact, taken a condom from the trash after sex one night, squeezed its contents into a Tupperware container and placed it under the ice in her freezer. She later transferred it to her deep freeze where she kept the large beef filets and racks of ribs.

Charlie's words made her think the lower deep freeze temperature would somehow preserve the quality of the sperm and keep it from thawing prematurely. But Violet feared it was she who was infertile. And even if she wasn't, she couldn't bear the thought of having a surrogate. Could someone else carry her kid for her in their uterus? The image of another woman bearing Charlie's child made her feel disgusted. She threw up in the back of her throat.

The lactic acid burned her throat like a glass of Charlie's scotch. She'd hated the taste, but used to pour a glass, after Charlie left, and swirl it in her mouth. The peaty burn left an aftertaste that reminded her of Charlie's kisses. His saliva, she used to say, tasted like a "bowling alley," but when he stopped smoking, the pure lowland singe-malt flavor was a welcome odor that instilled a courtly sense of romance in her.

Violet was crouched on her hands and knees in the cell. The concrete floor bruised her skinny knees, but her instinct propelled her to continue to pose like a prized hunting trophy. She wanted someone to take care of her. She was so accustom to being the breadwinner, she thought it would be nice to feel secure because of a man.

She looked at her reflection in the metal on the bed frame. The extended portrait made her look not only elongated, but colorful and lean. If she lived inside a cubist painting, she might be considered beautiful. More importantly, her reflection was narrow enough to fit through the bars of her cell. It gave her the idea to continue to deny the meals in the prison buffet line until she was thin enough to slide through the bars and out of this hellhole.

The possibility of feeling the air on her skin, driving purposelessly down PCH, Charlie's hand in hers, was the only motivation she needed to start this regimented diet. If she could starve herself for the rest of the year, her body would reducc itself by such a large difference that she would easily be able to maneuver between the bars and out into the dream life she remembered. One day at a time, and one meal at a time. It gave her a mission. A goal, with a glowing flame at the end of the tunnel. Once she got back to Charlie, she would let him do anything, live anywhere, she would give him anything, if only he would pledge himself to her.

CHAPTER EIGHTEEN

I could only handle two hours at a time in ICU. Janet had gone home to make her boyfriend dinner. For an hour, it was just my mom and I, and the flurry of nurses, and then I left too.

I lit up a Marlboro red and cleansed my mouth. When your mouth is dry and you can only breathe in the pollution from the Valley air, your first inhale tastes surprisingly like Campbell's chicken noodle soup. The similarity satisfies your hunger. I hadn't eaten in hours, and the day had slipped out from under me. I knew my mom would recover, but would she ever be the same?

The doctor said chances were good that my mother would return to normal after some rehabilitation. She would probably need speech therapy though. What I had imagined for her was much worse. I had envisioned her sitting in the same spot of our living room staring at the TV, drooling and calling out to me in a muffled tone, *Can I have some more noodles?*

The smoke from my cigarette looked like it was chasing the few stars in the sky. I followed the trails hoping they would tell me how to escape my life. Read the stars like some astrological premonition. I connected the dots in the sky and closed one eye. They formed the shape of a female silhouette. I thought it was my little sister, but the face was older, still angelic, and demure. I couldn't place her. I could only see her golden hair again, scampering through my mind.

I knew at that moment the answer was in her.

Her existence changed my whole day. I inhaled one last drag from my cigarette, flicked it into the street, glanced up at the stars and promised myself I would find her.

I went back into the hospital to go say good night to my mother. Visiting hours were over. I knew my mom would be happy to hear I found a woman. I had to chase down this angelic creature who I saw in my vision. Back up the elevators, down the hallways to the East wing ICU. My feet carried me like they were plugged into a magnetic moveable track. I tried to open the door, but the silver handle didn't budge. I tried again; the lever was stuck in its horizontal position. I pressed the tan intercom button and waited. A minute later a male voice came on.

"ICU. How can I help you?"

"My mom is in there."

"Visiting hours are technically over."

"I just want to say good night. Please, sir?"

He must have sensed the urgency in my voice.

"Sure," he said, and a moment later, I heard the door unlock.

I walked over to my mom's bed, leaned over her and kissed her cheek. "I love you mom." I took her hand in mine, "I found the girl I love, mom. I am going to get her. I'll be back before you wake up. You'll come back to me too, ma..." I placed her hand back against the bed, blew another kiss across the space between us and left to find my dream girl who I had only encountered briefly at the W Hotel.

Crossing back past the myriad of colored light diners, gas stations, and strip malls I decided to start my search for the mystery woman right where I left her. *No, she would never be back to that place.* I thought.

The air felt like an ashtray, thick and musty, moistened by a light drizzle that lowered into the valley. I lit up a smoke and searched the skies for a sign that might lead me to the woman I loved. Nothing showed its face to me in the night. I decided to drive to Las Virgines and take the canyon to the ocean.

The traffic lightened after the 405 overpass and finally I saw the green and white exit sign for the canyon. I exited the freeway, made the left and started my ascent. Guard rails leading to the apex of the hill provided safe passage to this weary pioneer, who needed to free himself from the cacti of the San Fernando and taste the cleansing salty air of the Pacific. The natural vortex created by hills on both sides of me kept the air passing coolly through my van, and nearly purified the putrid fumes of my exhaust.

The canyon broke out past a building made of glass patchwork. The regenerative harmony of the waves repetition brought a sense of calm. This was the escape that I had been looking for before I started the search into the doldrums of LA to find the girl with the golden hair.

PCH was vacant. A few passing strangers walked to and from the gas stations that offered late night service. The breeze was filled with the faint scent of tar and sand. It layered the air in tiers, its atmosphere changed at each height. My van morphed into a surf van, sand particles in every crevice of the built-in bed and the paisley patterned flannel sheets that adorned the mattress.

I had an old friend, Bennett Harbor who lived in the guesthouse of a very affluent family in the Colony. I always wondered how he scored such a sweet deal, but no one ever bothered to ask him. We only knew that his dedication to his job at one of the local surf shops didn't pay much, unless you counted the massive discount on boards. Bennett had decided to build up his collection instead of investing in his own piece of property, which the rest of the Malibu community and local surfers all admired, in a way.

Bennett had nothing to do besides surf, smoke weed, and fall asleep dreaming about the waves he would surf the next morning before work. I always thought his die-hard devotion would pay off, and he would become a pro surfer, own his own shop, or even work filming his own version of *The Endless Summer*. Instead, one day while Bennett was walking home from Surfrider beach to the colony with his 9' 6" Infinity, a local bus clipped the board and sent him spinning into the middle of PCH. He was run over so many times, the ambulance and police had a hard time identifying him. After his death the local surf community held a huge surf style funeral out past 3rd point, and all the locals, like Jimmy Hart, Stan Arnlaugher, and Leech "Svenny" Alan, were there to lead the ceremony.

They floated his ashes out on a 12' solid mahogany gun from the 1970's. When Jimmy lit the leis soaked in gasoline, the wood burned with a vibrant blue authenticity the same color as Bennett's eyes. I was there on one of Bennett's boards that day. I could feel him watching us, laughing at me as I tried to keep my balance on one of his short fishes.

Byron and Pam Lasky, the couple that owned Bennett's guesthouse left his room just the way it was. This included leaving the massive wood carved Hawaiian Luau statuette he had made in a wood carving class in Topanga. It outsized everyone else's in the class by a good four feet.

Over the years, the Laskys removed Bennett's stuff, item by item, and donated it to local surf shops for memorabilia. Byron and Pam became kind of like the father and mother of the whole surfing community. Byron had always been kind of a hero for us, but after Bennett passed away, it was as though their own flesh and blood was lost. He, too, went off the deep end every time he gave some object of Bennett's away, it was as if a piece of Mr. Lasky were going with it. The one thing they never touched, though, was Bennett's board collection. They built a small shed on the backside of their own two-story modern beach house that looked like a bamboo hut, furnished with a few shell wind chimes, and faded papier-mâché flowers left by ex-girlfriends as they stopped in every year after the accident.

The hut reminded us that Bennett was always surfing. Those of us who knew him well were given a silver key that granted us access to the colony gate from the beach. We were allowed to borrow the boards on good faith. Each ride was an homage to Bennett.

It never felt right taking his boards, but tonight I felt compelled to take a ride. *When it feels right man, it is right,* I heard Bennett say in my head. I never understood what the hell he meant, other than he believed that whatever he was doing day or night was right to him. “I guess that's what really matters,” I said. And it was like I was talking to Bennett.

It was late and freezing, but the combination of the darkness, sea salt, and the waves was inviting. I sifted through the middle console to find the silver key I kept attached to a Celtic knot made from old maritime rope. Sure enough, it was still there, stuck to the side of the plastic cup holder with a half-melted lemonhead.

I parked next to the old lumberyard and walked through a break in the wall, tracing the dirt path around the willows to the South entrance of the Colony. The gate had rusted, the iron spray painted over in black to conceal the weather damage. I put the key into the lock. It wouldn't twist. I struggled to turn it, and finally, by force or fate, the lock opened and I entered the vacant street.

The fog was stale. The night air was sitting stagnant over a privately owned golf course. My feet became heavier, the moisture soaking my socks. When I reached the ninth house on the left, I knew in a couple feet I would see the monument to my old friend Bennett. The ambient white light smelled of bamboo trodden with Havianas, soaked by massive amounts of salt from the ocean.

The air coming from inside smelled like sage: cleansing; warm, smoky, and pure. I touched the outside of the makeshift hut. The texture of the bamboo was brittle, and the fibers peeled off in my hand in shards.

The surfer's dream is the wave that is untouchable. Paradise lies underneath two thousand pounds of pressure at the bottom of the ocean, where the thundering roll of the crests pounding the coral beds sounds like an aquatic symphony. In dreams, there's never any scripture to show you the way to find these waves. The only map is in the darkened corners of an untapped imagination.

I knew if anyone was on this wave, it was Bennett. And here I was, looking to use one of his boards to travel into the depths of the night, the sea, finding the answer to give me guidance as my internal sextant.

I measured the loss of life that was perpetuated by aquamarine semi-precious stones glued to a Renaissance black oil soaked canvas on the wall in the silhouette of the great Bennett Harbor, and his nickname was spelled out. “H-A-R-B-Y.” His name was written in shells that had been spray painted gold.

The homage was more beautiful than the professionally taken surf photographs of him that hung around the inside, taken from his many clippings and victories in surf competitions. I sat for a moment on the sandy floor of the shack and stared up at the ceiling covered in dangling puffer fish, shells, and old rope, even a few mismatched pieces of lingerie. I didn't think there was a wave Harby hadn't surfed. After a few minutes I was compelled to grab one of the 9' 6” Stewarts and take to the ocean.

CHAPTER NINETEEN

"I want my purse back, you asshole," Jennifer shouted. Her brow furled, and the make-up she had caked on the night before cracked.

"I just want to see what kind of game we're playing here." A man in his mid-forties rifled through her suede Henri Bendel clutch. "Aha! What's this?" He pulled out a wad of cash.

"That's mine."

"I don't think so. This belongs to me. And what the fuck is this?" He removed a .22mm handgun from the purse.

"That's mine too, fucking put it back. You want me to fucking scream? Do you?"

"Calm down! I'm not going to tell on you. Don't worry." Jennifer slowly eased back into the conversation and weighed out her options. It appeared the best choice was to at least hear him out. "What do you want?"

"Well, now that's a good question. I think it's more like what made you think you could steal my money from me."

"I earned it."

"Was that the arrangement?"

“Yes, that's how it works. You got what you wanted.”

“You took a thousand dollars from me.”

“That's what you owe me, I don't usually do this.”

“So shouldn't it be less if you're not a professional?”

“I mean I don't sleep with people for money.”

“Yeah, I know what you meant.”

“Then no, I'm rare so it's more expensive.”

“Why'd you take my car keys?”
“What car keys??” Jennifer pretended not to remember the 911 Carrera parked downstairs.

“It's vintage you know?”

“What?”

“My Porsche.”

“Oh, that I had know Idea, I just needed to go to the store.”

“Oh, alright if that's all.” He was amused.

“So… what are you gonna do? Turn me in?”

“How about we come up with something else?”

“What? I don't think there's an easy fix to this.”

“You said yourself you don't normally do this.”

“That's right.”

“Me neither, and had I known.”

“Oh, don't pretend you would've paid straight up.”

“Maybe.”

“It was good, you're lucky.”

“To get robbed?”

“It was a trade. You know, barter system.”

“If I had known it was going to cost me my car, then I would've at least gone another time with you.”

“Is that all you want?”

“At this point it seems only fair.”

“Fine. How do you want it?”

“Is that where we're at? No romance anymore?”

“Give me a minute to freshen up.”

“Oh, right you probably expected to be on your way on the highway now in your stolen Porsche.”

Jennifer went into the bathroom and splashed water on her face. She took one of the plush hand towels and wet it with hand soap and water. She lifted her skirt and scrubbed her crotch with the rag in short circles. She dipped the other end of the towel in the remaining warm water, and rinsed off the soap and remnants from the night before.

In the mirror her reflection was dreary. The hustle had started to wear on her youthful appearance. She could still taste the swirl of olive juice in the back of her throat from the martini she'd had last night. She closed her eyes for a moment, opened them again and looked back at herself in the mirror. She tried to see the scared and innocent child she had once been. The light in her eyed faded. She went back into the bedroom.
\
“I was wondering if we were ever going to make this happen,” said the man stretched out on the bed.

“I'm sorry, I just wanted to look nice for you.” She stretched the corner of her mouth into a seductive smile. The man was already out from under the covers, stroking himself. Jennifer crawled up the bedding and put her lips around his cock. She almost choked a few times, but continued. After five minutes, the man had turned Jennifer's lean pale body around and placed her palms on the top of the low wooden headboard. He penetrated her, again and again, until it looked like he was about to explode. Tears ran down the side of Jennifer's face, but she didn't let him see her pain and disgust.

“Is that good baby?”

"Yes, Uhuu—O, yes… yes." She continued to fake pleasure. Finally he pulled out right before his orgasm. Rather than finish, he continued again and came inside of her. Jennifer lunged forward, not from the immense force, but from the loss of her pride. It vanished in an instant and sucked out with it the innocent child she was so desperately looking for.

"You were everything I hoped for that time," he said and lay back down onto the covers, fluffing the embroidered pillow to prop up his head.

"You really earned that car. Just tell the valet Jimmy said it was fine to take it." Jennifer was cuddled up like a ball of spoiled milk. She stood up, limping. Semen leaked out and down her leg. She grabbed her purse and picked up the make-up and hundred dollar bills that had fallen out when it fell off the bed to the floor.

In the bathroom Jennifer put her clothes on robotically. She grabbed the towel off the floor she used before, and flossed between her legs with the whole towel to wipe off the fluid from her skin. She sat on the toilet. Jennifer got up and took one last look in the mirror, but her image was unrecognizable. The sound of the TV came on in the other room, or maybe she just hadn't noticed it before.

"It's time to get the fuck out of here."

She wiped the rest of the tears from her face with the sleeve of her cashmere sweater.

In the bedroom, her exhausted Jimmy was snoring and sleeping with Fox news on in the background. Jennifer couldn't help herself. She walked over to him and stared for an extended minute, her disgust and anger pouring over him. She reached in her purse and pulled out the .22mm. She pushed it against his temple and pulled the trigger. The silver hammer clicked, "No bullets, asshole." She walked over, grabbed her pumps and left the room, moving towards the elevators, clutching the Porsche key in her hand.

The valet smirked at Jennifer, and she could tell this was not the first time a car had been traded at this hotel for sex. She brushed him off, and stepped inside the tan leather interior of the Carrera. She revved the engine and shimmied the shift knob left and right reaffirming neutral. Jennifer had driven a stick shift throughout high school, but had never had a Porsche powertrain with so much power. The thick black rubber burned off a layer and the smoke spilled over the valet that watched anxiously. The young girl who looked vulnerable was now controlling more torque than a single man could exert having sex for his entire life.

The wind was thick. It filled Jennifer's hair and weighted the ends. The straight panels of blonde were flattering to her angular jaw line, and when she adjusted the rear view mirror she caught a glimpse of herself. She looked different then she remembered. The warm air settled on her skin momentarily when she stopped for a traffic light. That sense of calm was immediately broken by the car's rapid acceleration.

She moved through the streets of Westwood, to Santa Monica, and down Channel road to PCH. A flurry of memories drifted in and out of her head. The only one that she could not shake with a sway of her head was her childhood crush. A boy who lived in a house with his mother in the middle of the famous LA Stairs. Generally known for the avid stair-climbers that ascended them on a daily basis, to Jennifer the stairs were the path to reach a feeling inside her stomach for a boy from Australia named Austin Richter.

The last time she visited Austin, he and his family were packing up the house to move back to Australia. As she secretly watched him through the window, a tickle on her leg made her look down. It was the largest cat she had ever seen. An Orange Marmalade-colored cat that looked like the Cheshire cat from Alice in Wonderland. She wanted more than anything to pick him up and take him with her.

Her fantasy was interrupted by Austin calling for the cat. Even now, Jennifer still walked the stairs the last day of every October to look for the cat, or maybe just relive the memory of her youth.

“What if he had seen me?” Jennifer couldn't stop repeating the question aloud. “We would be married, have kids, live in Tasmania, and ride horses.”

The cliché made her blush. She felt foolish for thinking it was possible for her to be married. She wanted to have someone to grow old with, but couldn't believe anyone would want to marry her. The self-esteem she'd once had had faded into the light of the street lamps that illuminated the windy turns down Channel Road. She blew past the last red light that lead to Rustic Canyon and sped down toward the endless ocean ahead. The sea was blocked only by grey cement barricades strategically placed by the city so no one continued driving straight off the highway and onto the sand.

The waves were barely audible under the sound of the Porsche accelerating northbound up PCH. Jennifer thought she could hear the faint cries of seagulls, but she knew they were only in her head, that she was projecting her desires again; a symptom Freud had warned her against. She needed to live in the present, Jennifer shook her head nervously, convinced what she was doing wasright.

Just past Big Rock, Jennifer stopped at a liquor store. She pulled in just past the flower shop and parked in one of the diagonal spaces in front of a yellow glowing sign 'Liquor.'

The owner, a beach-stained fifty year old man in a navy blue mesh cap with an eagle patch on it, watched her, curious. Jennifer didn't even notice. She moved through the aisles, knowing her true intention was to find a cold bottle of champagne that would calm her nerves. She caught the man behind the register eyeing her, and blushed.

"Champagne?" She said.

The man didn't answer. She couldn't have known it then, but her beauty silenced him.

She opened the refrigerator and found Veuve Clicquot on the top shelf. She took one bottle, and then she grabbed a second one.

"Is that all?

"Yeah, birthday party."

"Alone on your birthday?"

"No. My friends are already at my house."

"Are you sure you…?" Before he could finish, he lost his nerve. "Don't need anything else?"

"No, that's all."

He looked at her, the Porsche, and just couldn't piece together the puzzle. There had been many customers, underage like Jennifer in fast sports cars, and he had always quizzed them on their birthdays and astrological signs to see if they were telling the truth. But he didn't ask Jennifer any other questions. He wanted to help her. Helping her drown some of her sadness, he figured, was the least he could do.

Jennifer drove past Carbon beach, the affluent stretch of homes on the thin sliver of sand that connected the Malibu to Zuma. Before she could even continue to Zuma she saw red and blue flashing lights in her rear view. She contemplated accelerating, but decided to pull over and play the crying card, the innocent damsel in distress. She lifted her breasts so they stood even more prominently. One bra strap became visible on her right shoulder. She sniffled and let the tears trickle out.

Howard Munson had been the Malibu sheriff for 25 years, and had seen many young girls pull the same act Jennifer was pulling now. Fortunately, Howard had remained head of the department for so long because of the support from wealthy Malibu property owners who made generous contributions to him and his department every year. The contributions fueled a positive track record for Munson and a reputation for showing favoritism to young girls in high-priced automobiles that belonged to the kind donors to his own coffers.

This evening, Munson was training a new recruit to the ways of the small county, outside the norms for the typical LAPD standard operating procedures. Munson gave him preferential treatment because he was a distant relative and had served as a legal intern with a judge in Penticton, BC before moving back down to his home in Oxnard. The new recruit followed Munson's every move.

“Evening, Miss. Do you know why I'm pulling you over?” Munson gave her the chance to catch herself in a lie, admit to something she thought she might have done.

“No officer, I'm…” The tears continued to fall.

“Is everything alright, ma'am?”

“Alright?” She looked at him seductively, reassured by his concern. “I'll be fine. I'm sorry if I did anything wrong.”

“Well, can you tell me where you're going?”

Jennifer looked at him and thought about the thousands of destinations she'd had in mind: Point Dume, County line, or just off the 1 highway and down the cliffs of Santa Cruz into the crashing waves below.

“I'm visiting my family friends in the Colony.” She figured one of the ten different families she had grown up with would provide an alibi.

“Is that right?”

“Yes sir.” She looked down at her breasts and made sure Munson took a good look before she lifted her strap from her shoulder and covered them back up again.

“This is a nice Porsche.”

“Thanks, it's vintage,” she said, knowing he was on the verge of letting her go.

"Have you been drinking?" He asked, remembering he had the rookie on the other side of the car. Though he was too focused on Jennifer's indescribable beauty. She looked like one of the Hungarian dolls that his mother collected when he was a child.

"Officer, of course not."

"Should we test that?"

"I swear officer, I don't even like alcohol." Jennifer was obviously lying, but her blatant disregard for the reality of the situation, plus the fact that she had just pulled out of a liquor store parking lot was hilarious to Munson. He figured he had put enough pressure on her. Besides, if she was going to do something stupid, it was going to be after she finished off the liquor she had purchased, not before. By that point, she would not be on his road. Munson didn't want to fantasize about all the erotic predicaments she could find herself in after she was intoxicated, but he secretly couldn't help it.

"Don't lie. Just be safe, and don't drink and drive. We lose a lot of good looking children on this road every year."

"Sure," Jennifer said, and then looked at him, waiting for permission to continue on her journey.

"You are free to go, Miss… "

"Bannister."

"Right of course! Rupert Bannister. You're his daughter."

"Yeah."

"Okey dokey. Well, you tell Rupee hello for me won't you? We were sad to see him move up to the Hollywood Hills and leave Malibu."

"Will do, sir." She gave him a salute and fired up the Carrera.

"Damn, haven't seen Rupe since I was doing security on set for M*A*S*H up in the Malibu Canyon here."

But the Porsche was already pulling away.

"M*A*S*H you know that show William? Probably not, a little before your time."

"I've seen an episode or two," the rookie muttered, still captivated by the impression Jennifer's beauty had left on him.

"Doesn't matter. Different damn time." Munson was struck with a wave of nostalgia, remembered his first wife and how they used to lay back and smoke a joint of reefer and watch M*A*S*H on their 14" Zenith TV, adjusting the rabbit ears to get a clearer picture. This was years before Howard had joined the police force. Those memories always gave him a soft spot for the younger generations. It also made him a little more lenient on drinking and the recreational drug use in Malibu.

"Yes, indeed. 'Nother time, 'nother place."

"Right, sir."

"What about the girl?"

"Who? Bannister's kid? She'll be fine."

The cops watched for speeding cars careening into parked cars in the opposite direction on PCH. Munson was satisfied after their run-in with Jennifer and his trip down memory lane. Now it was time to get some revenue for the city and pull over a group of valley kids passing through looking for a party. Outsiders were not welcome, and he didn't want the transients to interrupt the equilibrium in the community that he tried his whole life to preserve. He would rather the sin stay all in the family, and he let the appearance of good be his guide for his logic.

CHAPTER TWENTY

The Pacific Ocean was freezing cold. The dark sand was a fair warning of what I could expect once I got into the brackish water. Fortunately, I had put on an old O'Neill wetsuit about two sizes too big that had been left behind by one of Bennett's old buddies. My toes sank into the wet sand, and the remnants of the last wave still frothed. I walked until my feet disappeared into the darkness of the water. The ocean swept me up, and I fell forward onto the epoxy-lined surface of the board. I buoyed right and left to confirm the boundaries of my balance before paddling out into infinity.

Once I was past the break, I felt a sense of peace. I turned and saw a few people walking on the pier, and fishermen still scuttling along the shoreline trying to catch the late night lunkers in the moonlight. I wanted to continue out into the darkness, but something inside me kcpt telling me that after I passed the reef barrier, the Great White Sharks that lived between Malibu and Catalina might come take a closer look at me. I decided to paddle toward 1st point; the short boarder's break twenty meters to the North shore.

There was no movement now on the beach. I felt calm. The rocking motion of the waves below the board was barely noticeable, and after about an hour, my body was numb with cold. I lay on my back and put my feet up on the board. Staring into the sky I could almost make out a handful of real stars. I had made it past the spoiled pollution of Los Angeles county and was now touching the natural world just beyond the cityscape. I was so unused to this kind of silence that I nearly fell asleep. The only thing that stopped me was a siren screaming down PCH. I couldn't pinpoint it's location but I knew the direction of the car was out toward Point Dume, a party spot for locals and underage Simi Valley kids, who gathered for drinking, sex, and some midnight full moon surf sessions.

I was glad no one had the idea to head out to Surfrider to party instead. The reef below was an obstacle that even the most suicidal surfers wouldn't try to handle in the dark, but I knew the cuts from the sharp rocks were the price I had to pay for gaining the serenity of the hum from the waves beneath me.

Closing my eyes I pictured my sister and I as children, playing in the sand with our multicolored mini-rakes, buckets, and shovels that our dad had sent us for Christmas. I never knew if he really did send these toys to us, or if our mom just signed the card from him. Either way it made us smile. We felt comforted just knowing he was somewhere in the world and cared about us. Minute details can change a person's entire perception, and as kids, the gesture altered our feelings of loss and abandonment, pacifying us for the rest of the year.

The nostalgia subsided and it was time to paddle in.

CHAPTER TWENTY ONE

The sand under Jennifer's feet was crystalline, thousands of minerals touched by water, separated, and swept in the tide to the land. The bottle of champagne fell to her side. The champagne bubbles slid in secession, limitless. Completing her walk on the beach was a handful of painkillers, which she used as a chaser for the Veuve Clicquot.

“Take this you bastards!” She yelled throwing the first empty bottle into the ocean. The crashing waves swallowed her words. She walked down toward the water. The water stung her legs. There were a few stars visible, and Jennifer reached out her index finger, shut one eye and connected the glowing dots to make a crown.

“There. I'm a princess.” She extended her arms and curtsied.

“Now, where is my prince?”

Looking out into the water, she thought she saw someone. Jennifer pretended she was on a float in front of her kingdom. She waved, cupping her hand and robotically turning it from left and right to acknowledge the crowd. It was time for her to give a speech.

“To all who come here today… I applaud you. Your generosity. For it is you that make me who I am, and all that I will be. I am fucking grateful…”

Jennifer raised the bottle of champagne to the sky, opened it firing the cork off, put it to her lips, and swigged a quarter of the bottle.

She looked around for the spot on the beach where she had parked the Porsche, but the few glowing streetlights blended together, and started to crisscross, forming a spectacle of yellow, “Jesus is that you?” she blacked out and fell to the sand.

A floating plastic bag washed up onto the shore. The waves played with the synthetic object, trying to submerge it. The figure behind the plastic bag, the person Jennifer had mistaken for Jesus, was moving closer to her. Jennifer's eyes twitched. Her body struggled to pump enough blood into her brain, hindered by the cocktail of pills she had swallowed. The medicine had performed its miracle, shutting down the parts of the body that allowed her to feel. Knowing she would never experience the future made her smile ever so slightly. She fell into unconsciousness, her body camouflaged among the brindle colored rocks.

Jennifer lay on the beach. The tide was coming in and the water tickled the bottom of her bare feet. She dreamt the frosty tongue of the ocean was the licking from her old dog, Trevor, the Spaniel she had had since he was a puppy. Trevor had developed a bizarre fungal disease that atrophied his limbs at the end of his life, but in Jennifer's unconscious Trevor was alive and well, squeaking his favorite chipmunk stuffed animal and waiting for her to throw it.

Jennifer picked up the stuffed toy and tried to squeeze it. A loud screeching noise came out from the plastic bubble inside. The screeching became louder and louder until she couldn't bear the sound. She dropped the toy and it fell down to the floor. The blackness returned and she drifted in and out of consciousness; intermittently illuminated by red flashes of light.

Surfrider's peace was broken when I reached the shore. It erupted in glowing red lights. I had drifted with the tides past the pier and underneath the pylons. The sound of the water underneath the pier blocked my view of the scene that was unfolding on the beach. I couldn't see what was happening, and I really had no desire to find out. I figured some poor late night fisherman had drank too much alcohol and been hit by a car.

I came out from the shadows below the pier. When I saw the golden blonde hair I could not mistake it for another's. I grabbed the board and stuffed it into the boulders. I knew the tide would retract back into the sea, so there was no risk of losing one of Bennett's favorites, although he would have understood. I walked, dragging my feet in the sand, as they were only beginning to gain feeling back in them from the numbing cold that stung like needles. The footsteps I left in the sand were shaped in parenthesis, broken by the staggering limp in my right leg.

I was within ten feet of the stairs when the sensation came back into both my legs. I grabbed hold of the white chipped paint railing and climbed up, leaping over every other step. I reached PCH and ran down the thin shoulder of the road, missing rearview mirrors of parked cars by centimeters, increasing my pace down the asphalt. The images were blurry, but felt more real as the blood pulsed through my veins.

There was a terror inside of me that grew with each step, not knowing. I had been in the ocean in a meditative state to pray for one more grace of her presence, and as much as I wanted to believe the paramedics were helping just another bleach blonde who had fallen down dead drunk on the beach after a perverse evening of exploitation at the Malibu Inn, I knew my intuition was correct. The girl's anonymity was fading with every car I passed on PCH.

I broke in the huddle of paramedics administering what appeared to be a saline solution into her blood. She was turning blue, but her hair was the same sandy blonde, plastered to her scalp now by layers of grit. The sand did nothing to diminish her beauty.

“Who are you man? Do you know her?” The paramedic in charge of putting flares in the street to deter the oncoming traffic was looking at me.

“Who me?” I didn't know how to answer. I didn't even know her name.

“Yeah, you. What are you doing over there?”

“She's my… my… girlfriend man.” I responded.

“OK, don't get in their way. She's pretty bad off.”

I continued to stare at her face. The pink flesh tones started to return to her skin as they lifted her on a gurney into the back of the ambulance. I tried to grab her hand as they slid her onto the tracks. My fingers just missed hers.

“Where are they taking her?”

The ambulance spewed moist brown smoke into the street as it sped off. The monoxide eradicated any fresh taste of salt water that still lingered. I wanted to smell her again, and have her scent cleanse me of the poison that filled my lungs. But she was gone, a siren screaming down PCH. I couldn't do anything else but scream, giving my frustrations back to the world. My yelling prompted one of the fireman's attention, and he came over to see what was wrong with me.

“Get the fuck away from me!” I lashed out at the fireman who was unaccustomed to completely erratic voyeurs wearing full wetsuits and yelling irrational phrases out of pure bliss and shock from the numbness of their limbs. “Buddy, be calm. I don't want to have to restrain you.” He looked back at me, surprised, and I could sense the fear behind his eyes.

“That girl means everything to me.” I didn't know what else to say.

“Well, you better go get her then,” he said. His advice was shortsighted, but right on the money.

I ran down PCH, back in the direction of the Colony, to get my van and chase down the ambulance that carried the girl I loved.

The long legs of the wetsuit came unrolled and flapped underneath my feet like oversized inflatable inner tubes. I stumbled and nearly clipped a huge yellow SUV. The next car was not so lucky: I knocked the side view mirror on a Porsche clean off. It did its damage to me too. I fell to the ground.

I was starting to sweat from the suit anyway, so I decided to strip it off, forgetting, in the midst of my pain, that I was wearing nothing underneath. I yanked the legs of the suit off and looked down at the pavement where the side view mirror lay. I wanted to somehow affix it back to the car, but knew there was no hope with the lack of tools or adhesive I had available at my disposal.

I thought that if I used one of the flares I could melt the neoprene onto the metal and solder the mirror back to its original position. The still frame image of the car with half of a melted black wetsuit coating the fender was enough to deter me from playing Mickey Mouse mechanic.

I looked at myself in the quadrangle mirror, and barely recognized the face that stared back at me. I wore an expression of panic, but there was something surrounding me. In the mirror, I saw my sister's reflection next to mine, the colors cloudy and washed out, like an image from an old family photo. I took the mirror and clutched it to my chest, wishing our images would stay embedded in the glass, etched into it permanently. I wanted to carry the mirror around as my own personal keepsake, an oversized wallet photo, or wear it around my neck like a locket.

Cars honked. Headlights illuminated the already embarrassing chain of events that was unfolding as a sideshow to the stopped traffic. I shivered. I started to run again, when I felt a force knock me back into the pavement.

“I got him!”

“Good work rookie. Another flasher.”

“I'll read his Miranda's.” The rookie anxiously awaited the sheriff's instruction.

“Don't bother, Bill. Just find out what in the hell he thinks he's doing, scaring everybody with that awful sight.”

“So, what are you doing buddy? Why are you traumatizing these people, huh?”

I was ‘traumatized' by the unorthodox restraint the cop had on my wrist. I couldn't help but chuckle to myself when I realized his hand was not only restraining me, but resting on my bare ass.

“Can you let go of my wrist?”

I felt his weight shift, and he looked up toward the older cop for his go-ahead. The other cop nodded.

I turned over and faced both the cops. They both turned away instead of looking straight at me, so I knew I would not have to worry about any further sexual innuendos or role-play. I huddled, bringing my knees in tight to my chest to retain the last bit of heat my body still possessed.

"I was trying to find the love of my life."

"Oh, is that all son?"

"I'm just so tired."

"So. Where is she, or he? Right, Bill." He nudged the younger cop and chuckled.

"She… She was in that ambulance."

"The drunk girl?"

"Is that what happened?"
"Can't discuss it, but let's just say, kid, you don't want to watch them pump the stomach of that girl. Poor Bannister's got a problem child to deal with."

"Is she going to make it?"

“Don't know, she was pretty bad off. Was barely breathing on her own. A local resident was walking their dog from Carbon over here, and spotted her. Lucky girl.”

The cop seemed reluctant to share any more information, and the Sheriff turned away. The guilt of the Sheriff didn't bother me, we all carry it, but his willingness to lie to me, a naked, in love, hallucinatory, and broken boy on the pavement, did.

I decided to give into my pressing desire to know where they took her. I was determined, and knew if I caught the officer contemplating his own interior guilt I would have a shot at prying the information from him.

“Where'd they take her?”

“Can't disclose that,” the young cop said.

“West Hills ER.” The Sheriff said, much to the Rookie's surprise.

“Thanks for being the last decent cop,” I said, and I meant it.

“No problem kid. Now go get her. I hope she's worth it.”

“She is, sir. She is the only thing I have left.” My voice trailed off as I started to stampede toward the stairs and back to the shoreline path. I knew it was the stealthily alternative way to get back to through the Colony's fence and guard tower deterrent. Halfway down the beach I realized I left the board behind. I knew that one of the local surfers would spot the board and recognize it as Bennett's', maybe keep it there like an homage to his memory.

I prayed silently on my jog back that my girl was OK. I had to trust modern medicine to save the only two women left in my life. This was an anathema to me, but I had no choice. I pictured the different ways each might die; knowing that playing these scenarios out would make them less likely to occur. The world doesn't like you to be prepared for the curve balls it throws you.

The top two ways to die were always drowning and burning, but at this point I felt like I was suffocating with a translucent bag around my head, staring in the mirror and watching the oxygen levels deplete in the bulging sensation of my eyes. I was like an antique diver wearing a copper ringed suit a thousand leagues down below the ocean's surface, the breathing tube cinched shut by the pressure of the water. I pictured the thick glass fogging up with the last warm breaths of life. I didn't have to see the face. I could feel my heart beating wildly as the air escaped, and my chest was heavy, experiencing an anxiety attack.

The ground was gritty as sensation returned to my feet. My toes already chewed up pretty badly from the extended run on the asphalt. Pebbles stuck in my skin, and there was a trail of blood behind me on the dry beach. The colony gate was still open, and I scurried through it and down the empty street. I could barely make out the direction of my van, but the vertigo was tempered by my commitment to track down this girl, who had once again reinvigorated my spirit and given me purpose, as she fell into the arms of the paramedic's unconscious.

I threw the dirty wet suit back into Harby's shack. I noticed the Laskys' lights on. I could hear them arguing. I didn't have time to make out the words as my quest had just begun. I was going after the only thing I could remember ever truly having a need for. I slid open the back and grabbed my clothes. I put them on my wet skin, they felt good. I jumped in my Chevy and cranked the ignition. The fucking starter wouldn't fire.

“Damn solenoid,” I guessed. I remembered a trick a mechanic from Palmdale had once taught me, and I grabbed my tire iron from the back. I got out and lay down underneath the side of the car. I reached deep into the middle of the car, next to the transmission, found the starter and hit it a few times with the tire iron.

The clanging must have been loud enough to disturb the pleasantness of the Malibu community because a few house lights down the block went on and off. Their arrangement lit up a runway, and traced a way out.

In the process of jumping back into the cab, I felt a nurturing hand touch my shoulder. It was Mrs. Lasky. She was beautiful woman in her late forties, and still had the most charming and elegant demeanor that enhanced her attractiveness.

“I almost didn't recognize you, Charlie,” she said and put her arms out to hug me like I was her long lost child. “I know I haven't been around. It's really great to see you.” “You too.” Her smile comforted me. Being a woman with the most acute intuition, she could sense my urgency was over a female.

Her intuition was of course undeniably accurate, and so she asked, “So, she must be pretty important to you?”

“She means thc world,” was all I could say.

“What's the lucky girl's name? Do I know her?”

I didn't respond.

“She's really done you over. Cat's got your tongue.” Mrs. Lasky continued.

“I actually don't even know her name.” I admitted.

“You're kidding Charlie, c'mon. You just don't want to tell me. Even if she is one of the girls who used to leave their bras in Bennett's ‘love shack' I won't judge you, you know that. Besides, I'm sure whoever she is, she's all grown up by now right?”

“Honestly, Mrs. L, I really don't even know her name. I know that must sound totally crazy, but I just know she's the one, if there is such a thing.”

“I believe you,” she said, which surprised me. I jumped back into the captain's chair and tried for a second time to get my trusty beast back on the highway. I wasn't sure if she had been crying, but her eyes were swollen, and I could feel her kindness and sympathy making its way through me, keeping me from falling apart.

“I have to find her. She's been taken to the hospital.” The urgency returned to the pace of my words.

“Well, go, sweetheart. When you find her, bring her by some time. You know we would love to have you here for dinner or something. Especially with the love of your life.”

“I know.” I turned the key in the ignition and the starter turned over, emitting a black cloud of oil from the tailpipe. Fortunately, the wind was Southerly so it blew it away from Mrs. Lasky who had a concerned look, as I pulled out of the driveway and down the street.

It didn't take me long to blow through the guard gate and back onto PCH toward Zuma. I knew the streets would be completely empty, minus a few lonely cops, and I knew where to find them: They were still tied up with explaining and taking statements from the local neighbors on Surfrider who spotted my innocent girl stranded in a toxic oblivion. I knew it was impossible to change someone who didn't want help. I didn't want to change her, but I thought the feeling of my hand on hers might prove to her that life was still worth living.

I had convinced myself that she was more than real, an incarnation of Aphrodite, a goddess without flaws. Now, I thought, she might die before I knew anything about her imperfections. Sometimes it is the imperfections that make a person even more beautiful. The glorification of perfect beauty is the fuel for superficiality, and if I were a member of the clergy in ancient Greece this idea of divine beauty as a flawless persona would be painfully bled out of my vein to cure me of the notion.

I wanted to know every detail that made her different from the sea of girls I had met throughout my life but didn't give a shit about. I had given her all of me. If she was gone I would float back out into the Pacific Ocean and intentionally forget to paddle back in. I would go so far out that even when my survival instinct kicked in to propel me back toward land, it would be too late.

The image of my sister returned. She was there now clear as day. Not just a phantom vision, or cloudy ghost. She was sitting there. My sister held my hand as I drove back over the hill. I looked in her eyes, and I knew it was the last time I would ever see her. It had been four years since her death, and in that time, she had shown me what was important. She had given me a gift, and now I had to figure the rest out on my own. I took one last look at her and she smiled at me. I felt goosebumps all over my body as she vanished back into the void. I would only have her guidance now through her voice in my memory.

The valley air was warm. The hospital was close by. I had to get to her room before anyone questioned me about our relationship. I couldn't handle going through what I had just gone through to see my mother. I needed to bypass as many of the gatekeepers as possible. If I could just reach her, I could provide some respite from the hospital staff.

The salt on my skin, the smell of oil burning off my engine, and the overwhelming scent of tobacco that stuck to my hands no matter how many times I washed them in peroxide would surely let her know that she was still alive, still part of the colorful world she so badly wanted to experience only now without consequences.

I entered the maze of hallways and made my way into the ER wing. I snuck around corners, nearly colliding with a few orderlies as I looked into each room, hoping to catch a glimpse of her blonde hair.

Down the last hallway, I smelled charcoal. I knew it was for her. In order to pump her stomach, the doctor would fill it with charcoal to absorb all the toxic acids. The thought of the black mineral filling her organs made me also want to vomit.

I walked into the room at the end of the hall. A nurse stood at the side of her bed monitoring her vitals. She finished up her checklist, and then tucked the clipboard back into a slot on the side of the bed and left. My girl sat there, a tube down her throat, and two clear prongs in her nose to assist with her breathing. She looked like a lab experiment in the future, a test for scientists exploring the different qualities that make a person beautiful, looking into her insides, testing her genetics to figure out if there was a common thread that tied all beautiful creatures together.

I walked to the side of her bed. I reached over the low side rail and touched the top of her hand with my fingers. It was cold. I didn't want to disturb her rest. I knew she needed strength to regain full consciousness. I decided I would sit and wait until she opened her eyes again.

I sat down and replayed the memories from the day over and over again, like a director watching dailies. I didn't have any control over the other actors, but I could watch the events unfold, and see what part I had played. It was then that I realized how little control I had over what had happened. The only choice I had made was to leave the circumstances that had me imprisoned in Bel-Air, captive to a woman with no mercy for me. I had faced the pain of my mother's sudden brain injury and crossed Los Angeles in search of some romantic ideal of love. I happened to find it, just as she was being placed on a stretcher. Now I was in a hospital again, with nothing left except the anonymous girl lying peacefully in front of me.

CHAPTER TWENTY TWO

I would like to tell you that when she woke up, we were inseparable. The truth is, when she woke up, her eyes rolled back into her head. When she finally stabilized herself and glanced at me, she paused, trying to figure out who I was.

“What are you doing here?”

“I came to find you.”

“Who are you?”

“Charlie,” I said.

“Charlie.” She repeated. The way she said my name made me smile. She accented the final ‘e' and made it sound like a word that never ended, like a concert that had stayed with her days later after the performance.

She fell back asleep. The nurse came in shortly after and asked me how she was doing.

“She seems fine to me.”
“Good,” The nurse answered. “We need to get someone else in this room. You can come with me and sign her out.”

I was nervous. I didn't know if she was ready to be signed out. She could barely keep her eyes open. And what was she going to think when I wheeled her to my van?

I still didn't know anything about her. I didn't even know her name. I didn't want to make claims about our real relationship to the nurse. I agreed anyway, even though I was reluctant, I knew she couldn't stay in this environment any longer.

I walked down the hallway to the nurse's station. The nurse handed me a clipboard with a release form on it. I figured it must be protocol, ensuring that patients be released to the custody of family, friends, or in my case a complete stranger totally obsessed with the notion of her anonymous existence. Nonetheless, I proceeded to fill out the form to the best of my knowledge. I paused when I realized the top of the form was already pre-printed with her information. Her name was Jennifer Christina Bannister, and she lived at 14236 Mulholland Dr., Los Angeles 90077.

"Jennifer," I whispered under my breath. It felt good to say her name. Just knowing it made me feel close to her.

"Are you all finished?" The nurse interrupted my fantasies about our future together. Something inside of me was certain we were meant to be together.

"Sure, I'm all set." I handed the clipboard back to her. She told me to meet her back in the room, and she would bring a wheelchair, as Jennifer would still be very weak.

I helped the nurse prop Jennifer up. She opened her eyes wide as she resisted our efforts to get her up and out of bed into the wheel chair. "Where are you taking me?"

"You have to get up, honey." The nurse said.

"It's time to go, Jennifer. I'll help you."

It was the first time I had said her name, and she looked back at me suspiciously. "I'm going to take you home." I was trying to reassure her. I was sure her family was worried about her current location. I wondered if the hospital had phoned them, and whether they cared.

"I don't want to go home," Jennifer said after a long moment.

"She'll be fine in few hours," the nurse said to me. "It may be a couple of days until she is 100%, but at least you can get her into her own bed to sleep the rest of it off." I just nodded and lifted Jennifer down into the chair. She was so lightweight; I could almost support her weight in one hand.

The nurse gave Jennifer the release form for her final signature to grant her release into my care. She didn't even look at it. She scribbled her name on the line. It wasn't a marriage commitment, but I took it as a sign of trust. I wheeled her out of the double glass automatic doors and toward the visitor parking lot where I had left my van. Before we reached the curb, security stopped me.

"We need that chair son. You'll have to help her out and swing around to pick her up." I agreed to do so, after confirming that Jennifer could stand up on her own.

She stood up, looked around and saw the guard eyeing her from the doorway, "You have a smoke?"

"Yeah, sure." He reached into his pocket and realized it was his lucky last cigarette. He offered it to her anyway realizing that she might need it more than he did. "You're giving me your lucky! Thanks."

He looked perplexed, confused, a piece of his childhood uniqueness borrowed for an instant. He lit the cigarette for her. She swayed, catching her balance as the rush of sweetened Virginia tobacco slid over her tongue.

“You know why they call it lucky, don't you?” Jennifer said.

“No. I guess I always figured it was because it's supposed to bring you fortune.”

“They used to include a cigarette in every carton, or wait, maybe every pack. I don't exactly remember. Anyway, they'd put in one cigarette that had a little piece of opium in it. You had to smoke each cigarette down to the end to make sure you got that one hit of pure bliss. And it made sure you never gave away any of your smokes.”

The guard shook his head. Jennifer pushed the wheelchair toward him, and walked down the curb to the van.

When she was younger, Jennifer had promised her mother she would never get in a van with someone she didn't know. She crawled up into the captain's chair and slipped a little bit. I jumped out and ran around to help her up.

“What a gentleman,” she said.

I had to laugh. I skidded out of the parking lot and put on some Janis Joplin. I figured there was nothing like *Pearl* to cheer her up and nurse her back into shape. We drove down Ventura Blvd until we hit Topanga. I jumped on the 101 and headed to the address on the form, which I concluded must be her parent's house.

Before we got to the freeway entrance, Jennifer grabbed the wheel and swerved across two lanes into the far right lane.

"That's the 101 North. We need to go south."

"I'm not blind, just a little queasy. Head north."

"Don't you want to go home?"

"Just go!"

I barely made the turn onto the on-ramp and thought I may have popped a rear tire as it skidded over the low red curb at theentrance. "Where are we going?" I asked.

"I'll tell you when we get there."

I wanted to argue, but began to realize this was all I wanted... to be alone with her on our own adventure. I decided to 'live' as she said, and go with the flow for once in my life. Jennifer did it so easily, rolling down the window and putting her hand out into the wind, letting it float along like a feathery white bird playing against the updrafts over the freeway.

I gave in. It took me all of about a minute. I relaxed back into my seat and listened to the wind hitting her hand.

CHAPTER TWENTY THREE

"Did it upset you that he had fallen in love with someone else?"

The therapist's words had resonated with Violet. She looked into the mirror behind the bars in the guard's room. Her reflection was tiny, but the glare of yellow light reminded her of Christmas spent with Charlie the year before. They were opening presents, listening to Tchaikovsky, and he was still sleepy, wearing a Santa hat and sitting below the tree.

Violet didn't celebrate Christmas, but it was important for her to have an excuse to express her emotions through material objects, rather than with physical tenderness. She wanted to give gifts that would lead to a prolonged embrace, possibly hours of intimacy, but in the end the result was always a timid imitation of the affection she so desired. It came in the form of hugs, or the more typical, "Thank you so much!" The response was never the imagined fantasy. In the simulated surreal light of Christmas morning, she once again put her faith in experiencing a moment of euphoria, where the gratitude matched her expectations.

Charlie was huddled over a pair of slippers Violet had given him. Charlie put the slippers on and wandered around the dark hardwood floors. He walked into the bar area, over the polar bear rug and behind the oak bar. He opened the fridge and found the eggnog. He poured a glass of the frothy beige elixir with his right hand, and simultaneously filled the glass with dark Caribbean Rum. He filled it to the brim, and took a big slug without hesitation like it was a health tonic.

Violet just stared. She couldn't get mad at Charlie, but she wanted more from him. She had provided him a home, clean clothes, and spoiled him with gifts and expensive dinners. The least he could do was to dedicate one day to the worship of her, she thought. Charlie had nearly finished the glass of nog when he drifted past Violet. The smell of his morning scent was intoxicating to her. "Where do you think you're going?" she said. Charlie looked at her, "Back to bed, I'm still exhausted." Violet was unhappy. "We still have presents to open," she said.

"Can't we do this later? I'm so tired."

"No, wake up. What the hell." Violet was irritated.

"Look baby, we can do this in an hour," Charlie said casually.

"Do what I say."

"What?" Charlie was taken aback.

"I mean. Let's just finish." Violet tried to recover, softening her demand.

She could smell the thin layer of sweat on his skin from the night before. She wanted to lick it off him oblige his wish to go get in bed, but they were still in the process of unwrapping presents, and she really wanted to give him a certain present this second.

"I think I see another present over there," she said.

"I don't think so, we cleaned house," Charlie said.

"I see one in the branches it looks like," she continued, and motioned over to the back of the tree. Charlie walked over behind the Noble Fir and forced the prickly green needles to the side. Sure enough, there was a small wrapped box. Charlie removed it.

"I didn't put this here."

"I know." She shook her head. "Obviously. I think Mrs. Claus put it there for you. Open it." Charlie didn't know how to respond. Something inside his stomach told him that by opening this gift, he was opening a commitment to Violet. He wasn't sure if that meant a ring, or other symbol of monogamy, but he knew that the entire process of hiding it inside the tree for this specific moment implied a deeper meaning then the pair of slippers he already had on his feet.

"Maybe we should save this for later," he said.

"No, no. I want you to open it right now, Charlie." She couldn't restrain herself from pushing him to open the gift.

"Ok, if you really want me to that bad." He hesitated again, but could see the seething smile of Violet for him to open the gift she had put so much energy into. He smiled sheepishly, and took the single piece of tape from the bottom of the gift. He opened it, and he found a black box with a gold crown on the top. Charlie had seen the emblem before, but never up close. He proceeded to snap open the jewelry box to find a Rolex watch.

"Do you like it?" Violet asked.

"It is really amazing. You didn't have to do that you know."

"Yes, I did. You are my prince Charlie. I want you to look like one."

Charlie was confused. As much as the gift was elegant, prestigious, and reflected a level of class he never expected to know first-hand, there was a reason he never wore watches. He didn't want time to catch him, and he certainly didn't want to be bound to someone else's schedule.

"Put it on. Let's see how it looks," Violet said, and helped him clasp the leather band. The gold on the fastener was sharp, and it speared through the leather eyelet with ease. Charlie withheld his appreciation. He was in awe of the gift.

"Now you'll never be late to meet me," Violet said.

It instantly transformed Charlie into a mature and even potentially wealthy looking gentleman. His boyhood charm still existed, but the enhancement of his overall prestige increased Violet's attraction to him. She decided she could no longer wait for him to embrace her fully and take her down onto the couch, so she wrapped her legs around him. "What are you doing baby?" Charlie asked, but he also knew that his acceptance of his new timepiece had changed his plans for rest of the day, and probably his life.

"Show me that you love me."

It was the first time she said it to him. Charlie was baffled by the concept of loving Violet. He didn't love her. The love that Violet wanted from him, he was incapable of providing.

Violet weighed just under one hundred pounds. Charlie carried her easily to the bedroom. He could feel her hipbones protruding. She tucked her head underneath his chin. In spite of himself, he was aroused. He took off her clothes, told her to turn over, and began to massage her back. He felt guilty after accepting the watch and wanted to return the favor.

The skin on her back was pale and freckled, the only part of her body that looked exactly its age. Charlie continued to rub her, and Violet continued purring until she couldn't take it anymore and reached to take off his belt. They began having sex. She scratched and clawed at him. Charlie clutched her tightly. Violet grabbed his lower back and pulled him in closer. Charlie was surprised by how good it felt. Other nights, he had allowed his mind to drift, fantasizing about other, more beautiful women to bring himself to ecstasy. This time he tried to think about more objective, non-sexual objects, so that he could last longer in this position that provided satisfaction to both of them.

"It's alright, honey," she said, looking him in the eyes.

"What do you mean?" Charlie was confused.

"Look into my eyes when you do it."

"What?"

"You can cum inside me," Violet said.

Charlie hadn't had unprotected sex since he'd gotten his high school girlfriend pregnant, and they had gone through the abortion process together. But it was too late. Even if Charlie had wanted to pull out, he couldn't have. He had done what he had promised himself he would never do again.

"Don't you feel better, baby boy?" Violet whispered to Charlie. She had the orgasm she wanted, and now, tired after the physical activity, proceeded to lie down and sleep.

Charlie didn't know what to say. He wanted to ask Violet if she was sure it was all right that they had had sex without any protection. She had mentioned something, once, about going on the pill, but he had no idea whether or not she had. He got up and went into the bathroom and searched the cabinets for birth control boxes. He didn't find any. He crossed his heart and said a prayer asking God to ensure that another life would not be brought into the world against his will. He went back and tried to go back to sleep. Violet's snoring kept him awake. Charlie didn't know if his prayer would be answered, but he hoped that the combination of birth control and religion would be enough to stop his sperm from ever creating a child.

Violet lay there clutching a stuffed bear her twin sister Destiny had given to her for their thirteenth birthday. The years of wear and tear had turned the toy into a decrepit and lumpy ball of limbs, sewn back together at the seams with a needle and thread. Charlie watched Violet hold tightly onto the tattered remains of her childhood.

Charlie didn't want to look back and see his life like that bear: broken, shredded, and ripped apart, held as a prisoner in the arms of a woman who wanted to possess him and did not understand that he needed a deeper connection, the loving comfort of a partner to explore life with.

Charlie got up, and went into the bathroom again. He saw his reflection, and didn't recognize the face that looked back. His jaw line was soft, his cheeks rosy red, flush and plump from Violet's rich truffle oils, as well as the shellfish and red meat they consumed on a nightly basis. He was bloated from head to toe. He felt grotesque. The thicker portions of his waist and lower back were especially noticeable in the mirror. He made hacking motions, chopping at the flabby skin with the sides of his palms.

Violet continued to snore soundly in the other room. Her snore was deep, and it vibrated along the wood floor. Charlie took a shower in the hottest water setting. He tried to rinse his guilt and dissatisfaction off beneath the water. His reflection in the mirror was a wake-up call. He was beginning to see just how far down he had allowed himself to spiral. He could hardly remember how any of this had begun, and he had no idea how it would end.

The water rushed over him. The soapy body wash smelled like ginger bread cookies, and the scent only made him feel more ill. As did anything that reminded him of the food he forced into his body simply to appease Violet. He had allowed himself to be compromised, and now he was too far down the rabbit hole to turn back.

She finished describing the fond memory to her therapist, before insisting on going back to her cell to continue thinking about Christmas with Charlie in peace. On her prison cot, Violet lay very still. This was the last memory she had of Charlie. She didn't know about the questions he had been facing, but she speculated that she had moved too quickly, forced him into a situation he hadn't been mature enough to handle.

She cuddled up closer to what she imagined was her stuffed animal, holding it like a newborn. As the fond memory faded, she realized the object she was nuzzling was her standard prison issue pillow.

Charlie's image faded from her mind, but the smell of his body against hers lingered in the fabric. Violet wept uncontrollably, her body shuddering. A guard working the graveyard shift noticed her convulsing in bed and called her name.

“Violet. Violet!”

She didn't respond. She continued to squirm.

“Open cell number 4421 dash E.” The guard called out to his counterpart who was busy watching late night television. The cell bars slid open, and the other guard entered the hall to provide back-up.

The guard who spotted her walked over to the bed, put his arms on Violet's shoulders and attempted to hold her still. The full force of his arms could barely contain her violent thrashing. “Can you lend a hand here?” The other female guard looked at him in disbelief. How was a thin, ninety-five pound woman giving him such a difficult time?

They managed to restrain her. The stoic look in her eyes sent a chill down the guards' back. It was as if he had become invisible. He had seen this look before when he first started four years ago in the eyes of another inmate who committed suicide, but it had never instilled such a sense of nervousness in him. She was unpredictable, and had crossed into a different threshold. This was the stage where the guards had to keep a watchful eye on the prisoner to make sure they did not try and end their own life.

CHAPTER TWENTY FOUR

Highway 1 up the coast through Santa Cruz was pure bliss. I looked at Jennifer; she was sleeping tenderly, her legs curled up against her chest. The sun had just set behind the green and brown hills, the yellow and orange poppy flowers still shown in the remaining light. The craggy cliffs sloped and bent around the isolated coastline. The road could have continued on forever, made it past the horizon and just wrapped around the entire earth. All the regrets I had about the life I'd led before skittered down the side of the four hundred foot embankment into the powerful waves of the Pacific Ocean below.

The low light made it hard to see the curves of the road. I decided it would be better if we pulled off to one of the viewing areas and took shelter below the bluffs. I forgot to change the sheets on the bed, but I figured with Jennifer's level of fatigue she wouldn't notice if I helped her into the back bed for a few more hours of sleep. At least she could spread her body out and rest in greater comfort than upright captain's chair. I found a designated viewing turn off and pulled over. I pulled the black handle to engage the parking brake for the van. The image of the two of us, locked in the confines of the van, sinking thousands of feet below the earth's surface, beneath the dark water, the last remaining bubbles of air trickling out, was enough to give me the sweats.

I eased Jennifer out of the front seat, swinging the captain's chair in a semi-circle, pulling back the thick purple velvet curtains, and placing her on top of the mattress.

"Aren't you going to give me a kiss goodnight?"

I looked down at her angelic face. My body told me to lean in and kiss her. I couldn't do it. Something prevented me from taking advantage of her current state. I wanted her to remember the first time our lips met. She turned her head and offered me her cheek. I leaned in. She turned her head and our mouths met. I felt her breath go into my throat. We held the kiss for a moment of time, paused, and then she rolled over and went back to sleep.

I stayed up on guard, in case some unsavory character out on the lone highway decided we were easy prey. I didn't want to wake Jenny up, but I needed to keep myself occupied. I decided to turn on my stereo in the back, plugged my headphones in, and put one earpiece in so I could still hear any movement around us.

In the middle of the night, it started to rain. It was more of a thick blanket of mist that collected and fell so the slightest audible drips were heard on the metal. The psychedelic rhythms of Grace Slick and Jefferson Airplane made me feel sedated. It was as if Jennifer and I were levitating over the highway, past the Ocean and out to the Channel Islands, living on the land, alone together.

Would you try some of my purple berries

I've been eating them for six or seven years
haven't got sick once

probably keep us both alive.

Paul Kantner's lyrics reinforced the vision I had of us living naturally, eating the fruits of the world provided by the land. The hippies had it right. You had to approach life naked, experience everything wholeheartedly, and remember how important the present was.

I had read the *Tibetan Book of the Dead*, or, at least, I had read the beginning part of it, about how the spirit travels through the Bordo. You wander out of your body looking for spiritual enlightenment, or to be welcomed into the afterlife. The celebration of death in Eastern religions baffles most Americans. It didn't confuse me. I had read the book when my sister died. It gave me more faith than the pastor at our local ministry who just told me, "Let's pray together."

I thought of my sister now as I watched Jennifer sleep. She brought me the same peace she had. I didn't know how I would ever tell Jennifer my secret that the ghost of my sister had still been with me up until yesterday.

My life replayed on a loop in my mind. It took me from the image of holding my mother's hand in the hospital, to seeing my sister, and then looking up and seeing this beautiful girl sleeping soundly in front of me. I knew I needed to protect her, to make sure that wherever she was destined to go I would be there, by her side. Even if she wanted to get rid of me, I made a vow, whispering, "Whatever happens... I will protect you. You are my angel, and now I will keep you protected."

I prayed a separate prayer to ask for help from some greater force to allow me to be able to keep my word. If I had to lose my own life for her, I would. It was the first time in my life that I was comforted by the life I had led, knowing that if I died now it would be protecting someone who I cared for more deeply than I cared for myself.

I dozed off and began to dream. Part of me stayed awake, unable to fully relax. I slept sitting up with my back against the bed. I wanted to cuddle with Jennifer, but I knew it wasn't right. I didn't want her to think I was taking advantage of her, or crowding her personal space. She was undergoing enough of her own physical and mental recovery, and those wounds needed to heal irrespective of my nurturing of her spirit back to health.

We barely had enough gas to reach the next gas station without having to back track. Once we made it out of the other side, I decided I would see how she felt about going inland through Santa Cruz and back out to go through some different small towns. I pictured each stop in the different towns, one slightly different from the next. I decided to write my thoughts to Jennifer. I grabbed a legal pad from the cabinet under the stereo. I started to write vigorously and without end. Every emotion, every thought I transcribed for her. It was real. I wasn't manipulating the words this time to get some desired effect. I was just writing, truly writing to her alone.

I didn't want the journey to end so easily. I struggled with my better judgment to deliver Jennifer back into the arms of her parents who I knew must be worried about her. She didn't seem to be a loner like me, abandoned by parents. She had a resistance about her that could only be the result of the consistent presence of two authority figures in her life. I decided to sleep again.

I finally fell asleep. I didn't dream that night, and the lack of dreams made me tired when I awoke. The groggy feeling quickly escaped me when I looked around and Jennifer was not there. *I didn't hear the van door open?* I looked out, slid open the velvet curtains, and saw the passenger side window was open. I yanked the door. I stumbled out, and there she was. Jennifer was sitting on the railing overlooking the ocean. The mist had lifted and the sun glowed.

I walked across the circular dirt path. I sat down next to her on the railing. “I didn't even hear you get up.”

"Shhh… do you hear that?" Jennifer placed her finger over my lips.

I listened, but I couldn't hear anything. I pictured the sounds of birds, or the voices of other people in the distance. A conversation carried by the wind.

"I don't hear anything."

"The ocean. You can't hear it from inside."

I listened, and then the sound of the waves pouring over the rocks below finally traveled all the way up the cliffs into my ears. The sound was so soothing; each time it reached us I knew it would last until the next wave's own uniquely similar sound reached us.

Jennifer put her head on my shoulder. I wanted to sit there forever, watching time pass. I could smell her hair every time I breathed. Baby powder, and a hay field freshly cut. It nourished me. Just the smell was so intoxicating that I could endure any fear I had of us plunging into the water. It was one of the only times I could remember ever feeling safe, present, and vulnerable.

"Lets go down to the beach," she said.

"I think we have to drive for a while to find an access point."

"I'm fine with that."

We jumped back into the van, and I started it up. The drive to find a beach was completely silent. I could feel her wanting to say something to me. I continued to replay over and over again in my mind the thoughts that must be funneling through her head. We had only been together a few days, and already the road to the rest of our lives was right in front of us. My only regret was the years of my life that passed before we met. I wanted the remaining days to make up for lost time.

I continued to think about what she was possibly contemplating the rest of the ride up the coast. When we finally descended into the Santa Cruz valley, you could feel the difference in precipitation.

“I'm sure we can make it down to the sand here.” She motioned to a street that seemed to head straight down at a forty-five degree angle into the sea. I followed her lead and turned down it.

“Nice.” She was right. I wondered if she had been here before.

The cul-de-sac was lined with vintage streetlights, potted plants and yards draped in pink and white Azaleas. We reached the beach, parked almost right on the sand. She jumped out before we stopped. I tried to catch her, but she was already halfway down the sand bar. I followed after her, taking out my wallet, and hurdling over the curb. She stopped when she reached the wet sand, just as the ice cold water touched her toes. I wondered if her feet had ever seen the daylight before now. I realized I forgot to take my watch off. The pearl luminescence was drowned in salt water, but it didn't matter. I forgot all about Violet until now. She didn't matter to me anymore.

Jennifer's eyes met mine. I looked at her one last time. We plunged underneath the dark blue water. Her face turned slightly purple. The chill traveled through our interconnected bodies. At one point I stopped knowing where my fingers stopped and hers began. We both surfaced, floating on the tide, pushed back to shore. Her underwear was soaked through. Her body was perfect. I did my best to force my eyes back to her face. She stared at me openly, lifting her hand to touch my stomach. She pulled me closer to her.

"Hold me," she said. I thought we were going to kiss, but the warmth of her skin against mine made me feel closer than if we had. Her heart was beating slowly, and I knew she was still weak from the experience in the hospital.

"We have to get you back."

She nodded. At least I knew she was aware of her inhibitions. I realized she must be starving. I lifted her up and carried her in my arms.

I slid the door open and placed her back on the bed. I moved in the direction of the driver's seat.

"Wait. Don't leave me."

"I'm not, I promise. I just have to get you a bite to eat. You need to get something in you."

"I don't need anything. I'm just cold. Come here."

I was ready to do whatever she asked me to, but I had to take initiative and get her some food and electrolytes before she slipped away from me again.

I lay her head back against the pillowcase and jumped into the front cab. We made it up the hill and onto the Main Street in no time at all. I pulled into the parking lot of a small café called the Wishing Well. Judging from the stares I got when I walked in, it was obvious I wasn't from around here. The café was full ofhippies, and I wished, for a moment, that I had the time to stick around and make friends. Before I made it to the front of the line, Bob Dylan's *One More Cup of Coffee* came on, and I knew I better grab some food before I was swept up into this wave of nostalgia.

I decided on a tofu wrap and a bottle of water. The cashier, a young girl of about eighteen with a head full of blonde dreads, suggested a few other packaged foods, "You definitely want to try the new cold pressed juices. The ultimate hangover cure. That water comes from this natural spring, so we call it Jesus water."

"Yeah, the juice and some Jesus water," I said.

"Cool. Is that it?"

"Food too. What do you have that I can grab real quick?" The urgency was starting to get to me.

"Umm… I guess you can grab those sandwiches. We just made them."

"Cool. Perfect." I didn't want to wait for anything to get made. I could only imagine how long it had already taken to carefully piece together those sandwiches.

My attention shifted, I heard the horn of my van honk and I saw Jennifer, her head resting against the steering column. She looked unconscious. I gave the pretty Deadhead one of my last twenties and told her to keep the change.

"It's actually twenty-eight dude." She stopped me in my tracks.

“Here you go.” I reached in my pockets and pulled out a ten and tossed it on the counter.

I lifted Jennifer's head from the steering column and tilted it back, pouring some of the beet colored juice elixir in her mouth. She swallowed voluntarily, so I knew her metabolism hadn't slowed beyond repair. I could see the color reappear in her skin. I wanted to lean in and kiss her cheek, but it was more important to get her back into a state of consciousness.

“Where were you?” she asked.

“I was getting us some rations,” I replied.

Her weakness was overpowered by her curiosity. Her slow blinking made her even more alluring. It wasn't the vulnerability, but the timeless sense that each blink could last for an indeterminate amount of time. I watched in awe, waiting for the next blink in complete anticipation. It may sound mundane to focus on the opening and closing of someone's eyelids, but when you are fascinated with someone, the unexplored details are the invaluable traits. I only wished I knew whether she felt the same about me.

I knew the attraction was there in a mystical way; a lowly traveler's love, always seeking out new destinations. Maybe all I was to her at this point was an indigenous species that was not yet categorized: a tortoise in the Galapagos, whom she could ride for her amusement. No! I couldn't imagine that I was only a vehicle for her whims. There was an intimacy that swelled between us, and when it reached its peak I knew our feelings for one another would unravel in unity.

When I looked up, a crowd of people had gathered around the van. I noticed a few of the old-timers from the café, but the rest of the crowd was made up of other transient locals whose faces were unfamiliar. Just then, a knock at the window. It was the cashier with the blonde dreads. I rolled it down as I lifted Jennifer into the back of the van so as not to provide the onlookers with any more of a spectacle.

"You guys alright?" She said.

"Sure we're fine. Just got a little dehydrated down at the beach," I said.

"Okay, well then you better get goin', because someone called the paramedics, and you know the cops'll probably come down here too."

"Right. Thank you," I said, and started the van down the street to cruise on a side street out past the city limits.

We were at the edge of town when I saw the lights flashing. I took a deep breath and held it in. I exhaled I started to whistle the Bob Dylan song from the café, "One more cup of coffee before I go… to the valley below." The melody was unfamiliar, but before I hit the bridge between the two verses, Jennifer woke up in the back and I could hear her humming the same tune, "Hmhm. Hm. Hmhmm…" I wasn't sure if her melody was layered, and slightly syncopated from mine, or if because of the distance between us it sounded like she was a few seconds behind my rhythm. I refocused on driving in a straight line to keep suspicions down about anything out of the ordinary occurring inside the van.

I looked down the road, and the lights were gone. Had he turned off? I know I kept the van in a straight line and under the suggested speed limit, but I'd imagined that would be the first thing a cop would look for when suspected illegal activity was going on. What you're supposed to do is make a few turns without your blinker, and pretend to be talking loudly to someone. This way they psychologically misinterpret the response of your gestures to being nonchalant, and you instantly transform from perpetrator to lousy driver who disobeys minor traffic laws; in other words, almost every driver in California.

CHAPTER TWENTY FIVE

Jennifer woke up half way down the 101 just where the stockyards began. She looked at the poor unsuspecting cows waiting to be slaughtered for consumption. The air was so filled with nitrogen it gave her a head rush.

"Where are we?"

"Just outside of Los Angeles. Still on the coastline," I said.

The Los Angeles County line was about fifty miles into Ventura, but something compelled me to push through the mileage and get us to the city limits. The fear of being caught back in Santa Cruz by a local sheriff looking to make his quota crossed my mind. It wasn't just the local police squad that made me shutter. It was the fear of losing my mother for good, if I didn't ever make it home. If I brought Jennifer back, she would serve as some magical talisman. She had brought me full circle, but I felt like I knew myself better, and my heart finally knew what it was like to love someone.

I lit up a cigarette. I hadn't smoked in a while, so it felt good. The light buzz made me drift a bit, and think about Jennifer. Think about what I had written to her. The words that meant so much to me and how I would give them to her. I didn't want her to think I was a creep, but needed her to know how deep I felt our bond.

No matter what circumstances we encountered, I was ready for them. I wouldn't let us be torn apart again like I had in our first meeting. The time between has felt endless and only bad things had happened to us both while we were apart. Now we co-existed, our union was a safeguard.

“Can I have a drag?”

I felt Jennifer's fingers on my hand, taking the cigarette from me. She placed it to her lips and took a deep, long pull. I watched her inhale, subtly playing with the smoke, moving her tongue through it as she exhaled.

On the side of the road was a sign. *Fresh lobster tails, $5 dollars each.* I couldn't resist. I made an abrupt turn across two lanes and onto the side road, tracking the hand-written signs to a little pick-up truck. A man wearing a sombrero sat in the truck's bed, using his long fingernail to shuck shrimp, one after another.

“Wait here. I'll be right back.”

Jennifer looked at me, and hopped out of the van anyway. She had changed back into her hospital gown, as it was more comfortable than the extra clothes I gave her. Her bra straps showed and she just held the top of the gown to her chest, as she hadn't been able to tie the string around the back on her own.

I picked out some stellar lobster tails, and turned to look at Jennifer. Her blonde hair was blown into her face, plastering the strands down against it. The light filled her bloodshot eyes, which glowed blue and green. My instinct told me to reach out and touch her, cover her up, and protect her.

“Damn those five tails look good,” I said. I handed the man a twenty, and tried to hurry away with Jennifer.

But Jennifer stopped him, poking through a crate on the truck's bed overflowing with strawberries.

“Are these for sale too?”

“Of course. How many do you want?”

Jennifer picked up one of the strawberries and examined it carefully. I was mystified by her; wondering what was significant about this one strawberry? Was she checking it for pollen? Or the proper hue to indicate the sweetness of the berry?

“Just one,” Jennifer said. “…This one.” She held it up like it was the perfect one out of the palette of berries he had.

“Just have it please,” the man said.

She took a full bite of the red fruit, the juice of the berry trickling down her cheek and onto her hospital gown, where it left an oblong pink shape on her collar.

I walked over and took Jennifer's hand. It was the first time I had been able to sense her strength since we left the hospital, and I acknowledged it with a half smile. Her pulse beat in my palm. I supported her, and she rested her head on my shoulder, looking at me.

Some of the strawberry juice was still in the corners of her chapped lips. I leaned over and kissed her. The roughness of her mouth felt good against mine. I continued to kiss her on the side of the road.

The van provided shelter for us. We continued back to Los Angeles. Just after we passed the county line, rain began to pour down. I decided the best thing to do would take Jennifer home and get back to the hospital to see if my mother was out of the ICU.

"I want to go to the mountains and get closer to the rain," Jennifer said during a break in the music. I was confused, thought she would want to be at home. I decided to follow her wish and stay living in this fantasy with her. I didn't want it to end either.

"That's fine. We have to make a stop first, okay?" I needed to say good-bye to my mom one last time.

"Sure. Where are we going?"

"We have to stop by the hospital."

"No way! We're not going back there."

"A different hospital. My mom is there, and I just want to say good-bye."

"I just want to go to Beachwood and go under the trees at the top of the mountain to sit in the hills with you. Then you can go stay with your mom. Please."

I thought for a few minutes, and realized that my mom was probably not even back to recognizing the environment around her. I stopped at an old phone booth to make a call before we reached the Hollywood Hills.

I found one of the last remaining pay phones on the side of Franklin. I called the hospital collect, and the operator accepted the call.

“Ms. Winters please. She's in ICU.”

The operator connected me to the main ICU line. A nurse answered, “ICU.” There was a pause.

“My mom, Marla Winters please. Can she talk yet?” I held my breath.

“Ms. Winters has been transferred from ICU as of (pause) late yesterday afternoon,” he said. I was relieved.

“Thanks man. I really do appreciate all you guys did for her. I do.”

“Sure thing,” he said.

“Can you connect me to her room?” I asked. The nurse patched me through to another nurse who told me she was resting, and they were still draining fluids from her brain.

“She still hasn't regained the use of speech. It will be some time before she recovers fully from her experience. We are, however, expecting a miraculous recovery from your mom. When are you coming to see her?”

I was in shock. The idea of my mom not being able to recognize me or speak normally sent me into a spiral. I hung up the phone. I was afraid to confront this situation, afraid to acknowledge the possible loss of the last person in my family who was still alive. The rain pelted the glass of the old phone booth. Before I could respond there was a dial tone and I was disconnected. I ripped off the cover of the decaying phone book to provide a makeshift cover over my head.

"Is everything alright now? You ready?" Jennifer asked.

"Yes, I'm ready."

We drove up into the Hollywood Hills.

CHAPTER TWENTY SIX

We continued far up Beachwood to look for a place to park. I had the impression that she knew where we were headed. She pointed down different streets for me to turn on. I continued to drive toward the top of the mountain. When I say mountain I don't want you to use a manufactured image of a mountain that you might see as an iconic image from the Rockies, but more so a hill that is taller than anything else except the four skyscrapers we have in downtown. The hills are brown, and occasionally in the 'once a year flood' like we were having that day, they fill-up with lush greenery that lasts temporarily, but for a day it's beautiful.

Turning down another windy street, we reached a dead end. "Turn left onto that dirt road," Jennifer said. I bumped the van over the curb and onto the thin strip of dirt that had turned to mud from the rain. I crossed my fingers that the rear weight of the van would not get locked in the mud. We were off-roading. The cacti around us formed odd shapes, crowding on the space. I stopped the van underneath a tree gave us decent cover from the downpour. The intermittent drops that fell through the natural barrier were a nice break from silence.

Jennifer grabbed my hand and pulled me into the back. We lay on the bed, staring into each other. I saw a fear that hadn't been present before. Her adventurous spirit was lost in this fear, her childhood sense of wonderment, tarnished by some boundary that possessed her. I placed my hand on her cheek. She clasped it with both of her hands and brought it closer to her body. I could feel the fear lifting. I could tell she felt safe.

The ecstasy we felt was unbearable. I had never felt so intoxicated. Every time she came, her sighs called my spirit to crawl one step further out of my skin and into hers. I finally couldn't hold it anymore and came inside of her. The smell of the rain and our sweat was invigorating. We both lay next to one another dazed and dreaming.

I wanted the sensation to last indefinitely. I knew, even while dreaming, that when we awoke it would be over. The first time you do anything is always the best, and there would never be a first time again. I turned to kiss her on the cheek. Her face was ice cold. Her eyes were still open, staring at the ceiling. I didn't quite know if she was relaxed, in a state of subdued momentary sedation, or if she was in another dimension.

I kissed her cheek again before getting nervous about the true state of her being; whether she was actually still alive or not. I decided to calm down and let the energy from having sex resonate over us. The pulsing sensation between us was soothing, each pulse of blood, and every breath was easily felt.

I could see her chest rising and falling. Her breasts were cold, so I pulled a blanket over her. I felt awkward staring at her naked body. Her freckles added something to her appearance that let me know she was real.

I decided I would take Jennifer to Tennessee's condo. I had the code, the key, and he was in New York, wrapping things up with his ex-girlfriend. It would be smart to take her there before turning her back over to her family.

“I can't take you home,” I said. The words rolled off my tongue inelegantly. The atmosphere inside the van didn't change.

Jennifer's eyes fluttered and she looked at me. She nodded her head, and I knew then that she felt the bond between us growing too.

The road back down through the Hollywood Hills had opened up. The low level clouds that buried the hillside funneled in a long thin strips along the side of the road. The 101 freeway was totally empty, except for a few off-duty public transportation vehicles. Deserted, the road felt different. It didn't give me a sense of loss even while it was completely abandoned.

Jennifer had fallen asleep. I was tired too. I could barely keep my arms on the steering wheel. I wanted an autopilot switch that would hone in on Tenny's condo, drive up the entrance, through the gate, and lock onto a magnetic track that guided us right into his garage. No such luck. I started to nod off when I clipped a real estate agent's sign on the curb. The loud sound woke me up. I shrugged it off.

I found the front entrance. Entered in the code he gave me. I couldn't remember exactly which condo was Tenny's, and my eyes were growing very heavy. I decided to park in the back, in the exact same spot I did before. That way, I could retrace my steps.

I wandered up the back steps to the door I thought belonged to Tenny. I tried the key he'd left me. It fit, but it didn't turn. I jiggled it into the lock. The key refused to move. I heard some commotion inside, and the door opened. In front of me was a woman, barely clothed, her robe exposing a bra full of silicone filled breasts.

“Can I help you?”

“I'm looking for Tennessee's unit,” I stuttered. I didn't want to look at them and be rude, but it was hard to take my eyes of them.

She took my hand and escorted me to the door next to hers.

“Here you go, honey,” she said.

I tried the key again, and sure enough, this time it worked.

“By the way… if you're bored later come by for a drink,” she said.

“I really appreciate it. I'm actually with my girlfriend. She's my only girl.”

“I respect that. It's nice to see a real gentleman. Most of these creeps will leave a woman for the next piece of ass in a second.”

“Thanks for the help.” I waved and went back to the van.

I was glad to be stationary for once. To be with her in a place that had hot running water and a full sized bed that I could hold her in. I went back out to the van to get Jennifer. I opened the passenger door. She was gone. I started to panic, and then I felt her hand on my shoulder. I turned to her, relieved.

“I was just looking at the city's lights,” she said.

I took her hand, “Well, we have a place to stay,” I said.

“Great, thank you.” She kissed me.

“For what?”

“For everything. This. Taking care of me. You know. All of this.”

“It's no problem. You said you didn't want to go home.”

“Home. Ha. I don't have a home now.”

“Sure you do. With me!”

I picked her up, twirling her body in the air, and carried her up the stairs to the condo.

“Something smells,” Jennifer said as we closed the door behind us.

“It's the chinchillas,” I said, holding a hand over my nose.

“Chinchillas? Cute.”

“Not really. I think one got out.” I followed a set of dirty paw prints behind the curtains. When I moved the bottom of the curtains ever so slightly, the little monster leapt out at me. I lunged back at him, flinging him back onto the curtain. He tried to climb the fabric, but his nails tore the Venetian silk to shreds. I couldn't help but feel bad that I allowed this creature to do so much damage, not to mention embarrassed that something so cute could make me so jumpy. Jennifer sat on the couch laughing hysterically.

“I don't know who's more scared of who,” she said.

I looked at the chinchilla that was huddled up in a puffy ball. Jennifer walked over to the curtain and reached out to pet my furry adversary. He waddled closer to her, sniffed her hand, and then climbed onto her arm wrapping around her.

“See? I told you. He was just scared. I don't blame him.”

I nodded, and went over to clean the bleeding scratch marks on my hand. The blood ran off my hand and into the stainless steel sink. The water cleansed my wound and revealed a minor scratch. With Jennifer nearby, I felt grounded.

I washed my hands again with the sandalwood soap. The scratch stopped bleeding. I put a few paper towels over it. I looked in the fridge hoping Tennessee had left a few beers, or if I was really lucky a bottle of wine. It was wishful thinking. Aside from an overstocked condiment drawer, there was no food and nothing to drink.

It was all coming together. We had become inseparable. I wanted to christen the moment.

“I'm going to pick up a few things from across the street. Do you want anything?” Jennifer had the Chinchilla on its back in her lap. It was actually letting her pet its stomach. She gave me a grin.

“Don't go. Please…”

“We definitely need a few things. I'll just be a second I promise.”

“Fine, maybe just some snacks, or actually mint flavored water. I love that stuff.”

“No problem. No wine or anything?”

“I'm good baby.” She stood up, came over to me. She gave me a sensual kiss.

I sighed, and looked twice in Jennifer's direction before I walked out of the room. The phone rang just as the door shut behind me. I decided it was better not to answer it. I knew if Tenny called me it wouldn't be through the house phone.

The distance to the store was fifty feet away, just close enough to walk. The night air was cool against my skin. Inside, the aisles of fluorescent overhead lights illuminated infinite consumer goods. I lost track of what I had come to buy. And then I remembered: *Mint water, alcohol. Simple. Maybe something to go with the lobster tails.* I found the items I needed, and placed them in a red plastic basket.

I found a bottle of Cabernet Franc in the shitty wine aisle. The smell always reminded me of smoking a cigarette right after it rains. It was a rare grape looked down on by the connoisseurs who called it ‘dirty', but highly regarded by those who understood. I couldn't believe I found it in this market. I learned the art of winemaking through a five hundred page illustrated coffee book and for some reason this wine from France spoke to me. I couldn't wait to share the wine with Jenny. I wanted to believe we could teach and share with each other for the rest of our lives.

I paid. I walked out of the market, and I heard a loud noise. It sounded like a firecracker exploding into the air. The sound echoed across the strip mall parking lot. I felt as if I had swallowed a vial of Hydrochloric Acid. Something was inside my skin. The burning traveled into my chest until I lost my breath and my sight blurred.

CHAPTER TWENTY SEVEN

The parking lot had filled with medics and police officers. Thirty minutes later, the detectives arrived. There had not been a single other shot fired in the area that night. The only report of criminal activity was a liquor store robbery off De Soto, but the detectives deemed it wasn't connected. The shooting had been an intentional act of malice.

Unless a family member showed up at the local district field office and raised hell with the administration these kinds of cases rarely ever saw the light of day. There was no question that this looked cut and dry to most of the cops.

But there was something left unanswered. The bottle of wine looked like a rare vintage of Cab Franc, which puzzled the detective. He had an above average understanding of wine, and he knew this grape was a rare one, with an earthy flavor. It was an uncommon choice for the average buyer.

There was no way that some innocent bystander wandering through the liquor aisles of a strip mall supersized supermarket would come out of the overpowered marketing of Mondovi and Napa Valley consortiums with a Loire Valley French-produced vintage of Cabernet Franc. This conclusion was as good enough a lead as any.

Fortunately, the patterns were easily discernable to the trained eye. Detective Sandoval wasn't convinced. He was better than any other detective, even though his track record didn't surpass all of his peers in the SF Valley. Perhaps it was chance, or his mind, or merely thirty years of looking at crime scenes that never added up. This wasn't a gang shooting, or a random misfire. It had the deliberation of a first time shooter written all over it.

The placement of caution tape, circling of helicopters, and flares surrounding the mall lasted for over five hours. Detective Sandoval was getting into his blue Chevy Caprice Classic, when he noticed a blonde girl standing on the edge of the caution tape in tears.

When Sandoval saw this girl, he saw beyond her beauty. He knew the faces of seemingly innocent bystanders could reveal a murderer, the next victim, or a close family connection to the victim of the recent crime.

Sandoval shut the door to the Caprice and walked over to the crowd. He made sure to zigzag so the blonde didn't flee. If he singled her out, he knew she would be gone before he could make it through the crowd. The zigzag strategy almost worked.

"Hey wait. Please!" He tried to camouflage his urgency. The caustic reaction of the blonde let him know she knew something about this case, something that might be worth exploring. Sandoval jumped into his car and drove across street, driving the perimeter in the alley surrounding the strip mall.

Jennifer was long gone. She had fled across Ventura Blvd and ducked into an office building parking lot. She stayed huddled in the shadows until she could figure out where to go. Her body convulsed wildly in the dark. She fell to her knees. The pain ran up her body into her limbs, expanding and contracting.

She crawled out when she heard the rev of an engine. Sandoval had found her creeping around. She spotted him and jumped up. She fled down a small crevice between the buildings. Sandoval ran from the car and headed to the passageway. He tried to breach the gap, but his excessive weight around his midsection kept him from sliding down the space. He stopped short at the edge of a brick building.

“Damn. I am way too old for this.” He grabbed for his walkie-talkie in his jacket. “Yeah, she's gone. Heading Southbound from 20691 Ventura Blvd. Suspect is a white female, blonde hair, about 5' 7” in jeans and white shirt.”

The description could have described nearly every girl in her mid-twenties in the valley. Sure there were a few things that set her apart: she was pale and she had real blonde hair, but these were two qualities that Sandoval had neglected to mention. He would follow the lead, see if other witnesses had anything consistent to say and hopefully they mentioned the blonde again. The brief chase wasn't enough. He knew from experience that people run from fear, not just from guilt.

Sandoval went back to his station in heart of the San Fernando Valley. It was already past eleven at night. The Valley air was still over ninety degrees. The back offices had window air-conditioning, but still felt at least over eighty, and the strips of tape attached to the AC unit were hardly moving. The water cooler was nearly down to empty. The only thing left untouched was the lukewarm decaf coffee in the break room. Sandoval decided it was better than nothing. It would at least keep him up for a half hour longer than he expected. The in-between being awake and falling asleep state had produced answers in the past, uncovered evidence, and revealed sources he didn't always see when he was astute mulling over details at the scene of any crime.

“Time to call it a night, Sandy.” A fellow officer said as he passed by his desk. Sandoval looked up, and then back out onto Kittridge

Street. The streetlights were dim. He thought of going for a walk, but he felt his body lifted weightlessly from the seat behind his desk and float out of the window. He tried to feel the ground below him, but his grasping of the air did no justice to the defiance of gravity he experienced. His body passed through the windowpane, a jelly-like membrane and he continued to float into the empty street.

There was no one out on the street. No early morning runners, no dog walkers, not even the stray homeless waking up for the day. He looked down the row of streetlights and saw the silhouette of a young girl. He recognized her. When the light filled his head he saw another image next to the girl, it looked like a man, outlined in chalk, and he knew it was his victim from earlier that day. *It had to be... they were lovers maybe?* He thought, the image pressed on and in the background he saw animals walking in a pair, they were not dogs, or cats, but looked like rodents crawling wildly on all fours. He didn't know what in the hell he was viewing. The devout religious man inside of him wanted him to write the image off as Edenic, but his logical brain forced him to use rationality to reverse psychologize the extraordinary circumstances.

Sandoval felt a warm tingling sensation in his hands. He looked down, and saw brown liquid all over his fingers. He blinked. His desk was covered in coffee. His case file was soaked.

"Almost on my way out. Thanks for noticing."
He spoke to an unseen force above him, maybe the Police guardian angel, God, or maybe just himself.

CHAPTER TWENTY EIGHT

Sandoval went back and retraced his steps. He figured the girl had not gone far, being on foot. His brief nap allowed him to make a few more connections in the case. Sandoval hoisted himself up from the desk chair and made his way into the hallway. The hallway was empty. It was a sight he was accustomed to.

Sandoval stopped at the vending machine for some cherry-flavored fruit snacks. He popped one in his mouth and closed his eyes. The taste reminded him of the pipe tobacco his father used to smoke when he was a kid. The smell lingered in his memory. The way it saturated everyone that happened to be in the room. After his father died, Sandoval kept his belongings in a wood shop he'd built in his garage. When he would work on his hobbies, the smell brought back the memory of his dad.

He kept his father's old reclining chair in the living room. It made the entire house stink like cherry tobacco. His wife made him remove it soon after they moved in together. When they got divorced he moved it back in from the garage, but it just didn't smell the same.

Thinking about the chair led him back to the chewing of the cherry gummy. It tasted good. Sandoval pulled an electronic recording device from his pocket and spoke into it, "What was the motivation behind the shooting? The victim seemed like a good kid with refined tastes. Possible scenario one picking up a bottle of wine for the blonde (pause) heading back to see her. Perpetrator intercepts victim. Shots fired." He put the device back in his pocket. He had shoveled in a handful of the remaining gummies, and eyed the vending machine.

“A condo complex!” He blurted. He knew she must have retreated into a complex to hide from the helicopter light. He decided to check it out. He trashed the empty bag of cherry gummies, and dashed to his car. He drove out of the parking lot, and turned left to Ventura Boulevard.

Sandoval squinted, trying to adjust his eyes to the change in light. He turned abruptly down the same alley he had followed the blonde-haired girl down four hours before. The alley led to a dead end. His path was blocked. He wanted to call it in, go grab a quick combo meal and hit the sack. He persisted on despite his urge to home and get in bed with a glass of whiskey. He backed out of the alley.

He looked up and realized he was at the service entrance to a high-end luxury condo complex. ‘Deliveries Only' read a sign on the door that led to an underground parking garage. A passkey was required, but Sandoval slipped past the gate on foot and into the complex.

His face was swollen with fatigue. Sandoval pressed his fingers against his temple. He had a migraine that he couldn't get rid of. Whatever vows of secrecy the blonde had taken, he knew that if he put her under enough pressure, she would crack. All it would take would be continual questioning; confusion was always the best information-gathering tactic. It was never about what was said, it was about what a suspect neglected to say, the silence in the details they consciously forgot to mention, that allowed him to connect the dots.

He approached the main entrance of the condos. The indoor plants outside the glass looked real. He tried to shred one of the leaves on a ficus, and it didn't tear. “A fake,” he said. “I knew it.”

“Are you waiting for the elevator?”

He looked up to see the face of a woman who had quite a lot of plastic surgery, her oversized breasts being the biggest dead giveaway.

“No. Just waiting for someone.”

“Do you need some help finding them?” She insisted. He realized she was trying to engage him in conversation.

“I think I should be alright by myself. If I need something though, or my friend doesn't come down, I will holler.”

She had the most captivating figure, if you were into fake, that is. Her body was tucked perfectly into every spot of her curves, and the breasts she was wearing nearly filled the space between the two of them.

“If you holler, I won't hear you, but someone will. Everyone's real helpful around here, and we know everybody.”

“That's perfect. You may be just the person I was looking for.”

“Really? Shoot, Lone Ranger,” she said. He wasn't sure if she was picking up on him being a cop, or if she just used Western allusions often.

“I'm looking for the daughter of a friend of mine. He's in the hospital, and well he said she lived here with her boyfriend.”

“What does she look like?”

“Blonde, young, blue eyes. Actually, I'm not so sure about eyes. My friend has brown, but his wife has bright blue eyes. Probably about five foot six. Does that help at all?”

“Nobody in this building looks like that, sorry. You may want to try next door though. My friend Marina lives there and she was talking about some new girl. Miss Natural she called her. Blonde I think, too.”

“Ms. Natural, eh?”

“Yeah, you know. No fake stuff, all *naturale*. Guess some men still prefer the plain Jane types.”

“I'm sure they're missing a lot.”

“Of course they are. I don't need to convince you do I? I mean my boyfriend doesn't come home for at least an hour.” Checking her fake Rolex watch, and then sizing him up, trying to determine if he would be any good in bed.

“I really can't stay,” he said anticipating her inquiry to save her the embarrassment.

“Don't flatter yourself, honey. I wouldn't even dream about it. You couldn't handle me any way. I would hurt you.” Her forward attitude was a welcome change from the awkward blind dates he had been on; the constant rejections he had faced at his local bar.

His divorce had caused him great dismay, and put a Scarlet A permanently on his forehead in the small community where he lived. He was close enough to smell the vanilla and tobacco hints of her perfume. She was soaked in the scent, and the combination was intoxicating.

“What if I said yes?” He said, and she stared at him. The elevator arrived. She leaned in and put her finger on his lips and ran her nail on his teeth.

“Maybe next time, sweetheart.”

She got in the elevator, smiled and looked down at the floor. The doors shut and she was gone. Sandoval realized he had more important things to do than feed his ego. The lead she had given him could be useless, but he thought it was worth a shot. He mulled over his past cases, thought about the different angles, the flashback of moments he'd missed.

He walked out of the complex to cross the parking lot. The other building of condos looked slightly older. The new paint covered up the blemishes in the plaster. He could hear a waterfall, but couldn't see any pond or fountain. He continued walking to find the front of the building. He really couldn't distinguish between the building's front and back, and entered the side. He noticed a steep set of stairs leading up to a pair of ground level units.

Before he reached the door of the first unit a woman who could have been the plastic surgery girl's doppelganger came out. Her nose and chin job was coated in a fresh coat of make-up. Sandoval couldn't decide which was more appealing, seeing the reconstruction in the raw or this woman, with her flawless paint job and perfect doll face. This condo complex was filled with society's sexual exiles. *It must be housing for the adult entertainment industry's old recruits*. He couldn't figure it out. His internal questioning was interrupted by her exuberant personality, which stopped his cynicism.

"Can I help you?" she said.

"Sure can, I think. I was told you might know a young blonde girl who's been staying here?"

"We're all young and blonde."

"Yes, I know of course. I'm sorry, let me say I'm a detective actually looking for someone. A relative of a victim in a case."

"I figured you weren't here for a rub and tug," she said jokingly. Sandoval chuckled, feeling suddenly shy in spite of himself.

"So, any young girls? Natural blondes? May not fit in so well with the more developed women who live here."

"Developed? Hmmm. I don't know if I like the way you put that."

"It wasn't meant to be derogatory. You're beautiful. She's just a little like a child is what I meant to say."

"More natural you mean?"

"No, just smaller. You would notice her."

"What's her name? That might help me remember. Maybe one of my friend's daughters or something who hasn't realized the power of her sexuality." He blushed, and she cackled. "I'm kidding."

"I actually don't know her name."

"What kind of detective are you? Sounds like a wild goose chase, honey."

"That's what it feels like."

"Oh, there, there, Mr. Detective, don't you cry. You need to have a sense of humor."

"Too many years on the job."

"Yeah, well today is your lucky day."

"No more luck, please." He figured he would have to stave off another attack on his manhood.

"I've seen the little lovebirds you're talking about."

"Lovebirds?"

"Yeah, the two passionate young kids. So cute, aren't they? I haven't had that kind of love in a long, long, time."

"And the blonde?"

"Yeah, they stay in my neighbor Tennessee's condo."

"Not anymore."

"What? What do you mean not anymore. Are they in trouble?"

"I hope not."

"Oh don't fuck with me. I just helped you. Tell me, what the hell happened?"

"He's been shot. Charlie has."

"Charlie, oh my God! That's him. He's the cute boy. Such a sweetheart. Is he going to make it?"

"Pray for him."

"Jesus… is that what happened tonight? We saw the chopper earlier, didn't realize it was a shooting."

"The poor girl, I'm sure she's going insane."

"I'm sure. Have you seen her tonight?"

"Earlier, yes she came out with one of Tennessee's chinchillas."

"How long ago?"

"Gosh, I don't know. Hours ago, I guess."

"You said that unit?" He pointed.

"Yeah, my neighbor." Sandoval took the instruction, and as a precaution unclipped his holster under his wool blazer. He still didn't know what had happened. He only knew she had no place to go, and that it was impossible for him to be too careful. He walked over to the unit and peered into the window.

"Hey, what are you going to do?" She was still following him.

"Listen, please be quiet. I'm not going to hurt her. I know she's probably scared, and don't want to startle her that's all. I just want to talk to her."

"I've heard that before. If you're lying to me… I'll fuck you up for not having any type of warrant."

"Look, shhhhh! Alright? I'm not going to hurt her. You have my word." He approached her. When he stood upright, she realized his six-foot frame was rather intimidating. She adhered to his demand, and stood back to watch.

He didn't see anyone inside the condo. Suddenly, the curtain moved. He decided to have use his new doll friend help him gain access to the unit.

"Come here," he said to her. She pointed to her chest. He nodded. "Go knock on the door. See if you can get her to answer."

"Why should I help you?"

"Because I want to help her, and if you want to see the two lovers live happily ever after, you'll make that happen."

"Like their guardian angel."

"Sure. Whatever."

She agreed and knocked on the door, "Honey, are you in there? I need to borrow something? Sweetie, can you come to the door." They waited, and heard a rustling. Then they heard an engine start in the parking lot. It startled them, but Sandoval stayed by the window. A van drove out of the lot. He looked briefly; saw a young boy with a hat on driving out of the gates.

“Alright, I'm going in.”

“Wait!”

“What is it now?”

“Don't break it. I have a key.”

“Well, why didn't you say so?”

“Because I didn't think you were going to break the door down.” She brought the key to him. He turned the lock, and opened the door. Something sharp grabbed his hand. He pulled out his gun without a moment of hesitation and aimed it at the object.

“What the fuck is that?” The hissing chinchilla had latched onto his elbow. He struggled to pry it from his hand. Finally it let go, leaving a substantial tooth mark in his hand, which began to bleed.

“Why would anyone buy these nasty things?” The neighbor had left him alone in the condo by himself. He decided to explore the unit, to see if there was any sign of where she had gone.

The quasi-domesticated chinchilla had left the unit in shambles. The fridge was open. It was empty except for a few condiments. He checked the envelopes on a nearby desk. He thought maybe the owner of the unit was tied to this. The name on the envelopes was Tennessee Sterman. The name gave him another link to track down his mystery blonde. Sandoval narrowed it down: she was family, a lover, or possibly just a local neighbor looking after the chinchillas.

The desk was overloaded with bills addressed to Tennessee, post-it notes, and a long, hand-written letter in a woman's script. The brief letter seemed like an important find. It had been written in haste, and it said:

We have never met. I know you were a friend, a dear friend from what I understand. There has been a serious accident, and well Charlie... he is in the hospital, he was shot they think. Going there now. Please come as soon as you get this.

Always,

J.

The brevity of the letter meant "J" was definitely not who Sandoval thought she was. *So who was she staying with?* The friend was Charlie, and how had they gotten to Tennessee's place? Sandoval searched around the house for car keys, a garage opener, anything to tell him what type of vehicle J might be using. If Tennessee lent them his condo, his car was probably somewhere around here too. Sandoval ran down the carpeted stairs into the connected individual car garage. There, he found a BMW, hood cold, which meant it hadn't been driven recently. He couldn't figure it out. How had they gotten here, and what were they doing staying out here at Tennessee's place?

He remembered the van that left the parking lot. What color had it been? He couldn't remember. His mind was moving in circles. The thousands of different suspects' cars he had seen in the past crept on him. The flashbacks of random cars started to narrow.

“The Van!”

He couldn't help but blurt out the answer. He didn't expect the girl to be in an oversized vehicle as her get-away car. *It had to be the victim's car*. But he wasn't looking for a victim. He was looking for a witness who could tell him who had pulled the trigger. The motivation for this shooting was calculated. He knew it. There didn't appear to be any motive for J, just a lot of shock and fear. These two emotions coincided with a witness passionately wrapped up in something she didn't understand.

He was intrigued by the lack of explanations. Sandoval relied on the laws of logic to guide him. Logic trumped the absurd in cases involving violence. The act itself was a crime of passion, but the planning, and the choices that lead up to it always happen according to a formula. The formula was what concerned him.

CHAPTER TWENTY NINE

Violet was a wreck. Her months of isolation had finally begun to break her. Her body was so frail from starving herself. The color of her skin was a muted green, caused by malnourishment. Her body smelled so moldy that not even the starch in the cell's bedding could cover it up.

The days were dragging out. Even the memories of Charlie did not warm her anymore. The New Year was approaching. She decided to write a letter. She wanted to make reparations with the people she'd wronged. She decided the first letter would be to her twin sister. If she could manipulate her into doing things for her on the outside, it would help her to make resolutions with the people she'd hurt. *I went into this a lamb, but I'll come out a lion,* she thought. The words reflected the myth of spring. In Los Angeles, a city with no seasons, they were hollow.

She craved Charlie's touch one last time. Before he left she had said to him, "Let's be open with each other, we can at least do that." Charlie conceded. They slept in bed together the night before he left. It was the first time she felt he really understood her. She decided to pleasure him. She thought it would connect them again, cement their bond; no matter where he traveled beyond her reach, he would feel her around him. This was her hope. Before he went to sleep, she said, "Touch me."

Charlie just lay there contemplating what these sexual gestures meant to her. It was too late. His hand was down her panties and she was near climax.

“Look at me. Look at me when I orgasm.”

He looked into her eyes and saw nothing.

Violet opened her book of letters that Charlie had written her before he left. She read the letters page by page. Before he left her, the letters pointed to a future of happiness, marriage, and even children. She made jokes about her ovaries drying up, about how she didn't really like kids, though she promised Charlie she would, “Make one for him” if that was what he wanted. The way she phrased it made Charlie choke. He loved kids, but just didn't see them in his future with Violet.

A loudspeaker cracked the silence. “Line up for count.” The bars to her cell slid open. She stepped forward to the railing, and put her pinky on the bar. She envisioned leaping over the thin pipe railing onto the grey cement, three floors below. She wouldn't kill herself, but the fall would damage her knees permanently. It might stir up some pity at the parole board's next meeting.

She thought of her brittle bones, the poorly illuminated hallway, and the memory of her last court trial. The smell of wood freshly cleaned with lemon-scented Pine Sol filled her nose. The scent made her think of doing housework back in Bel-Air. She took pride in the fact that she didn't need maids to clean her beautiful craftsman home. Just a small bump of cocaine and an old Phil Collins track, and she was a cleaning machine.

The court trial had been a complete disaster for Violet. She couldn't control her emotions, and the prosecutor's remarks sent her from a state of despair, to a place of anger.

She thought of all her friends that should have stood up for her. The many weekend benders they'd had together at her house. She had provided a place to party for the whole weekend, making friends in the dismal hours of the night, high as hell. As long as she continued to provide the venue, they had maintained their friendship, finding their way to her house every weekend.

The house. The house she had brought back to life.

When she purchased the house, she found a broken sewer line, and psychedelic mushrooms growing in the garage. The putrid scent of mold lingered everywhere. The property was a steal. It stayed on the bank's books for months until Violet decided it was the buy of a century. She put all her savings in, borrowed some money from her boss at the firm. “Just carry the paper for the first year, refinance and you're golden,” he had said.

Violet didn't understand exactly what he meant, but he was the king of Beverly Hills real estate, and she trusted him. She jumped into the mortgage and had been carrying the “paper” ever since. She only pulled equity for reasonable purchases and didn't over extend herself until Charlie came along. His presence made her feel youthful, but more importantly, he made her feel loved for the first time in her life.

It wasn't just the constant affection, or the willingness to befriend her circle of party people. It was the little nuances he appreciated about her. The half wink of her right eye, her quirky smile, the way she was so nurturing. Her generosity never went unnoticed with him. He always said thank you, and kissed her. The culmination of his gratitude and these minute details made her love him. It was the spirit he brought to her life. It was also the challenge to keep him in her possession.

Her dream of Charlie drained out of her, leaving her to face her reality. Around her, the cell was dismal. On its blank walls, she could see all the empty years she would never get to fill. That is if she survived prison.

The inmates serving life in prison were the biggest threat. They swooped in unexpectedly to catch weaker inmates and beat them, usually in the small corridors behind the laundry. Violet's first fight managed to deter even the more ruthless inmates. Her first week inside she nearly strangled to death one of the two hundred pound intimidators who made fun of her broken heart. Afterward, she decided to tattoo a picture of a heart with a crack in it over her left breast. She wore her wifebeater just low enough that it was always visible. Rather than serving as a sign of weakness, it was her badge of courage. It showed that she had nothing left to lose just like those serving life sentences. She had a state of mind that the rest of the incarcerated women respected.

What mattered to Violet's prison shrink, and what the courts wanted to know, was whether or not she was sane enough to re-enter society. In order to answer this question, they had to retrace her thoughts, examine the circumstances that made her violent.

It took Violet months to admit any wrongdoing. She constantly professed her undying love, saying that only love could provoke someone to act so irrationally. It was this plea under the Crime of Passion statute that gave her such a light sentence. The case itself was a drawn out process where secrets of their relationship were revealed, elaborated, and portrayed as a holy consecration of love.

CHAPTER THIRTY

The trial took place on October 21st, 2009, almost six months after the incident. The timing seemed fitting, it was right on the cusp of Halloween, Charlie's favorite holiday. He was still in a coma, but starting to show signs of life. His intermittent blinking, and nightly scratching of his fingers against the hospital bedding gave the neurosurgeons hope he would regain consciousness again.

The district attorney was excited. This was not a typical racially motivated homicide related to gang violence, but a murder that read like it had been torn from the pages of a screenplay. Simon Rifenbark graduated Southwestern Law School in the late seventies. He'd dreamt of a career in business affairs at one of the major studios, but that never panned out. A couple of wrong turns, a few passionate marriages that ended in divorce, and a twenty-six year old son living in the Valley were all he had to remember those early days of ambition by.

Now he had this case, part love story, part violent affair. He didn't believe in coincidence, but he did believe people crossed paths for very specific reasons. It was a philosophy that lent itself to success in his profession.

The court smelled like body odor and reused mop water. Simon wore a wool suit, too hot for the room. Honorable Randall Cunningham presided over the case. Judge Cunningham came from old southern blood in Atlanta. He had witnessed a lot of his friends thrown in jail by ignorant cops who had nothing better to do than hassle innocent young men. Those cops motivated young

Randall to pursue a career in law. "To know the force used against you was the surest way to rise above it." He repeated this mantra in the face of every obstacle he confronted, from racism to finding his own mother dead in the back of the family car after a heroin overdose. The culmination of this life gave him a hardened edge that also let him sympathize with the less fortunate, and granted him a certain level of understanding beyond the limits of the law. He was fair and had become one of the best on the bench.

A few jurors made preemptive decisions and dismissed the case as, "another damn shooting." Others just shrugged, fiddling with their hangnails, and licking their chapped lips as the orders were given to the court. When the opening arguments began, Simon Rifenbark went to bat huge for the prosecution laying down the facts.

Aside from getting his name in the paper, Simon was driven by the idea of seeking redemption for Charlie. Charlie was still in a coma in the hospital. After six months. Simon wanted to prove that justice did exist, and he would be the one to deliver it.

"The honorable Judge Cunningham presiding, all rise." Simon leapt up to his feet, as did the defense lawyer, Melanie Kessler. Melanie was a highly ranked attorney from Beverly Hills, and a friend of Violet's. Her track record was flawless. She had made partner after only six years at her prestigious Century City law firm. Melanie took the case as a favor to Violet, who kicked in a large portion of her commission when she sold Melanie her first house so that she could afford it.

Simon gave Melanie the once-over. Melanie paid him no mind, knowing she could, with full confidence, expect the jury to eat from the palm of her hand. Violet was placid, sitting as elegantly as one could at their attempted murder trial.

It was time for Simon's opening statement.

“Ladies and gentlemen of the jury, this case is simple. The defendant, who is sitting right over there, gunned down her lover in cold blood. She bought a gun, stalked him, and when she had a clear shot, shot him. Why would someone do that, you ask? Because Charlie, the victim who has spent the last six months in a coma, had moved on. He didn't want to be in a relationship with the defendant anymore. He broke up with her.” Simon walked back over towards the defendant before continuing.

“The defense is going to argue that this was a crime of passion. That it was justified in some way. That Violet's broken heart is a reasonable defense to attempted murder. Don't let them fool you. Don't let her fool you. She may look small and harmless, but she isn't. She's dangerous. She's a lonely older woman who preyed on a man half her age, and then tried to kill him. So follow the evidence. Follow the facts. Follow the law. Don't let her fool you the way she fooled Charlie.”

Simon concluded his opening statement. He had them, at least for now. He confidently made his way back to his seat. It was the defense attorney's turn.

Melanie Kessler straightened the top of her custom fitted blazer and approached the jury. This was her courtroom now.

“This is an attempted murder trial. That's right, Violet is on trial for murder, and you get to determine her fate. It's entirely up to you. She was betrayed, hurt, lied to and ultimately used, stolen from. These are real, very real offenses. She was so hurt, she was driven out of her mind. She was driven out of her right mind by the alleged victim. That's what's called a crime of passion. And it does not qualify as murder. She didn't want to kill anyone. She had never even held a gun before. Through this case you'll understand how Violet was robbed and taken advantage of before being thrown away. Have you ever been hurt? Abused? Used? Thrown away? I bet you have. What Violet did, she did because of Charlie's own actions. Please consider what she went through and show her mercy. She's been through enough."

Melanie knew this case would be difficult, but the foundation she had just set convinced her success was not beyond her reach. She would go on to use every theory from Jung and Freud and brew it up alchemically with the teachings of the post-modern legal philosophers to poison the jury in Violet's favor. But first Simon had his chance to make his case. He called his first witness. Detective Sandoval.

Sandoval stood up and walked towards the stand. He was ready for his vacation. He was leaving that night from the Port of Los Angeles in Long Beach on a cruise to the Mexican Riviera that he had won over the phone.

Simon was anxiously awaiting Sandoval's testimony. He was relying on Sandoval to paint a picture of all of the events in Simon's favor.

"Detective. Please tell us how you found out about Charlie Winters."

"I was called to the scene of a shooting off Ventura. The officers at the scene first called it gang related, but that isn't how it appeared to me."

"And why is that?"

"A few reasons. The victim wasn't your typical gangster."

"Please tell me, how was he not typical?"

"He didn't fit the profile."

"And why not?" Simon pushed. He needed Sandoval to get specific.

"If you're asking me what threw me off, the first thing was the bottle of wine he had bought at the store right before he was shot. It was a pretty rare bottle. You normally wouldn't find something like this at your generic mom and pop store. Whoever bought the bottle searched for it… must have been looking to celebrate something special."

"So this wasn't gang violence. What was it then?"

Sandoval was getting excited. He loved telling juries, or anyone who would listen, about how he pieced a case together.

"Well, the bottle of wine led me to survey the crowd. The second step, after looking at the evidence at the scene of a crime, is to look around and review the people at the scene. Many times, the perpetrator, or a quality witness is right there watching their loved one."

"Was that the case the night of May 3rd?"

"Yes sir. I looked up and saw a young blonde."

"There she was, this blonde, her face had lost its color… bleach white. I knew she had to have had some involvement. I didn't know to what extent, whether she was a friend, family, or in this case the victim's lover."

"How did this young woman's expression help you figure out that foul play was involved?"

"It wasn't about foul play. It was only that I knew there she was my witness, that she had some information that would open the door to discovering the shooter's identity and motivation."

"Got it. Ok, so you did eventually track down this young girl, who had been exposed to this horrible act of violence against Charlie?"

"Yes, her name is Jennifer… Jenifer Bannister. She was so afraid to talk with me. The majority of our questioning was difficult, filled with sobbing, a lot of tears. She was in shambles, totally distraught."

"Objection. Relevance!" Melanie jumped up and shouted. She didn't want the jury feeling sorry for Jennifer.

"Overruled." The judge was intrigued and wanted to hear more. Melanie sat down, defeated.

"Sure, I think we all relate to loving someone so much it hurts." Simon looked around the courtroom. Some of the jury members were nodding. He felt a rising sense of hope.

"But did Jennifer help you discover the shooter?"

"Yes she did. Once she told me about Charlie's previous relationship with the defendant, I knew I had my shooter."

“Thank you Detective Sandoval. That's all for now.”

“Defense, your turn to cross,” said Judge Cunningham.

Melanie stood and marched right up to Detective Sandoval.

“Detective. So you've based a lot of your position, that Violet is responsible for this crime, on Jennifer Bannister's statements. Isn't that right?”

“I mean, well, yes she was my witness. That's how it works, you find a witness—”

“Thanks that's enough.” Melanie cut him off. She needed to show the jury that she was in charge. “Jennifer was hardly a credible witness. As you told me yourself, she had multiple run-ins with the law. She was arrested once just this last year for public intoxication wasn't she?”

“She was troubled.”

“Oh, I agree completely. I'm sure her life as a famous Hollywood writer's daughter was very difficult. It must have contributed a great deal to her trouble.”

“Objection. Relevance.” Simon knew he could get this one.

The judge interjected. “Sustained. Miss Krassel, if you don't get to something relevant very quickly you are going to need to change gears.”

“Your honor. The point here is that we have a ‘troubled' girl, who, the Detective has just pointed out, was arrested just this last year. I have records showing her last hospital stay was because she almost overdosed on a beach in Malibu. The pattern here is that she has never been in control of her emotions, her life, and how can we trust that? How do we know that she isn't the shooter?"

Now Melanie had gone too far. Simon screamed. "OBJECTION!"

Before the judge could rule, Melanie smiled and took it back.

"Withdrawn." She didn't need the testimony to stay in the record. She had planted the seed of doubt in the jury and that was enough.

CHAPTER THIRTY ONE

She came back to me. I had to experience true love and a bullet hole in my belly, but my sister was sitting beside me again.

"I thought you were gone. Gone for good." These were the first words I had said in months.

She held my hand in hers. She put it up to her milky colored face that had grown pale as she descended further and further into the afterlife. The fatigue I felt subsided as she spoke to me.

"Mom's okay, too. She's with me."

I sighed, leaned my head against the starchy sheet, and felt the tears drip down my face. My skin was dry. I now knew mom didn't make it. The doctors had lied.

"I bet she's alright. Better than here. Anything's better than here," I said. She shrugged and continued to look at my eyes. I was conscious, but the room was blurry, pulsing with the sunlight of the morning.

The nurses entered. My sister faded away. The overweight nurse carried a tray with syringes and a few vials. She rolled one of the vials in her hand, took the syringe and put it into one of the tubes connected to my vein. I relaxed, and within moments I was asleep again. But the slumber was far from natural. I could see my surroundings, but it was as if I saw them in a dream.

I continued to drift in and out of sleep, noticing different faces. A nurse with a mole on her forehead continuously entered. Her hair was a mess of black substructures, edging down her back. Her uniform had teddy bears in neon colors, reminding me of the Grateful Dead's many psychedelic logos. I kind of wished for the vinyl I had of *Terrapin Station* right then. I prayed it would come on over the muted speakers embedded in the wall.

I wondered whether I was going to die. I had only visited hospitals in my life to see death take over my loved ones. Their skeletons just laying there coated by the thin ethereal tissue, but nothing else remained inside. The person's spirit vanished and became another form of energy.

"Whang…wham… whan," The horrid sound of the loudspeaker and alarm announcing another secret code. When the alarm went off, a few staff members entered my room. I figured they must be here for me. I was the code this time. Had my heart stoppedbeating? Was my mind still working on overdrive while my body was dying?

The light I saw was not the pathway into heaven. It was the intensive electro charge zapped into my heart by the defibrillator. The emergency team witnessed life return to my body. A smile on my face. I was content to lie there and lick my lips, a white chalky substance formed in the corners of my mouth. "Thanks," I said. It was the first truly audible thing I had said to anyone living over the last few months of care. It wasn't that I couldn't speak, but that I hadn't had the energy. The electricity must have given me a crazy boost. I could feel charges of positive neutrons wiggling though my blood.

"Well, look at that. The kid is back."

I nodded and shook my head. I got straight to the point. "So what's next, can I get out of here? I need to see someone."

They all looked at me like I was speaking in a foreign tongue. They didn't understand. The driving force behind me had changed. I had become a compassionate human who needed to find hislover. But before I could say anything, they put restraints on my wrists. I thrashed and fought, but they only tightened my cuffs.

I looked down and saw blood seeping into my hospital gown. The staffers began calling down the hallway to someone. A large orderly came in with a shot and stuck it into my IV. I felt the sedative take effect. My eyelids grew heavy. My eyes closed. The sensation in my stomach subsided. When I swallowed, it felt as if shrapnel was tumbling inside my throat and tearing the inside of my stomach lining. I could only imagine the pain without my morphine drip. I slipped away into my mind where my only memory was of Jennifer. I had left her, waiting for me. The last female in my life, and I had abandoned her.

I searched for an explanation as to why I never made it back to Jenny. I remembered making love again on Tenny's couch. *Maybe we didn't?* I couldn't discern what was real and what wasn't. It was one of those moments where it all came together for a brief second and then vanished. I remembered why this silly life was worth living.

Jennifer asked me back in the Van if I believed in life after death.

"Like heaven?" I asked her.

"No, no not like heaven. I mean where do you think your spirit goes when you die?"

I had to think deep about that, picturing the apparitions of my sister, my previous atheist beliefs. I turned to her and said, “If a person's soul still has a purpose, like some unfinished business then I think they get to stick around for a bit. If not then… hmmm their energy spreads out and joins some parallel dimension I guess.”

She nodded intently. She weighed out all my words to really think about what I was saying, imagining the two different scenarios I proposed for versions of the afterlife.

She spoke in a near whisper. “I think people just die. Their bodies I mean. Their souls get trapped if they aren't pure.” I looked at her, trying to figure out which part of what she said was fatalistic and which part actually embraced the idea of having a spirit. I couldn't expect a Hindu perspective of reincarnation, but I would have preferred a little more optimism in her views.

It wasn't my choice. I couldn't tell her about my sister for fear she would run away. I feared that this perfect union between us would somehow crumble because of my insane anthropomorphic visions of my sister. I kept the dialogues I had with the ghost of my sister to a minimum while I was with Jennifer. Since I had arrived at the hospital, my sister was the only one who had visited me.

I came to three weeks later. Tennessee and Cindy were standing in front of me. Tenny had what looked like a box with a bottle of tequila in it. I wanted him to pour it in my mouth, to eradicate the taste of gauze and syringes that filled my pasty breath. I was sure they wouldn't let me have it for at least a few months. I didn't want to go the rest of my life without another Cadillac margarita.

Cindy had brought me a smoothie. She caressed my hair, which had grown long and ratty. “I can't believe you let them grow your hair so long. You look like Jesus.” She laughed, and adjusted my pillow so I could sit up and see them.

“What a shitty ride, guys.”

“What the hell happened man? You fuck the wrong chick this time or what?” I laughed, but the pain in my groin area grew the harder I laughed.

“No sir. Just wrong place, wrong time.”

“Did they tell you what happened?” Cindy let her journalist's spirit take control. I could tell she was sad, and that she had been crying for a few hours before coming to visit me. Her eyes were wide pear shapes, and the corners had sleep in them.

“They're worried about you man,” Tenny said.

“What? Dude. I'm feeling pretty good,” The drugs were really potent and I could hardly speak without shutting my eyes for a lot of the conversation.

“The doctor thinks the bleeding in your stomach stopped,” Tenny continued.

“That sounds good to me.”

I was locked inside a hospital, in a bed with an infection, but I decided that having the presence of people around me was a better feeling than being dead. I thought about the final moments of my mother's ICU journey. She must have taken a bad turn. Decided this life wasn't worth it.

It hurt me. I faded back into the sedation of my morphine dream. My eyes glazed over, and my sight was hazy. I saw a beautiful woman, my angel. She was climbing out of a hole in the ground, and taking off the halo on her head. I watched her take her robe off. She had the most beautiful body. I started to get dizzy and the vision changed as my dizziness escalated to nausea. The sick feeling woke me to looking at the scenic view outside my hospital window. The grim exterior convoluted my existential experience with reality. I was getting another series of shots by a nurse. She too was white robed, but looked nothing like the angelic figure I saw moments before.

I didn't want to die. I still had a zest for life, a deep passion. I wanted to see people, be hurt by them, and love them. Most of all I wanted to be with Jennifer.

Cindy was gone, but Tennessee was watching some movie on the television in my room. The pain in my stomach was overwhelming. "Sorry, I'm such bad company," I finally said. I figured it was more of a burden for him, than me. My body had become a physical anchor. It was completely incompatible from my thoughts. It continued to ache and press on independent of my thoughts.

"I'm sorry I ever introduced you to her, man."

"What do you mean?" I was groggy.

"Violet dude. That bitch. I swear if I ever."

"What are you talking about? You mean Jennifer? Where is she?"

"No, Violet. She... she's the one that shot you."

I was confused, and delirious from the meds. I believed him, but there was nothing I could do but lie my head back down and close my eyes.

"It's not your fault." It was all I could manage to get out before dozing off again.

I was dying, and intellectualizing it made me feel better. It took away the monotony of falling asleep permanently.

CHAPTER THIRTY TWO

The trial was almost over. Simon's attempt at keeping the tenacious young defense attorney at bay was failing. He sensed the jury's sympathies shifting in favor of Melanie's merciless defense. Melanie's work had done more than enough to provide reasonable doubt in more than half of them.

Jennifer was the only person left on the roster to be questioned in front of the court. Simon was betting he could use her emotionally driven testimony to sway the jury over the edge. Melanie planned to tear her to shreds.

The commotion was broken up by Simon, "We will now hear from the last witness in the case, Jennifer Bannister." The judge nodded his head in approval jotting a couple notes on a yellow legal pad. Simon turned around looking for Jennifer. She wasn't there. She had promised to arrive early. It had taken him weeks of prep to convince her to take the stand. Jennifer had agreed to do it for Charlie, but now she was nowhere in sight. Melanie chimed in, "Looks like your white knight is a no-show Rifenbark."

"If your witness is not here in the next minute, we are going to need to move on to your closing arguments." Judge Cunningham said.

"Can we take a brief recess your honor?" Simon pleaded. The judge looked up his attention was to the back of the courtroom, "Looks like you won't be needing that recess counselor." Everyone turned and Jennifer came in through the door, flush and in a hurry.

“You had me nervous there.” Simon took Jennifer's bag and threw it under his table. She went up and raised her right hand before sitting down behind the stand.

“Ms. Bannister. Please tell the court how you met Charlie Winters?”

“We were both at a hotel lounge. I felt uneasy that night, really nervous for some reason.”

“Relevance.” Melanie asked.

“I am trying to provide the court with context on their relationship.”

“Proceed.” The judge let him continue his direction of questioning.

“Out of nowhere came Charlie. He was in a really desperate state, and didn't look very healthy like he had been sick or something.”

“Can you clarify?”

“Yes, like he had been throwing up. His face was off-color, but he was really sincere. He put my nerves at ease and we had this amazing conversation. Our connection was unusual, but unlike anything else I had ever felt.”

“In what way was it unusual.”

“He wasn't fake. Like everybody else, he was just sad. I thought maybe he was going through a break up.”

“Objection! Speculation.” Melanie interjected.

“Sustained. Please omit the last sentence.” Cunningham requested to the court recorder.

“How do you know that Charlie loves you?” Simon was reaching, but the court needed to hear it.

“We were soul mates. He didn't even know my name after we met. He was carried off by her (pointing at Violet) and then managed to find me in the hospital. He sat by my side and then drove me up the coast. We are soul mates, meant for each other. To be together forever.” Jennifer started to get teary eyed.

Simon knew that the idea of ‘Soul Mates' might be a little abstract for the jury to follow so he dug deeper, “What else made you know that this love you both had was real?”

“Real? It isn't something you can explain. It's the feeling you get for someone and then they tell you ‘I love you with all my heart'. That's what he said to me before he was shot by that witch.”

“Objection your honor!” Melanie was frustrated and ready to question Jennifer to dissolve this illusion in front of the court.

“Sustained. Anything further counselor?”

“No your honor. We're finished here.” Simon felt confident in the last compelling words of his witness.

Melanie prepared her cross-examination. She had been rehearsing this for days in anticipation of Jennifer taking the stand.

"Ms. Bannister. We're happy you're here to clarify a couple things that I think we're all curious about."

Jennifer was uneasy, but ready sitting on the edge of the chair.

"You said that you know someone loves you because of a feeling right?"

"Yes, and the words they say to you to try and articulate something so deep."

"Sure, exactly. So if I say that you're my friend and I buy you a drink and tell you what a great person you are…"

"Love is different."

"Enlighten us."

"It's the rarest and most pure thing on earth."

"Let me be more specific. Don't you think it's a contradiction then that Charlie loved two women in this courtroom? You and my client?"

"No, he didn't. She used him and played the part."

"Look at these letters. Do these look like he was 'faking it'?" Melanie presented the letters written on different types of paper in zip locked bags into evidence.

"He's a good writer. He can make you believe anything."

"Maybe that's what he did to you too. Make believe."

"I know he didn't, but I don't care what you say. I wasn't the one that shot him over it. She fucking did!" She pointed at Violet again, who was staring at Jennifer with an amused expression.

"Where were you the night of the shooting?"

"I was waiting for Charlie to come back to me from the store."

"You were in the Valley too? Right across from where he was shot. Why didn't you go with him to the store?"

"Because he went alone."

"Objection. Relevance."

"I'm just showing that she may have not just been inside playing good girl."

"Sustained." Judge Cunningham was getting tired of the circles of questioning by the defense to an uncertain end, "If you don't have an end in sight Miss Kessler I suggest you find something else to bring to the table."

Melanie decided she would rest as well. She had done her job and caused tension and doubt in the courtroom. She was also able to get Jennifer to look agitated and not the picture perfect identity she portrayed.

Simon went through a lengthy closing to prepare the jury for their deliberations. He wanted them to remember that this was not just a love story, but a young man was shot by a successful business woman who had full, conscious knowledge of her actions. She was possessive and wanted something she couldn't have, Charlie.

Melanie kept her closing statements short and sweet, convoluting the love between Charlie and Jennifer and making it seem like he lead Violet on, used her for her money and then ran away. It didn't justify shooting him, but it might give her a lesser sentence under the Crime of Passion Law. The jury was escorted out of the room. All that was left is to wait for a verdict.

The chatter in the courtroom was lulled when Judge Cunningham came back into the bench. Melanie took one more look at Simon and straightened up in her chair. Violet was grinding her teeth and looking directly into the California State seal behind the judge's bench. She stared at it, running her nails along her pants. Judge Cunningham came out from his chambers and sat down. The jury followed into their jury box. They all sat down except the foreperson. She stood up and she read the verdict. Judge Cunningham confirmed Violet's sentencing.

CHAPTER THIRTY THREE

Jennifer nibbled her cuticles. Her nervous energy and anxiety was taking over her body. It was frenetic.

A montage of images: She and Charlie exploring each other's bodies, traveling up the coast, the smell of salty air, licking the taste from Charlie's skin. She began to cry. The tears were painful and stung her dry skin.

She lay completely naked on her bed. The heater in her parent's back house was turned up to eighty degrees. Her pale body was covered in perspiration. She wiped off the sweat with the red t-shirt she had taken from Charlie's van.

She paused, placing the shirt over her nose like a bandana to keep out a toxic gas. She inhaled deeply sucking in the smell of Charlie. The scent was so good; it combined the old smell of his van, the teak wood cabinets, musty beach air, and Charlie's skin after sex. Jennifer reached into her side drawer and took out a thin pink vibrator, placed it between her legs and arched her back over the side of the bed horizontally. She moved as if he was with her, touching her, embracing her the way he always did; protective, loving, and sacred.

Jennifer couldn't reach an orgasm. She was too deep in thought to relax. She rolled over and lit a cigarette. She put Charlie's shirt over her chest and set an ashtray on top. She smoked, calculating each breath, exhaling rhythmically. Her heart beat much faster, raising and lifting the ashtray.

She had shut down sexually after Charlie was shot. The trial took another toll on her. It clouded her memory of their love. The passion they enjoyed was holy; She did not want to share the intimacy with anyone else. She didn't want to be touched or held. The thought of another man's arms around her was revolting. She didn't want to believe that Charlie was going to die.

She stopped taking her anti-depressants, flushed the cocktail of generic drugs prescribed to her down the toilet. It was scary to disconnect from the routine of popping a few in the morning. She had stopped the few days she was with Charlie, and it was the best moments of her life.

Her parents pleaded for her to go back on her medicine. They thought it would be too difficult to deal with their daughter without it. She was their glue, and if she came unwound they feared so would their relationship.

Jennifer had spent the first two months after the shooting running away, and sleeping by Charlie's side in the hospital while he was still unconscious in a coma. Each night, she would hold his hand, her fingers tracing the IV lines to his palm. She couldn't help but feel like he was a robot with all the different tubes pumping fluids into him for survival.

"Come back. Come back to me." She whispered the words into his ears, trying to lure him out of the coma and into her arms again. This was her routine for two months until she gained the courage to visit the suspect in the shooting who was being held in prison. She didn't know her, and didn't want to know her. She had avoided going to see her, but the burning questions in her mind forced her to make the drive. Against her parents' wishes, but with their endorsement, she went to go visit Violet.

Jennifer's parents loaned her their car and she made the drive down Mulholland and out to the prison. The cream interior provided a capsule for her thoughts to bounce around in. "I know it was me all along who he loved. Why did this woman think it was her right to take it from us?" The question came out of her mouth and the words stung her chapped lips.

The hour drive to the prison was endless. She transitioned from freeway to freeway and tried to outdistance the traffic by turning onto side streets. She pulled over near Penrose Avenue when she couldn't see straight anymore. Her obsession with discovering the truth about Charlie made her blind with anger.

Jennifer hit the steering wheel with her right hand, repeatedly thumping it over and over again. The images she kept replaying in her head would not simply go away. They replenished themselves in more distinct and vivid forms, as she continued to think about their road trip, the celebrated sexual encounters, and their first real kiss in the Pacific Ocean in Santa Cruz.

The road grew more and more desolate. Business parks, strip malls, and a few fast food restaurants popped up at regular intervals. The sameness of all the buildings made the deep valley difficult to distinguish. Navigating this sea of suburbia seemed hopeless.

Jennifer maintained her head, despite fading in and out from fatigue. She didn't want her intuition to be right. The memory of Charlie at the W Hotel. Honest, yet completely anonymous. The witty banter and sexual tension that had made their first encounter stick in her mind. It may not have been love at first sight, but his presence in her life had set off a flurry of romantic fantasies. Their connection was pure and truthful. She needed to validate how pure their connection had been.

She quivered, and woke up from the daydream to find that she had arrived. The outside of the prison was yellowish plaster and aging brick. She had expected to see a lot of guards and other personnel surrounding the gates, but the area was vacant. The entrance to the lot had a single guard stall. A thick beam blocked the entrance. The guard shack was a small box, and the windows were made from reflective glass.

"Name, and Government issued ID or passport."

Jennifer was taken aback by the guard. She didn't realize she had already pulled up to the gate.

"Let me get it." She was unprepared for the prerequisites to get into the prison. She reached awkwardly around in the backseat for her black leather bag.

The guard reached down and took the blue wallet sized documents, flicked through the pages of multi-colored incomplete stamps from foreign countries to find one with Jennifer's picture on it. He looked at her picture and then stared at her for a long pause with familiarity.

"Can I have my passport back, please?" Jennifer said, breaking the officer's silent judgment. He was nervous, fidgeting with the passport, before handing it back to her. He pressed the button to raise the beam that blocked the entrance to the lot.

Jennifer also paused, looking for another sign of encouragement to signal safe passage inside.

In the parking lot, she passed a number of open spots between other cars, worried she might make the turn too wide, or some other visitor would dent her parents' car. She did one more lap around, her head rocking back and forth. She turned the air conditioning up.

After she parked, she stayed in the car and kept it running. She hoped the walk into the prison would be short. The auxiliary fan went on overdrive to compensate for the heat outside in the Valley. She got out of the car.

The air was humid, and the smell surrounding the jail was like laundry detergent. A modern building, sparsely landscaped with succulents and brown trees. The parking lot had one tree; a baby spruce that looked freshly planted and was already wilting in the heat.

Jennifer made her way to the front entrance of the prison. A voice came out from a small stainless steel intercom box on the wall. "Name?"

Jennifer felt uneasy. Her name felt heavy on her tongue. Her mouth was so dry she could barely speak. *Why was she here?*

"Jennifer, Jen. Bannister." She paused, feeling a sense of accomplishment in getting the words out.

"Name of the prisoner, ma'am?" The voice came back garbled and full of static. "Violet. Prisoner #22367-1." A loud beep. The higher tones clipped from the threshold of the speaker. The glass door slid to the side. Jennifer stepped in, and the door slid shut behind her. A red light above her head blinked rapidly next to a camera. The light turned green and the other door slid open.

The noises, and butchered sentences of the English language caused an immediate headache. A nauseating rush of blood reddened her eyes. Her arms acted independently from her body. She signed an entrance form and continued down the hallway in the direction of the visiting area. Each hall was no different than the next, and the monotony made it easy to lose track of what direction she was going. There were no maps on the wall, no information center with a red arrow saying 'you are here'.

She was a trespasser in this place. Strict rules governed her every move. But Violet was here. She was behind the glass waiting for Jennifer. Jennifer wished she could run. She sat down in the plastic orange chair.

The glance she gave to Violet behind the curls of her beautiful wavy hair was sadistic. Violet was hardened, and barely acknowledged the glancing blow. The floor was uneven, and Jennifer's chair slipped, forcing her to break eye contact first. Her blonde hair fell over her face.

Violet pointed at the phone. It hung on the wall next to the glass. Jennifer hesitated. The pulsing negative energy of the prison made it difficult for her to lift her hand. Her sweater began to feel heavy, wet. The idea of actually lifting the phone receiver and putting it to her ear seemed impossible. She situated her chair and lifted the receiver.

"So, this is overdue," Violet said.

"I didn't think there was really a point."

"But you wanted to know?

"Know what?

“That he loved me. That you weren't the only one.”

“No! I mean, that's not what I care about.” She straightened. Jennifer didn't want to show her true resentment and rage for Violet quite yet.

“Well, what? You want me to tell you more about the letters he wrote to me? Or did you just come to see me in here? Because I'm fine, you know. I'll be fine when I get out of here, and I'll always know the truth about him.”

“I want to know why.”

“Why? Little girl, you would never understand. You couldn't possibly.”

“You think I'm some little girl, like I couldn't possibly know what you know? But it's sad you know.”

“What's sad?”

“When you get out of here you will be even older than you arenow, alone. You'll have to buy some animals to keep you company. A pathetic old woman.”

“Listen you little bitch. Don't come here to insult me. I can hang up whenever I want, and you'll never know shit.”

“I'm sorry.”

"No you're not. Listen, I know, I was young and naïve once." The slight dig made Jennifer uneasy. She swallowed her pride and listened to what Violet had to say.

"He cared for you, I'm sure of that without a doubt. Broke my fucking heart, chasing you. You're beautiful, pretty, young. What's not to like? I'm sure you enchanted his little ass. He had a good thing. I bought him everything. I tried to keep the blinders on him, but he couldn't do it."

"Well, I didn't ever see him do that. Looking at other girls, I mean."

"Other women, sweetie. No actually, you're right, his affinity was for young girls when he got loose."

"Got loose? You act like he was in a cage. I don't get it."

"No, but we lived together. We had a life together."

"He sure didn't seem domesticated when I met him for the first time."

"Oh really, and where was that?" Violet was growing unnerved, but she was also curious.

"The W Hotel."

"The W Hotel." Violet repeated. When would Charlie have been there? She tried to pinpoint the night. Then she remembered. She left him in the car with Valet. *How long had he been down there? He must have been flirting with Jennifer the whole time.* Violet tried to think hard, and the visual image of him flirting, laughing and kissing someone else made her repulsed. She stood up.

“Wait, please. I just need to know,” Jennifer said.

“What do you want to know? Why I fucking shot him?”

“How do you know he loved you?” Jennifer's eyes filled up with tears, hoping that it wasn't true. She was searching for something deeper, some sense that the love she felt was real, that what Violet had with Charlie was just a lie.

“Ha. That's what you wanted? That's all you wanted to know?”

“Yes.” Jennifer paused. “Please tell me.”

“You know… you feel it, in your stomach. You know there is no one else that will understand, this thing you both have together. No one else.”

“Then I didn't have it.” Jennifer looked sad, but a smirk of joy hid behind the tears.

“I knew that, honey. You didn't need to come here to figure that out,” Violet said, certain she had destroyed the dreams of this pretty young girl. She felt free now. She didn't have to share the nostalgia, the passion.

“Violet. One last thing.” Jennifer felt Violet's vindictive stare. She stood up to look her in the eyes. They stared at each other, neither one blinking. Jennifer lowered her hand, lifting her shirt ever so slightly to reveal the bulge in her belly.

When Violet saw Jennifer's stomach, she jumped into the safety glass. Her face turned vicious, her skinny jaw chewing at the air, her throat letting out inhuman, guttural sounds. "Seven months today." Jennifer hung up the phone and walked away.

The exit from the prison felt better. She wiped her eyes again, knowing she had somehow vindicated her love for Charlie, and Charlie's love for her. He had written many love notes, captured the hearts of other women, but none shared in the glory of creating life through their union.

CHAPTER THIRTY FOUR

The pain subsided for the first time in weeks. I sat up in bed. The window was sealed shut, but I could still feel the warmth from the sun outside.

You're looking good Mr. Winters," the doctor said, holding up my most recent X-ray. They sent some radioactive dye through me to make sure the contusions, and internal hemorrhaging had stopped.

"When will I be out of here?" I had only one thing on my mind, or rather, one person.

"A few days more now," he said.

"Couldn't be soon enough doc. You know why?"

"Why?" He actually answered me.

"Never mind."

"Just rest, okay? That's the best thing you can do until you're 100%."

"Yes, sir. I'll rest up, then get back in the saddle." He looked one last time at my charts. "Aha," He said. The doctor signed a few things, checked a couple boxes, clicked his black and silver Mont Blanc pen and put it back in his front jacket pocket.

I clutched my shirt like something was missing from it. I didn't have a pen, a favorite item to validate other people, check boxes of their life and walk away. I looked up and saw a few white lilies next to the bed. A hand-written note on the back featured a detailed charcoal rendering of the two of us. We were together, and it was like a depiction of Adam and Eve. Our faces were so vivid.

The room smelled of the lilies, and it reminded me of her pale powdery skin, the few freckles on it, and her hair that smelled like hay. The combination of smells made me sweat under the hospital sheets. Life didn't seem so bad anymore. I wanted to change things. I knew I was meant for more than going back to the Valley, working to make processed meat taste good inside a soggy fake sourdough bun. The thought made me sick. I couldn't picture it. It just didn't fit into the frame.

People talk about new beginnings, rebirths, the pilgrimage and holy awakenings, and I guess I finally got to be one of those people. I always hoped I would be. You just don't know until it happens. I woke up that day feeling different. Those banal, trying days, each one worst then the next, were done. I kicked them away. The life that lay ahead of me would be lived alongside someone I truly, deeply loved.

The feeling continued, but the sounds of the hospital equipment started to drown it out. I tried to hold onto the memories, protecting them from the noise of the machinery. Night came quicker than expected. The hospital was quict.

I wanted to get better. I wanted to get out; I know I had wronged Jennifer. I had wronged her by not being honest about my past. I wanted to embrace all the sweet nuances of her spirit: The slight snort of her laughter, the tear that would sit in the corner of her eye, the patches of freckles on each of her cheeks when she smiled, her almond eyes, the blonde eyelashes that bordered on beingwhite, the sensitive skin that would turn to goose bumps with the slightest touch of my hands on her forearms.

During the nights I could think about all of these details, remember why I wanted to live, to get out of here and be whole again with my other half. Some people traveled to the ends of the earth to find their spiritual purpose, to find out who they really were. My purpose was right here in Los Angeles. We didn't have to search anymore; we could end the journey to nowhere, and be in one another's lives for a long, long, time hereafter. I couldn't wait for physical therapy. It was strange to think of something that would probably be so damn painful at first, but it would be worth every part of the biting pain to be a partner, a contributor to her continued happiness.

The stagnant air hanging over my bed was suffocating me. I couldn't stop my thoughts from spinning. I'd have paid anything for a can of WD40 to douse that small bearing on the wheel of the gurney that passed my doorway every ten minutes squeaking.

Part of me wondered if the Doctor's words were true about getting out of here. *Was I really recovering?* I felt that I would never leave the hospital. They say when you reach the end of your days you see a light, a glowing tubule of light coming for you like a gateway. But I didn't see any light. So maybe I wasn't dying after all.

Another squeak from the gurney down the hallway pulled me out of the immeasurable silence of the hospital, and into the present. I was scared to die. I began to cry. Tears poured out saturating the top of my Hospital gown. Images passed in front of me, portraits coming into view of the many people I had actually loved, and hurt over the years. I had not meant to harm them.

Once, I locked my sister in the bathroom for an entire afternoon, telling her I had lost the key. Really, I had just been holding the door with my hands. I persisted until she pulled so hard, she fell backward on the other side into the bathtub, cracking her head. She'd had to get a series of stitches in the back of her scalp. I heard the thud, and still I held onto the door. I just hadn't been able to convince myself to let go.

Now I realized why I hadn't let go… it was out of fear. I didn't want to see what my actions had done to her, the pain that I had caused someone I loved so deeply. I couldn't have known I was going to lose her.

I wanted to go back and open the door and let her out. We would get some Yoo-Hoos and share them with straws. She liked the strawberry one, so I definitely would have given her the strawberry one. Mom used to make sure we always had a few in the fridge, even if that meant taking some Hershey's syrup and mixing it with whole milk in an empty Yoo-Hoo bottle, shaking it up and screwing the cap back on really tight. It tasted good enough to me with the same richness as the original. Sometimes if you let it sit for too long, the milk and chocolate would separate, but you just had to give it another shake and it was back in perfect harmony.

My mom was next, her face younger than when she was in the hospital, she looked like I remembered her in the old Polaroid from her wedding in North Dakota. Her hair was long, all dark brown and silky. I could see the reflection of happiness in her eyes, a glow that had dulled after dad left us, muted to a tender softness, fading out a little bit every day. I lifted my hand and tried to touch the image of my mother, to embrace her one last time. The vision vanished in my hands. I returned to the present, my face crusted with dry tears.

I wanted to see Jennifer. I tried to focus on the dark air, scrunching my face and blurring my vision, trying to force her image to assemble in front of me. I started to drift again, and then she came, in perfect angelic spirit. She looked so real I could feel her breath on my lips. No words were exchanged. Her blonde eyelashes opened and closed. She looked down and then she, too, disappeared like the others. Had I wronged her too? No. It wasn't possible. We had something untouchable. Our love would triumph. I was sure of it.

I went back to sleep. It was almost early morning and I needed some rest.

CHAPTER THIRTY FIVE

Destiny's hand clutched the syringe handle tightly. Her hair was straightened, her eyelashes covered with chunky mascara. A nicely dressed man in a suit approached her from behind.

"Excuse me is that you?"

"Do I know you?"

"No, I don't think so."

The man continued to look at her like he was seeing double.

"You sold me my house remember. A year ago on Stone Canyon."

"No that wasn't me."

"You could be her twin sister."

"I am, actually. Sorry I need to run, but I'll tell Violet you say hi."

"Please do."

Destiny nodded. She walked off and found a nurse.

"I'm looking for the East wing, recovery. I mean my boyfriend is in recovery," she corrected herself. One of the nurses looked at her.

“No problem. Take the lobby elevators up one floor. Walk down the corridor following the signs, and follow the bridge over to the other wing. Visiting hours are over, though.”

Walking away from the nurse, she continued to the elevator in the lobby. The wait for the three different elevators was inordinately long because two of the elevators were out of service for maintenance.

It was a minor deterrence. She persisted. She peeked into open rooms as she scurried to the other wing. The signs ceased. She ran her hands down the wall looking for some type of directory to pop out.

There was a constant flow of orderlies coming from one hallway. The nurse's station had to be near. She didn't want to be noticed or cause any type of scene. She prepped herself by shaking her head, cracking each vertebra in her neck. The sound was jarring.

“Hello, I'm trying to find my brother.”

“Visiting hours are over, I'm sorry.”

“Yes, I know. I'm so sorry I just flew in from New York to see him.”

“Well, you'll have to come back tomorrow,” the nurse said with an exhausted look.

“Please. Look, I know you're not supposed to do this, but I have to see him.”

"I can't. It doesn't work like that." The nurse stuck to the policy.

"I'm begging you." Now the tears fell. At first one at a time and then more fluidly. The nurse paused and looked around, seeing everyone changing shifts, and her replacement walking up.

"Okay, fine. What's the name?"

"Charlie… Charlie Winters."

"Room 305," the nurse said in a low voice. Destiny hid her overwhelming excitement by ducking her head and tucking her hands into her jean pockets.

"That way Miss." The nurse stood up and motioned with her head the opposite direction.

She didn't pay any attention to the nurses carrying their late-night snacks in paper bags. Her pace quickened, but her body seemed to float along the floor. The only change was in her expression, her eyes squinting, exaggerating her wrinkles. Her tongue twitched nervously along the bottom of her top row of teeth.

The door to Charlie's room was closed. She took a deep breath and her body trembled as she inhaled, growing an inch taller in height. She pushed through the door. The light poured in with her, brightening the black room. Charlie's breaths were slow, drawn out and consistent. The distance to the bed was only five feet.

It wasn't the drive there, or the hallways, or the lies she had to tell the nurses, but these last five feet that proved to be the most difficult. She took her heels off and walked barefoot across the linoleum floor. It was cool to the touch. Her footsteps were almost silent. Charlie lay completely still. When she got close enough she could see his eyelids fluttering in deep REM.

She watched him for a few minutes. Each second dragged on. Destiny looked at him and felt a growing desire. She reached under her jeans into her panties and began to rub herself. Charlie twitched and rolled onto his other side. Destiny froze and stepped away from the bed. She reached into her back pocket and pulled out a translucent brown bottle and a syringe. In the bottle was Phenobarbital a solution used to stop seizures in epileptics. With the syringe in her right hand she pierced the top of the bottle and filled it up to 45 mg. She took the syringe and stuck it into Charlie's saline I.V. tube. She gently pushed the liquid into his blood stream.

Charlie's body twitched a few times. His mouth opened and closed. Destiny looked at her watch, and watched the minute hand tick away. After a minute had passed, Destiny climbed on top of Charlie, mounting him. She was careful not to press down with all her weight, but he struggled nevertheless.

She began to ride him. This aroused Charlie, and his eyes opened. Her hand was on his skin. His breathing was heavy and a stream deep moans escaped. His eyes opened. He tried to lift his hands, to caress the face of the woman on top of him, but was stopped by his restraints.

Charlie blinked rapidly. Every time he blinked he saw a little more clearly. This woman wasn't Jennifer. Jennifer was nothing like this woman. He remembered the face, "Destiny, what are you..." Charlie mumbled.

The words were broken. His eyes rolled back in his head and he couldn't see straight from dizziness.

The realization that he had Destiny on top of him crippled Charlie. Anger and disgust flooded his veins. He struggled to call out in fear, “Nurse! Please.” His voice came out crackly and muffled. No matter how hard he tried to scream for help, he couldn't. “You think you can do this to my sister. Then just fuck me and leave me asshole.” Destiny grabbed the pillow and shoved it over his mouth. She held it down, her full weight on him now. The sound of his stitches snapping was like corn starting to pop. Blood seeped through the sheets.

Destiny pushed the pillow down with all of her strength. She felt Charlie's body go limp. She lifted the pillow. She looked at his face. He was still, but still breathing. She began to cry. She looked down and saw a pool of blood between her legs. She couldn't believe what she had just done. She jumped up, and wiped herself off with the sheets. She pushed the attendant button for the nurse, removed the syringe from the IV and darted down the hallway.

Charlie lay there, covered in blood and motionless.

CHAPTER THIRTY SIX

Jennifer sank back into her parents couch, tilted her head and tried to forget the whole journey with Charlie. She didn't really want the memories erased, it would make it easier if she didn't care for him so much. She couldn't bring herself to go back to the hospital. It killed her inside to see him like that. Her deepest fear was that when he was better he wouldn't feel the same about her. He might not love her the same. He might not be happy about the baby. She breathed deeply, sighing, as tears leaked out of both of her eyes. Her pale skin was flush red, and her hair was in shambles.

The electric fireplace was on full blast. The warmth it gave off did little. She could hardly feel it. Goosebumps ran up and down her arms in the isolated room. She sat in front of the fireplace and placed her hands on the thick glass. She beckoned the heat to penetrate the window and burn her hand. Jennifer removed her hand from the glass it was swollen and red. The heat had permeated the thick safety glass and burned her slightly. She hardly noticed.

Jennifer went into the bathroom and turned on the bath. The rumble of the water reminded her of the waves in Santa Cruz tumbling over the rocks below. The white porcelain claw-foot tub echoed the sounds. The harmony made her feel calm in a way she hadn't since their trip up the coast.

Her pants were on the floor. She was down to just her black tank top. She looked in the mirror, eyes swollen, hand throbbing. Her focus was on the weight she had put on over the last month, a stark reminder of her childhood eating disorder. She tried to accept it, but didn't remove her tank top so she didn't have to see her stomach.

The food she had eaten in the hospital was all junk food. She had been relying on her old favorite, Spudnuts donuts, to keep her in good cheer. Donuts and a Dr. Pepper had served as a kind of anti-depressant. The food had put a nice layer of pudge around her torso. It was hardly noticeable on her petite figure, but it made her uneasy and uncomfortable in her own skin.

The phone rang. Jennifer waited for her parents to answer it, but it just kept ringing. "What the fuck," she said. "Fine, fine. I've got it." She walked half-naked to the phone. She pressed the speakerphone button to answer.

"Yes, who's this?" There was a pause. After what seemed like twenty minutes a male voice came on.

"Is this Jennifer, Jennifer Bannister?" The man asked. "This is Detective Sandoval, do you remember?"

"Um, yes. Obviously. You hunted me down."

"Right, yes I'm sorry." His voice trailed off.

"I don't care. You caught her, so whatever."

"Well, yes we did. I mean, we had her as you know."

"What in the hell does that mean?"

"Let me explain."

"I've been seeing Charlie every week. He'll be OK, so I don't care. It all worked out OK?"

"I'm sorry to say this, but Charlie has died."

"What?" She had seen Charlie hours ago.

"I'm sure this is a shock. It was a shock to us too. My team has been at the hospital for the last few hours."

"What happened? Tell me, right now." Her eyes filled with tears.

"He was murdered," Sandoval finished. He waited for Jennifer's response, but he only heard heavy breathing.

Jennifer hung up the phone.

The tears wouldn't fall. Her face was the color of a dark plum. Hatred welled up inside her. Heart-wrenching pain tore through her, and she fell to the floor. Jennifer curled up into a ball and began to cry. A new sense of loss filled her, worse than any she had known before. The thought of losing Charlie again killed her. What little had been left of her was now permanently destroyed.

There was a knock on the door, a pause, and then another knock. "Jenny, sweetie... Are you in there?" Her mother's voice was hesitant, but persistent. Jennifer heard her fidget with the door handle and try and open it. They had removed all the locks in the house years ago during Jenny's high school eating disorder, when they thought she might be a suicide risk. The problem now was that Jennifer was in the master bedroom, the only room that still had a lock on the inside.

"Jenny, it's your mother. Can you let me in sweetie?" She tried to stay calm and not overreact. She put her ear to the door, and couldn't hear anything inside the room. After a few minutes she heard the sound of Jennifer's heavy breathing. She practically ripped the door handle off, but still couldn't get into the room.

"Jennifer! Let me in right now. This second."

She heard the sound of glass breaking. She flung her small torso into the heavy wood door, but it wouldn't budge. Finally, the door opened. Jennifer stood there, half-naked, tears running down her rosy face. All the color had drained from her body, except her flush cheeks that looked painted on.

Her mother entered. She saw the broken glass from the fireplace all over the floor, the flames pouring out being fueled by a clump of paper. Her mother tried to remain calm. She got a towel and wrapped it around Jennifer, covering her exposed body. She pulled her close and could see her stomach protruding. She didn't say anything.

"Everything will be alright sweetheart. I promise," her mother said. Jennifer watched the fireplace, her eyes fixated on the crumpled papers that were burning.

"He's better off not being in so much pain. You need to look at all the positives."

"He's not better off. You think so, but you don't know. You have no idea what love fucking means!" Jennifer shoved her mother, nearly knocking her over.

"Jenny, I didn't mean it like that."

Sure. I'm sure you didn't." Jennifer burst into raging tears again, "Please just leave me alone."

"Please, baby."

Jennifer ignored her mother and turned away, dropping her towel and exposing herself again. She dragged her feet on the stone floor, scratching her toenails against each ridge. Jennifer drained thebath. She liked the sound, but the memory was gone now. She pressed her pelvis against the cold granite counter top, pulled on the handle of the polished silver shower handle and let the water warm up. The steam filled the bathroom in minutes.

She opened the window by cranking the handle attached to the curved arm with the slider and breathed in the fresh air, looking at the empty street below. She waited for Charlie's van to pull up. She kept seeing the flicker of a Chevy emblem behind the leaves of the tree.

The steam bellowed from the window like smoke from a fire. Jennifer coughed. The vapor filled her lungs. She wiped the fogged-over mirror with a hand towel, and drew a circle around her face. The line on the mirror faded quickly, and she took off her top. She looked at her arms, traced the line down her body to her belly button. Her belly button was enlarged, and her child shown as a large bump inside her stomach. Tears flowed, pouring down her chest and onto the floor. *Charlie was another father who would never see his child grow up.*

Jennifer's tears soothed her. An enlightened, glowing look filled her face. She couldn't figure out how she had become so contented by the thought of this life growing inside of her. Jennifer had never wanted kids. She had never been able to figure out how to hold them or treat them to make them feel comforted. Her maternal instincts were also growing inside her. She was preparing mentally to bring a child into this world, and raise it on her own. Their child, the only trace of her dead lover — lived inside her.

She showered, the beads of water tumbling over her belly. Jennifer rubbed her palms over the bump, caressing it. She wanted to remember her life with Charlie as one of pure love. The moment when Charlie had been shot renewed her. She had woken up. This pregnancy would be a kind of rebirth. She faced a real chance to start over, and give all she didn't have to another life. She would embody his spirit and love it unconditionally.

Jennifer stopped the shower abruptly. She stayed behind the glass, drip-drying, the cold air felt good. She stared at her contorted reflection on the chrome handle. She sat down on the tile floor, soaking up the last bit of heat held from the stone surface. She fainted.

The banging on the shower door began minutes after her blackout. Her mom had unlocked the bathroom door with her key. She burst in to find Jennifer still on the floor of the shower. She wrapped her daughter in a dry towel. She tried to lift Jennifer, but her frail muscles could not even begin to retrieve her from the shower floor.

"Honey! Rupert, get down here now!"

Mr. Bannister was busy experimenting with some new hologram software he was working on with an old business partner. He looked at the computer screen, waited, saw the algorithm save correctly, and heard his wife screeching for him again. He stopped what he was doing, pulled his hand back, threw on his Crocs and clunked down the stairs.

“Oh, my god! What happened? Is she breathing?” He didn't lean down to pick her up. Instead he went over to the phone and dialed 911. Before the operator could speak, he began to shout into the phone.

“Please! If you have a heart! Hurry! It's my daughter.” Tears ran down his face. He went back into the bathroom and helped his wife lift Jenny's body out of the shower. He carried her into the other room, placing her directly in front of the fire. He turned up the setting on the electric gauge to high. The flame puttered and went out momentarily. “Damn. Stupid fucking electric fire.” Rupert rubbed the towel on Jennifer's wet air, and wiped a few daubs from her face.

“Wake up baby. Wake up sweetie. C'mon.” He slapped her cheeks lightly. Her breathing was slow, but consistent. Jennifer's parents were not going to let her leave them. She was all they had. Her mother started CPR, pressing on Jennifer's chest as tears streamed down her face. Lightly at first, and then harder and harder until Jennifer's pale cheeks were rosy with life in them.

“Stop it. Dammit, stop pressing her chest so hard,” her father urged.

“Wake up, Jenny! Wake up for your mommy. “ She grabbed Jennifer's face. Her wedding ring caught Jennifer's cheek and it began to bleed.

“Look what you did now. Look at her. She's bleeding. I can't do this. Go outside. Wait for the paramedics at the top of the street. They'll never find us down here.”

Their street was a small enclave, and there was a strong chance that without her mom to flag them down they would never find her.

Jennifer's mom was waving a flashlight at the top of the street facing Mulholland. She kept the beam on the asphalt to make sure she didn't blind the ambulance driver. She paced back and forth in front of the street. The minutes continued to go by. She would pace a few steps, then look up and shake her head in disbelief. She sat down on the ground near a white stucco wall.

After what seemed like an hour, she couldn't take it anymore. Her small fragile body was barely warm enough in the camel brown cashmere sweater she wore. She kept her pace up and ran back down the steep hill into the house.

Running up the front steps, she could hear voices. She looked into the living room where Jennifer had been lying. No one was there. The floor was still wet from where Jennifer had fainted. The drops of water led across the stone floor and up the pine stairs. She ran up them to see her husband Rupert and Jennifer sitting at the table having tea, looking at her as if nothing had happened.

“Hey mom,” Jennifer said.

“What in the hell. What are you two doing?”

“Mom, calm down, I'm fine. I just fainted.”

“How am I supposed to calm down? Oh my god I thought—”

“She's fine dear,” Rupert said.

“Fine? What about the paramedics?

“We called them and told them not to come.”

“Yeah, we were just talking. I had a lot on my mind,” Jennifer said.

“Is that right?” Her mom was still confused and scared.

Jennifer looked away from her mother and down at her Jasmine green tea. She looked up again to see her mother's eyes still on her, unconvinced. Her mother's mute stare stirred something inside of her. She snapped forward in her chair, and tears began to pour from her eyes again.

“Baby?” Rupert said, concerned. “Baby, what is it?”

When she didn't respond, he got up and walked over to her, placing his hands on her shoulder. Jennifer nudged his hands off, and finally looked up at him.

“I'm pregnant. I'm having his baby.” She stared now at her mom, knowing that her father couldn't possibly relate to this feeling.

“Really, you are?” Her mother tried to pretend she didn't know. Jennifer's mother had been lied to so many times over the years that it was difficult for her to grasp that finally her daughter was telling the truth. “You are pregnant?”

Jennifer nodded. When she spoke her words came out muffled.

“I'll be a good mom.”

Her mom cuddled her into her chest. Jennifer's tears wet her sweater. She held her daughter for what felt like the first time since she was born. She didn't let go. She pulled her child to her, and they began to cry together.

Rupert walked away and back into the kitchen. He took out a beer from the fridge and cracked it open, swallowing the whole thing at once, something he hadn't done in twenty years. The rush of alcohol to his head made him dizzy, and he swayed back and forth, grabbing hold of the kitchen counter for balance.

CHAPTER THIRTY SEVEN

In the living room, modern art hung haphazardly, as if it had been flung against the walls. The central piece was an old work of Jennifer's from high school. It overshadowed a lot of the more expensive artworks. The washed out colors did a good job of hiding the blended lines. "I always loved that one," her father said. Jennifer sat up and looked up at it, even though she had seen it thousands of times.

The tension in the room was still high. Finally, Jennifer spoke.

"It's a boy."

Her mother's mouth dropped. She got up and walked to the kitchen. Rupert looked at Jennifer.

"Well, sweetheart, congratulations! We're very proud of you."

Jennifer looked at him, but couldn't help staring at her mother who was in the kitchen drinking a full mug of water, as if now she was going to faint.
"Your mother is too. I think she's just a little overwhelmed by all we've been through tonight. It's hard on her," Rupert said. He folded his fingers under the arm of the chair, holding on tight to brace himself for Jennifer's reaction.

"Hard for you? Are you serious?" Jennifer started to cry again.

"I'm sorry. I can't imagine, honey."

"Mom? Are you happy for me?" Jennifer said.

Her mom walked back into the living room and sat down. Jennifer sat, anticipating her words. The phone rang, breaking the silence.

"I better get it," Mrs. Bannister said.

"No, dear. You two talk. I'll get it," Rupert said. He got up and rushed to the phone.

"Yes, aha. Oh, sure… Hard to believe. Yes, she's here." Rupert's voice was still prominent in the room.

"Who was that?" Jennifer asked.

"The detective. You know, Sandoval."

"What in the hell could he possibly want right now?"

"He wanted to talk to you, but I told him we were having a family meeting."

"I'm guessing he didn't take that too well? He seems like a pretty determined guy with nothing better to do than ruin my life."

"He was really helpful as a witness."

"He couldn't do anything to save him. To even keep him safe!" Jennifer shouted, holding back tears.

“I don't think anyone could have predicted this. He was nice enough to call us and tell us personally what happened. He didn't have to do that.”

“Who cares about him? He fucked up. Look at me. Can't you even see?” She stood up and did a one hundred and eighty degree turn.

“See what?” Rupert said. Jennifer was shaking, livid with fear and rage. Her mother could sense her pain.

“I can understand you're really hurting right now, honey. We want to celebrate the life in you.”

“What?” Jennifer was taken aback. For the first time Jennifer could remember, her mother was trying to connect to her. She walked over to her mother, who was still sitting down, fell into her lap, and curled in a fetal position. She needed to feel her mother's touch on her skin. She didn't cry, just pressed her nose up against her mother's chest and sighed.

“My baby.” Her mom brushed Jennifer's blonde bangs away from her face.

Before the embrace between mother and daughter could be fully realized there was a loud knocking at the door.

“Who the hell is that?” Jennifer said.

CHAPTER THIRTY EIGHT

Rupert went downstairs and answered the door. Detective Sandoval and a younger female officer in plain clothes walked in. Jennifer could hear their voices. She couldn't make out the words, but from the intonations she sensed the urgency.

"Mom, I'm leaving," Jennifer said, pulling away from her mother's embrace. Her mom tried to hold her closer. She had waited so long to share a moment with her daughter, and she was not going to let her go now. Jennifer misinterpreted her love for restraint. Her instinct told her to escape. She jerked upwards, pushing her mother's feeble body back into the chair.

"If you love me, then be quiet." Jennifer put a finger up to her mother's mouth.

"Jenny, please. They're just trying to help you."

"No, they aren't. They just want to ruin me and take my baby." She started toward the back door. The footsteps up the stairs grew louder, and she increased her pace. She opened the French doors and headed towards the side of the house. Someone grabbed her arm. The young female officer anticipated her flight. Together with Sandoval, she had come around to catch Jennifer as she made her escape.

"Jennifer, please. We need to talk." Sandoval intervened.

"Oh, do we? I don't have anything to say to you."

“I can do most of the talking, but I need your help.”

“What's the point? He's, fucking gone. Nothing you can tell me is going to bring him back. You couldn't protect him, he's gone now.”

Jennifer pried her arm out of the female officer's grip. Sandoval motioned to the officer that it was OK.

“You're not in trouble.”

“Why don't you leave me alone? Have you run out of leads again? Want to chase me down back alleys in the Valley some more?”

“No. I really don't. I just want to share some information, provide some much-needed closure for you.”

“I had closure. At least I thought I did.”

“Fine, maybe not closure. This won't be the end of it. But I can give you some answers. Don't you want to know?”

“I don't think so. Not now. It won't do me any good to hear about how you fucked up. You fucked up.” Breaking down into tears again, Jennifer walked slowly back into the house.

“We thought we had it all figured out, I'll tell you. This seemed cut and dry in the wake of the shooting. Outside of you being the elusive witness in this case, the rest was a wash. The problem is… we really didn't plan on Destiny.”

“What the hell? You think this is fate?”

“No, no. You mean, you didn't know either?”

“What are you talking about?

“Violet has a sister. Her name is Destiny.”

Please don't continue to drag me down with your bullshit. My piece of mind lives inside me now. I don't need you to come over here and spoil it for me.”

“She's an identical twin.”

“I don't understand. What are you saying?”

Detective Sandoval straightened out his shirt, tucked it in and sat down on one of the big white linen chairs in the living room.

“Oh, please make yourself comfortable. You think I want to sit down with you, hear a lecture and then what? You're hoping to extract some more information from me? Watch my pupils dilate to see if I'm lying too? You are lost. You are totally lost. And to be honest, I'm not at your disposal anymore. I'm done, I'm gone. Oh, you didn't hear? I'm leaving tomorrow for Northern California. I have my own life to think about now.”

“I just thought you would want to know we might have the wrong girl in prison.”

“Do I care about her, her twin sister? Destiny. Once upon a time, I might have, because I had a soft heart, but that's changing. It's not just me anymore I have to think about.”

"Her jealous sister may have done the shooting. She is twisted and we think Violet took the fall for her."

"Then they should both be in prison for the rest of their lives. What do you want me to say."

"I know this is hard for you to hear right now, but Destiny and Charlie apparently had something going on."

"You mean he fucked her detective. Is that what you're trying to say?"

Rupert jumped up and interjected. "Detective, please. If you're going to continue like this you can leave our house."

Jennifer acknowledged her dad's attempt to stand up for her. "I really don't care what Charlie did in his past. I accept that. We had more love shared between us in a few days than most people have in a lifetime of marriage, boredom, and…" She started to cry and couldn't finish.

"Please help us then. Did Charlie ever mention Destiny? We heard reports from the neighbors that she was always going up to the house. Sometimes peeking in the windows. A real stalker type."

"I really don't know. Can you please just leave me alone!" She yelled at him.

The conversation ended. Sandoval had hoped to learn more about Jennifer's relationship with Charlie. Had he ever mentioned Destiny and his relationship with her? How she would stalk him at Violet's house in the hills? Sit outside for hours, even let herself in and anticipate Charlie coming home; strategically wearing sexy lingerie or making sure he was always just getting out of the shower? Sandoval raised his eyebrow disturbed, and frustrated by her lack of response.

Jennifer lay still in her room again, caressing her stomach. She rolled out of the couch and went outside to her old room. She saw Charlie's pale face, his reddened cheeks, his dark blue eyes staring back at her. The image comforted her by telling her everything would be all right. His presence was enough to settle Jennifer's stomach.

She was never going to let what she had had with Charlie die. Sandoval could think whatever he wanted about Charlie's past. It didn't matter. Nothing could override Jennifer's dedication to her lover. Everything else—the murder, the trial—seemed manufactured to lead her to this point where she could have a child.

She reached underneath her bed. When she couldn't find what she was looking for there, she paced around the room, checking the cabinets, shutting the pine wood drawers with greater force each time. She searched her memory. Finally, on the top of the bookcase, her long fingers grasped the worn corner of a manila envelope. The envelope flipped over the side. Jennifer grabbed it before the contents could spill. The envelope was addressed to Jennifer and sent to her with a strange return address and no name.

She curled up into a ball in the chair and rested the envelope on her knees. Her hair was starting to dry and the bright overhead track lighting made the highlights at the end of each strand glitter. She bit her upper lip. When she opened the envelope, the contents scattered onto her lap.

She stuffed them all back in, except for a few small pieces of paper the size of post-its. They were all covered in writing and small doodles. Mixed in were napkins featuring restaurant insignias. One said Café Bizou. She read one of the square cut outs on yellow legal paper, "Hi Sweet Pea, I just went out for a bit to get some cigarettes. I'll be back soon. Don't miss me too much :)." Charlie wrote the note to Violet. Jennifer was so disturbed by the notes; they made her sick. She received the envelope after Violet was incarcerated.

"Looks like Destiny sent these to me. That jealous whore."

Jennifer's eyes welled with tears. She sniveled, but stopped herself from crying. "It's not worth it. Come on, girl. She did this. She's trying to manipulate you."

She put the notes and letters back in the envelope. "What do you think the detectives will have to say about all these notes?" Jennifer flung the contents of the envelope all over the floor of her room.

She ran into the bathroom and came out with a zippered make-up pouch. She unzipped it and pulled out a pack of Parliaments and a lighter. She bent down and picked up one of the napkin notes with lipstick on it. She twisted one end into a tight spindle and then she lit it on fire.

Jennifer took out a cigarette. She hadn't had one since she found out she was pregnant. She tried to use the lit paper to light the cigarette, but it burned down too fast. Jennifer let the twisted lit paper drop on the ground of letters. The paper ignited. There was a loud banging against the door. She spit the unlit cigarette out of her mouth.

"Honey, open the door. Open the door right now!" Her father yelled.

Rupert tried hopelessly to get the door open, dropping his keys on the ground. Sandoval pushed him aside and kicked the door handle.

The vintage hardware snapped sideways. A few more kicks, and the screws snapped out of the wood. The door swung open. The fire was spreading across the ground quickly, consuming the dried pieces of paper crinkled up on the floor. Sandoval grabbed the comforter and threw it down on the scattered burning papers, trying to smother the flames. Rupert ran in and grabbed Jennifer. Wrapping his arms around her, he pushed her into the corner of the room and out of the way of the burning embers.

Sandoval put the flames out and looked at Jennifer. She was still crying. She stared at the few remaining pieces of paper, those that had only been singed at their edges. The look on her face was stoic. Jennifer's mother walked in, and hardly recognized her daughter.

The distance between them had returned. She couldn't reach out to Jennifer. She couldn't understand what motivated her to do such irrational things. Sandoval finally broke the silence.
"What in the hell was that about?"
\
Jennifer stared at him. Her eyelashes fluttered, and she fainted.

Rupert caught his daughter's weight in his hands. He set her down on the Eames chair next to him, propping her head up with pillows. Sandoval picked through the ashes, and came up with a piece of white paper, the only one left untouched by the fire. He blew off the black debris and began to read the words.

I am leaving. This was never meant to be. We were never meant to be this serious. There is someone out there for you, like there is someone that is really my soul mate out there. Maybe we never find them, but we have to look. Thank you for taking care of me.

Sandoval finished reading the words and looked at Rupert. "Who is this for?"

Rupert looked down at Jennifer. Jennifer started to move. She looked up and saw her dad's face looking directly at Sandoval. Before he could say anything Jennifer spoke. "Don't say anything, Dad. I swear."

It was too late. Rupert was already shaking his head. "Those are letters that Charlie wrote for Violet. When she found out that he had left her for my little girl, she flipped out. Somehow found our address and mailed those to us. It was pretty sick and twisted if you ask me."

The detective stared at Jennifer, waiting for a response. Jennifer didn't mutter a word. She knocked the letters from Sandoval's hand onto the floor. The ash that clung to the sides of the remaining pages crumbled to the ground.

Sandoval picked up one of the pages again. He began to read. *You will always be my sweet pea. I will never let you go, you treat me so good. I would be a fool to let someone like you go. Bye. Love you.*

Jennifer started to cry. She shook her head. "You just don't understand. He manipulated her. He used that old bitch."

Her dad barely recognized his sweet daughter. She had never used such crass language in front of him before. He couldn't figure out whether to hug her or cry.

“Jennifer, please come here,” her father said.

Her mother pressed nimbly against the frame of the door. She wanted to block Jennifer from leaving, but she also wanted to be there for her. Jennifer paused with her hand on the door. Turning, she looked coldly at everyone in the room. She couldn't help but feel that she was surrounded by strangers. Even her mother was against her.

She shoved her mother aside and walked out into the street. Sandoval's assistant detective followed. Sandoval gathered up the remnants of the burnt paper on the ground. He looked up at the Bannisters. “I'm sorry this is the way it went down. Definitely not our intention.”

Rupert was angry. “We tried to help you. You fucked this up, look at Jennifer she is completely destroyed. She was fine before you got here! We were talking, she hugged her mother, which hasn't happened in as long as I can remember. We had tea, I mean fuck. Aren't you better at breaking the news? And questioning? What kind of amateur shit is this? I used to write a police show, and maybe our sources weren't always reliable, but this doesn't seem like the right protocol for something so sensitive.”

“I apologize sir. But you need to calm down. We are doing what we can here. Maybe you can get her therapy.”

“Her mother's a psychiatrist.”

“That's not what I meant,” Sandoval said.

"Well, I don't know what you mean anymore."

"We need to take her in to ask her some other questions about her knowledge of the incident. I promise you we will take care of her."

"Bullshit." Rupert said. It felt good to stand up to the cop. He adjusted his collar. "I'm going with you."

"I would advise against that sir. She's more likely to talk to us than she is to you."

"Unless she's under arrest, she's staying right here."

"It's too late Mr. Bannister. She's already with my deputy on the way to our station. You're welcome to ride with me down there." Sandoval was lying. He didn't know where Jenny was. Jennifer had given his deputy the slip and she was driving around Mulholland looking for her.

"Fine. Where is my wife?" Rupert went outside to confirm that what the detective said about Jennifer leaving was true. The deputy's car was gone. He went into the house and found his wife sitting there, crying and looking at a photo album filled with old pictures of Jennifer.

"Could I have been a better mother?" She looked up, but Rupert was already moving back out of the house with his windbreaker in hand. He paused and looked back. A long moment passed before Rupert spoke. "We both could have been better. I love you." He headed to the passenger side door of Sandoval's caprice. "I'm going down there honey. I have to help Jenny."

Rupert got in the car. They backed out of the driveway and onto Mulholland Drive. The twists and turns rattled the doors of the beaten up Caprice. The smell of mold and old cigarette smoke wafted from its beige cloth seats. Rupert rolled down his window to get a little air. Sandoval lit a cigarette.

“She's going to be fine. Jennifer was the key ingredient to this. Those letters, I mean, this kid was one hell of a little heartbreaker. Sure pulled a number over on these girls.”

“I wouldn't go that far.”

“Oh, really? What else would you call it? This twisted introvert becomes a rogue girl hunter in Los Angeles convincing them that he loves them and wants to be with them forever. He writes them love poems, holds them at night and makes them feel safe. Then he just leaves. Gives them just enough of a taste that they chase that feeling forever.”

“Are we talking about love or addiction here? My Jennifer is no addict. It's not in her DNA.”

“Love man, if you want to even say this warrants such a title. Shit, I was married for ten fucking years and that love is something totally different. Kids, right?”

“Yeah. I guess. She is different. They are different.”

“Right, like all kids. Think they know what love is, knock their high school girl friend up. Wind up in Planned Parenthood getting an abortion a month and a half later. Same cycle. I see it all the time.”

“How did you know?” Rupert was confused.

“Like I said I see it all the time. My daughter was the same way.”

“No, I mean about Jennifer's baby.”

Sandoval sat still. He was approaching the light at the bottom of Beverly Glen and Ventura. He rolled up one of his sleeves and extinguished his cigarette in an old diet Coke can in the cup holder,

“You're telling me Jennifer is pregnant?” He thought back and remembered the baggy sweatshirt covering Jennifer's stomach.

Rupert looked out the window. He nodded.

“Holy shit. This story just gets better and better.”

CHAPTER THIRTY NINE

Jennifer climbed down the steep embankment of the backyard. She snuck into the house. Jennifer couldn't contain her anger. Her face flushed red. She grabbed her parent's car keys and took off. In the living room, she passed her mother, crying.

Jennifer stopped at the kitchen. She grabbed a knife from the cutlery in the wood block on the counter, and tucked the blade under her forearm.

The Jaguar skidded out of the driveway. Jennifer sped through the turns on Mulholland and turned down Laurel Canyon straight through West Hollywood. The sun was starting to go down, the light settling into the Hollywood Hills. She drove down into the flats, past Wonderland and the general store. She accelerated with no hesitation. She was possessed. She sped through Sunset and down past Wilshire through Koreatown, where she turned on Pico.

There the cosmic notion struck her. The force almost knocked her back out of the car. What she had realized was that Violet and her sister, Christine, were interchangeable. They both aimed to poison her love, to slaughter the passion, the bond that she and Charlie had formed. The thought infuriated Jennifer. Her innocent demeanor washed away from her face. It was replaced by waves of hatred. Her body jolted as she came to a stop. She didn't notice the car in front of her, a Volvo station wagon with a busted right taillight. She remembered looking at it during the long pause she had before the light changed. The jagged red edge looked like the devil's face. She slammed on the accelerator when the traffic signal changed color.

Houses blurred in the rearview mirror. Her only objective was to get to Destiny's house. She knew where she lived. A fatal flaw that Destiny made in sending her those letters on behalf of her sister. The return address stared at her from the manila envelope on the front seat. She knew vaguely where it was. *Stay Strong Jenny, you have to*. She was further frustrated with the drive in traffic to get to the 90019 zip code. The area was familiar to Jennifer. She had seen a few plays with her dad at a little theater down the street called the Black Dahlia.

Jennifer's pale skin reddened. She had never wanted to hurt another person so badly. She hadn't felt the desire for vengeance before. The drive to hurt another person was foreign to her. The consequences seemed insignificant. She justified it further in her mind.

Jennifer turned left off of Pico on Sierra Bonita where Destiny lived. A few local kids scurried home before the sun dropped behind the Hollywood Hills. Otherwise the street was quiet. Jennifer crept down the last block, eyeing the addresses painted on the curb, looking for her target. She found it. She took a deep breath and tried to steady herself. Her body trembled with excitement and anger.

She took one more look at her face in the rear view mirror. She grabbed the handle, lifted it and swung the car door open. On the hill the doors weight fell back at her. She caught it before it could bang into her leg. She reached to grab the knife on the front seat and then she remembered there was something better in the back of the car.

Jennifer walked around to the car and popped the trunk. Inside, she reached for the emergency kit her father always kept in there. She fished around until she dug up the extra large white metal box with the Red Cross label on it. The case was vintage, a prop from one of his sets, but when she opened it and removed the flare gun, her nerves settled. She stopped shaking and cocked open the handle. Inside was the flare cartridge.

Jennifer concealed the gun behind the popped trunk to aim with the large round orange barrel. The grip was oversized and barely fit in her tiny palm. She fumbled, and the gun dropped back into the trunk. She started to cry, but pulled herself together. She grabbed the gun and tucked it into her bag. She turned and walked across the street to the address on the envelope 1316 S. Sierra Bonita. Jennifer walked up casually to the front door. She peered inside. It didn't look like a young family's home. The décor didn't fit. Everything was antique and there weren't any family photos on the wall. She was confused and stood unmoving. She finally walked around the side of the house to look through another window.

Jennifer rang the bell. Destiny would not be expecting her and she could shoot her point blank. She waited, shaking nervously. Her palms were dripping sweat. No one answered. *I guess I will just have to wait until she gets home*. Her heart was still pounding, but she was relieved she didn't have to shoot her in that moment.

Sirens came roaring down the street before she reached the street and could get into her parent's car. She assumed it was the cops coming for her. She jumped behind a large ficus hedge in the front yard. It wasn't big enough to conceal her, and she leapt to an oak tree instead.

An ambulance stopped at the house right in front of her. She was breathing heavily. She didn't want the paramedics to see her either. Jennifer inhaled deeply and sucked in trying to mold to the tree. She realized the flare gun was sticking out from under her shirt.

She tossed it into the bushes. The EMTs got out of the ambulance and ran inside. Two kids were out in the front yard.

After what seemed like a long time, Jennifer walked out from behind the tree and started to the sidewalk. She was ready to call it a day and come back later. Her curiosity led her to walk down the sidewalk instead toward the paramedics. Jennifer stood anxiously in the driveway. She peered into the house and tried to catch a glimpse of what was going on. A few other neighbors came out and congregated in the street next to her. One of the neighbors, an older woman with reddish hair walked over to Jennifer. "He probably beat her so bad this time she needs to go to the hospital." Jennifer looked up at her confused.

"What are you talking about?"

"Oh, we can hear it sometimes."

"The beating?"

"No, just Christina screaming, and throwing things at him."

"That is horrible." Jennifer knew this was the right house.

"Yeah, sure is. Especially for those two boys. They're going to grow up and be totally screwed. Pardon my language.

Jennifer just nodded her head. The stretcher was coming out. The EMTs were carrying it down over the front brick steps and onto the concrete path that lead down the driveway. They had an oxygen mask over the body. When it got closer she could hear one of the EMTs on the radio, "No, her heart is stopping. We can't get her blood pressure up." The stretcher was being pushed passed

Jennifer when the arm of the woman fell out from under the sheet. It was covered in white patches, diet patches. She noticed the face of the woman, she looked just like Violet only so emaciated and her skin was greenish colored. It was Destiny, she was nearly dead.

CHAPTER FOURTY

In the afterlife, you can still see your loved ones grind through the misery of existence. You watch them going through the motions of grief, dealing with the rubble you left behind. I would only watch Jennifer, my dreamer, and the child of ours that she carried inside of her.

Would I have cared so deeply if I had still been by her side, beaten by the shitty curve balls thrown my way? Probably not. I would have done something to fuck up the beautiful partnership we had forged on that drive up the coast. Now, the feelings we had would never go away. They would persist in the body of our child.

I knew she would have a baby boy. She would even name it Charlie Jr. It could not have been more perfect for me, and for the kid. If I had been around, I would have taken him down the wrong road. My tendencies towards self-destruction and self-pity meant that I was too selfish to raise a child. My identity was all fucked up. I barely knew what I wanted. Having grown up with no father around to give me any insight into what being a man meant, I'd spent my life working on cars and sleeping with women, the only two things I was good at. There was no way to break the cycle of the disaster that was built into me. Now, Jennifer would raise our child on her own, instilling her generosity and insight into him.

Jennifer could do it. She had the means, and a family that would stand by her and give her what she needed to keep my little boy safe. Maybe they would get out of the city. Go to the desert or the countryside and live in peace.

I knew the manic pulse of Los Angeles would always beat inside my child's heart. He would be drawn to it, try to wrangle the city only to be consumed, just like his father. But with me out of the picture, at least he stood a chance.

I wanted to hold my child. The one thing that doesn't change is the love. Love works like a magnet. It exists separately from everything. It spirals around each being and then produces the intelligent offspring that is just the manifestation of all of our collective energies working to save and perpetuate the existence of the whole. The whole: All of us, you, me, my sister, my love Jennifer, and now the seed of my child, growing. The unborn life that would carry on my name and belong to my legacy.

In Jennifer I saw the light. The light was her innocence. Our union was endless, eternal, and no one could take that away. The cops tried to drain us dry, the hospitals and doctors fed us prescriptions and pumped our IV's full of solutions to keep us hanging on the threshold. They were all determined to take away the one thing that kept life worth living. The love that would never die. I saw that now.

I felt my sister's hand. Our blood, or life force, was flowing through us and I could feel every inch of her being, and she could feel every inch of mine. I had been able to see my sister back when I was still alive, but this was different. Something greater than my own ego that dictated everything around us.

Here we were again together at last after all these years. I'd lost the love of my life. Now it was about getting back to my blood. My sister's energy was warm. It gave off a glow as it pulsed and danced. She spoke. “Did it hurt when you left?”

I paused. “They had me pumped full off meds. Don't think I had the strength to feel the pain.”

“Good, I was worried that it wouldn't be so easy. They say it hurts when you pass in a hospital because they try and keep you alive.”

I stared into the space around me. “Yeah, well I didn't feel a thing.”

For the first time I relinquished control over my mind. I let go and felt the light pouring in. All the thoughts slipped from my head, and I only felt the warm vibrations all around me.

CHAPTER FOURTY ONE

They stood by the oak tree on the cemetery lawn off Balboa. Jennifer was in tears. Her parents tried to console her. Cindy and Tennessee were there, dressed in black. The priest began the final prayer:

"This is not a time to be in mourning, it is a time to remember –To reflect and see the friend who we have lost and who lived such a full and everlasting life. To soldiers who leave this Earth we say they 'fought the good fight' and acknowledge their sacrifice and bravery for the rest of us. While I did not have the pleasure to witness firsthand Charlie's bravery I can see the impact he has made on all of your lives. It is in this place of darkness that we must all come together and celebrate his life. As we move forward with a place in our hearts reserved for him. For this blessing we say amen. Glory be to God and God Bless you.

Everyone bowed their heads. The priest held up a rosary and made the sign of the cross. Charlie had been gone now for months, and the funeral felt almost like an afterthought. Only Jennifer still felt his presence, lingering nearby. Her heart was still broken, and she still felt overwhelmed by loss.

"Only time, dear, will heal you." The priest was speaking to Jennifer. The words did nothing to alleviate her sadness. She squirmed in discomfort and nodded at the Priest, continuing to hold back her tears. She blew her nose. Crumpled balls of tissue were scattered at her feet.

Giving in to the pain, she broke down. Tennessee tried to console her. Jennifer's father moved his body closer to Jennifer and glared at Tennessee. Rupert Bannister had lost his child, his only daughter, to the boy being lowered into the ground. There was nothing Tennessee could do.

Rupert moved away from his daughter and sat down in the white plastic foldout chair. He straightened the navy dark blue plaid shirt under his black suit. His wife reached an arm around Jennifer's shoulders.

"Please don't, Mom," Jennifer said. She nudged her mother's hand away. When the ceremony ended Jennifer stood up and looked at all of Charlie's friends. "Won't you miss him? I mean you are all lucky to have known him, even just a part of him. His spirit, he knew that there wasn't much more after this life. You know he did it! He went for it. You should all hope you make it. Make something real happen. Love someone."

Her words drained away. It was apparent that Cindy was half-heartedly listening, looking around at the trees following a crow that flew, but also silently judging Jennifer and her choice to keep Charlie's baby. Tennessee was taking large gulps from a flask that had once belonged to Charlie, the sunlight bouncing off its metal casing directly into the priest's eyes.

Tennessee spoke. "Can I say a little something?" He had never been good at composing anything meaningful, but when he spoke after drinking, he always spoke from the heart.

"First, I love you. I love you Charlie!" He was almost shouting when he reached the stage. He was so tall that he dwarfed the priest. He stood with his back to the sun. The glare around him concealed his tears that started to flow.

“I have known him for longer than anyone here. He struggled a lot. His dad left him when he was a kid… Lost his baby sister, and his mom. I am just grateful he found a new love. His love for Jennifer renewed him. I could see a different light around him.” His speech was starting to lose its direction. Rupert reached towards him and motioned for him to sit back down.

“You didn't know him. Charlie was a good person. He saved us all. I bet no one knew that. He's going to have a beautiful baby with your daughter, sir. She loved him. That's some real love right there. I love you Charlie, I'll miss you man… and that's all I can say.” He wiped his eyes and blew his nose on the sleeve of his jacket.

Even if some of the melodrama was the booze talking, there was a lot of truth to what Tenny had said. Charlie had been selfish at times but gave his love to his friends—there was no debating that— his spirit was still alive. The casket was lowered and dirt was poured on. A sense of calm returned to the funeral. Jennifer looked down at her stomach and then up at the freshly poured earth covering the casket. She bowed her head one last time and said a final good-bye.

“I'm not going to just lay down. Does anyone else see what'sright? Don't you get what has to happen now?” she cried suddenly. Everyone turned to stare.

Jennifer looked at Charlie's friends in the eyes. They waited, attentive and alert. “I don't want to be so fucking down anymore,” she said. She ripped off the black veil she had on and headed toward a California oak tree near the top of the grounds. There, she dropped to her knees and produced one solitary tear.

Finally Charlie's friends caught up to her. Tennessee was running, but being out of shape and slightly buzzed made the journey up the slightly ascending field of gravestones difficult. He almost tripped and fell a bit, apologizing each time.

The remaining guests at the funeral had no desire to wander up the hill and deal with the crew surrounding Jennifer. They were mainly Charlie's friends, but a few of Jennifer's friends had shown up to comfort her. They stroked her blonde hair, which had come out of its neat bun and was getting messy. Jennifer brushed her friend's hands from her shoulders.

"Look I don't want sympathy. You know what I want?" She jumped up and nearly fell as her left heel snapped off from the weight of her baby. She kicked off the other shoe to make herself level again.

"What I want, I want to be married." There. She had said it. She felt a wave of shock roll through the small group around her. She watched her friends turn to one another to see if they were missing something. The expressions of discomfort reaffirmed that they all heard the same thing.

"Jen, I'm so sorry sweetheart, but you can't marry him he's gone," said one of Jennifer's friends.

"You think I don't know that? I can marry him. We're soul mates. Do you believe in that? Huh! I don't care if you don't believe in God you better believe in souls."

She surveyed the faces of everyone around her, trying to figure out who was a believer and who wasn't. "Fine. If you believe we have a soul then stay here. If not then go back with everyone else."

Tennessee was the first person to raise his hand, "I believe Jennifer. I'll stay."

In spite of herself, Jennifer was relieved.

"Will someone help me?" She collected branches from under the tree. No one understood why, but they followed. Jennifer piled the sticks up under the tree.

"Great, now who has a ring on?"

She looked down at all of her friend's fingers. The ring Cindy was wearing wasn't exactly a wedding ring. It was more of a Native American turquoise style ring. But Jennifer didn't care about the design. It was the symbol she was after.

"Can I borrow it? Just for a little bit?"

Cindy looked at her. Despite her gut telling her to just hang on to the ring and walk away from this, she was slightly intrigued. "Sure, take it!" Cindy took the ring off of her index finger and handed it to Jennifer.

"Alright well, we need to split up the parties. Girls and guys get on each side, except you Tennessee you are going to be the minister."

Tennessee was ecstatic. "I would be honored. Just tell me what to do." Jennifer nodded. She lined the party up by sex on either side of stick pile.

"Does any one have any objection to this?" She looked around.

Fear and confusion spread over the faces of her friends. She was acting like a completely different person. Her pace, her insistence on getting something she wanted at the moment she wanted it, were all things she had been taught not to do growing up. But her parents weren't there to stop her now. They were still down near the gravesite looking at their daughter disapprovingly from a hundred feet away.

Had they known she was forging a marital bond with the late father of her baby, they might have interrupted. Instead she was free to do whatever she wanted, and this was her compulsion. It wasn't tradition that drove her to want a wedding. It was the bond, like a pagan ritual, that would connect her with Charlie eternally.

"Alright I hope everybody is ready." She looked for Tennessee, who was making sure the stick pile was stacked up properly. "Tenny are you ready? I need you at the front here." Tennessee complied and walked to the front of the two groups. He was starting to feel a little drunk, but kept it together.

He leaned his back up against the tree for some temporary support. He wandered over to the makeshift pulpit near the collection of sticks. He picked up one of the larger sticks and used it as a cane to help support him. Jennifer repositioned him so that he was facing down the path.

"Where is my veil?" She searched the ground for her black funeral veil. One of her makeshift bridesmaids pointed. She picked it up from where it had fallen on the grass, and clipped it into her hair.

Jennifer quieted down, and gestured for Tennessee to begin.

"Hey, why don't we just go get the priest to this? He is much better suited for this type of thing than I am" Tennessee asked. He spotted the priest getting into his 1980s maroon Volvo station wagon. “Excuse me sir! Please wait one second.”

Tenny was waving his cane in the air and walking over to the car. He reached the Priest as he was trying to shut his driver's side door. Everyone in the funeral-party-turned-wedding party stood in their places while witnessing the ambush on the priest. Tenny shoved the cane to stop the door from closing. “I'm not a religious man, but I know the importance of having you bless this marriage. Please I beg you Father for your help here.”

“Okay, son. I will come with you and offer my blessing for your friends.” Tenny was relieved he didn't have to lead the ceremony, and walked with the priest up to the tree.

The priest walked up with his head bowed. The energy around him was unusual and kinetic.

Jennifer greeted him anxiously. “Let's make this official then.”

She nodded at the Father. As she started to walk down the path between the tombstones like pews at a church her parents' voice interrupted her perfect harmony. “Jennifer, stop! What are you doing?” They came running, waving their hands, trying to stop the unorthodox ceremony.

Rupert grabbed Jennifer by the shoulders. “Jenny, honey. I know you want him back, but you can't do this.” Jennifer looked at him, her eyes glassy. She turned towards Charlie's grave. “Look, I just cannot support this. We are behind you and your baby 100%. We will do anything to help you, but not if you go through with this. It just isn't right.” Mr. Bannister looked around at the arranged parties, and even the priest. He shook his head and pointed at the

Father, "… and you! I cannot believe you would participate in this nonsense."

The priest tried to step away, but Tenny gave him a look that was convincing. The priest stayed where he was. Rupert Bannister and his wife shook their heads disapprovingly and began to walk toward their car.

"You're not going to your own daughter's wedding?" Tenny asked. Rupert turned around and prepared to say something, but continued to shake his head, acknowledging how powerless he was to change Jennifer's decision. He lowered his head further, His wife looked back at Jenny, trying to connect one last time with her line of sight. She wanted to believe that her daughter would still come with them.

The ceremony continued. Her parents left the funeral grounds in their Jaguar, speeding, kicking leaves up everywhere. Jennifer walked down her makeshift aisle. She stopped in front of the priest and Tennessee, who was standing watch like a fanatical altar boy. The priest began to speak.

"We are gathered her today to consecrate the union of the beloved Jennifer Bannister and the late Charlie Winters." He stopped himself. "I can't do this, I'm sorry." Jennifer pleaded. "I beg you, please Father." She looked at him again and tears began to fall. "Alright, alright. Yes… gathered here to celebrate the love of two very different people's lives as they come together in holy matrimony." The priest's words continued, but no one was paying attention.

Instead they were looking at each other. Were they perpetuating a false reality? Aiding Jennifer further into a delusion that would make it even harder for her to acknowledge the truth?

“May we have the ring, please?” Cindy walked over and handed over the Native turquoise piece to the priest. “Please put out your hand, my dear,” he said.

Jennifer reached out. At the moment the priest slid the ring onto her finger, she staggered backwards, as if she had been hit with a pulse of energy. She rubbed her stomach and felt it deep in her loins.

“I now pronounce you, husband and wife.” The priest finished. He turned and walked off. Everyone else started to disperse. A few of the girls congratulating Jennifer were stunned by the heat they felt radiating off her body. She was starting to sweat profusely from her forehead and down her neck. She continued rubbing her stomach and walked away.

She grabbed her purse and took out the pack of Parliaments. She took out the lighter tucked inside the pack. She lit the cigarette and casually flicked it into the pile of leaves covering the stick pile. A few people saw her light the cigarette, and noticing her very pronounced baby bump, turned away in disgust. They didn't see that she flicked it into the leaves.

Her remaining friends stood in small pockets talking about what they had just witnessed. Tennessee was the last person to leave. He was also the first to notice the fire starting to burn from underneath the pile of leaves. “Holy hell! There's a fire!”

The wedding party ran in all directions, colliding into one another as they tried to find a clear path between the gravestones, but Jennifer stood perfectly still. Her face remained angelic against the fire. She swayed left and right. “Someone call the fire department!” A voice from the crowd yelled.

The flames grew until they reached an overhanging Sycamore. The white bark browned, blistered, and cracked before it burned. The flames rushed up towards Tennessee. His drunkenness caused him to hesitate. He felt paralyzed. He collapsed to the ground.

Jennifer was happy to see the air engulfed in smoke. The fleeing of her friends gave her satisfaction. "You have to burn a forest down if you want it to grow back again." Her words were interrupted by the fire engines roaring into the cemetery and down the road toward them. Tennessee started to get up. Jennifer watched, as the Sycamore branch above him cracked with a hissing sound and fell, knocking him back to the earth.

"Oh, my God! Someone help him," Jennifer said, pointing toward the area where Tenny lay knocked unconscious under the burning embers of the broken branch. She stared, pointing and screaming at the top of her lungs, but her raspy vocal chords cut in and out.

Firemen in yellow uniforms blanketed the field surrounding the fire. Water blasted from their hoses, putting out some of the flames immediately on impact. Jennifer grabbed hold of one of the fireman's arms and tried to drag him to where Tenny had gone down. The fireman tried to contain her by restraining her arms. She lunged forward and struck the fireman in the face.

"What in the hell was that?" The fireman said to her.

"Listen to me," she shouted.

"You need to calm down first. Then we can help you."

“I don't need any fucking help. My friend is lying under the fire over there. He's trapped.”

“There is no one over there.”

“Look!” She pointed to where she had seen Tenny go down. The fireman trudged around to the other side of the smoldering ash.

“Hey Jerry, you guys find anyone over here?”

“Nope, nothing yet. If someone's in there they aren't coming out looking very good, I'll tell you that much cap'n.”

“See I told you, little girl. Nobody is in that mess.”

“I saw him! You need to get him!” Jennifer yanked her arm out of the fireman's grasp and ran into the pile of ash and embers, kicking up sparks as she crossed through the aftermath.

Her ankles were getting burned by the embers that floated and clung to her stockings, melting onto her skin. She tripped to where Tenny was, and fell face-first, right into the arms of a waiting fireman. There was no sign of Tennessee. She started to feel the burns on her leg – the pain was real now.

She paused. A nauseating calm passed over her. Stuck in the middle of this tragic scene, she was static. Everything around her moved in hyperspeed. None of it mattered. The beat of her heart was visible in a pulsating vein in her forehead. Smoke filled the air, until there wasn't a pure breath left.

www.ingramcontent.com/pod-product-compliance
Lightning Source LLC
Chambersburg PA
CBHW030546310726
48979CB00010B/2050/J

* 9 7 8 0 9 9 6 0 9 6 4 2 3 *